A HANGING M~~

with best wishes

[signature]

A HANGING MOON

LEOPARD'S BANE BOOK 3

PHILL FEATHERSTONE

Cover design by Cathy Helms, www.avalongraphics.org

Typeset in Palatino by Opitus Books.

ISBN 9781739350734

Also available as an ebook, ISBN 9781739350741

Published by Opitus Books, Sheffield, UK.

www.opitus.net

❀ Created with Vellum

FOREWORD

A Hanging Moon is the third book in the Leopard's Bane series. It can be read on its own, but for anyone unfamiliar with the background, this is the context.

Book 1, *The Poisoned Garden*, is set in the ancient city of Chamaris, a wealthy community controlled by a small number of very rich men. Their leader is Karkis. He is ageing and going blind and must look to his legacy. He has two sons: the elder, Ragul, by one partner and the younger, Peglar, by another.

Ragul is sturdy and athletic. He is also a show-off and a bully. Peglar is quiet and bookish and often suffers at the hands of his stepbrother. Karkis also has a daughter, Malina, by his first partner, but as women have no rights in Chamaris she doesn't figure in his consideration of an heir.

Peglar by chance meets Yalka, a poor girl from the slums, whose view of the world is very different from his own. She is like no one he has ever met, and he is attracted to her. For her, Peglar may be a 'posh boy' but he has qualities that she respects, among them a willingness to listen to her denunciation of the corruption and privilege rife in Chamaris and a desire to improve matters.

Before their relationship can come to anything, Vancia, the mother of Ragul and Malina, who is desperate for her son to inherit everything, devises a scheme to discredit Peglar. The plot succeeds and Peglar is exiled from the city, with a price on his head. Almost at the same time, a fire destroys the area where Yalka lives, and kills her younger brother. There is evidence that Ragul has had a hand in this.

Book 2, *The Rhymer's Daughter*, begins with Yalka and Peglar both homeless. Because of the substantial reward offered for his capture, Peglar must go far away and he joins the crew of a freighter, The Morning Glory. A little way into the voyage the ship is attacked by pirates and Peglar is caught. However, his captors don't at this stage know who he is and he is able to arrange for himself a passable existence.

Meanwhile, Yalka and her grandfather move to another city some way off. They are gradually settling down when Yalka is kidnapped by slavers and sold. Her buyer turns out to be one of Ragul's men, who has a plan to use her to lure Peglar into a trap.

The story continues in *A Hanging Moon*.

1

VANCIA BATHES

In her bathing chamber in the Palace of Chamaris, Lady Vancia lay naked in a scented pool. Candles lined its marble edges, their flames dancing on the water. Beyond them, her waiting women stood in silent attendance. In an alcove, a eunuch gently plucked the strings of a baglama.

Vancia rolled in the water, relishing the sensation as it caressed her body. She snapped her fingers and two of the waiting women stepped fully clothed down the steps into the pool. Each took one of her hands and together they led her out to where another two women wrapped her in towels soft as down. She stood for a moment, allowing them to pat her dry. Then with her elbow bent she made a circular movement of her right hand, her forefinger extended beside her shoulder. At once and in silence the waiting women gathered their robes around them and withdrew. The eunuch put down his instrument. He knew what would happen next. It was always the same.

At the end of the pool was a huge mirror that filled

almost the whole wall. Vancia stood before it. Then, with a shrug of her shoulders, she let the towels fall and regarded her uncovered body. She was pleased with what she saw. She was no longer young but her skin was smooth and clear and her breasts firm. The triangle at her crotch was soft and downy like a girl's, a thin veil both covering and enticing. She turned sideways and admired her profile, her flat stomach and trim behind. The eunuch watched, impassive.

'Would you say I am an attractive woman?' she said.

The eunuch had his answer ready. 'Undoubtedly, My Lady. Lord Karkis is indeed a lucky man.'

Vancia snorted. Karkis, her husband, was old and almost blind. Movement was increasingly difficult for him and it had been a long time since he had last visited her bed.

She raised an eyebrow. 'Do you think I should take a lover?' she said.

The eunuch left a practised pause before he answered. 'Many men would be eager, My Lady.'

It was what Vancia expected to hear. 'Who do you have in mind?' she said.

The eunuch pretended to deliberate. 'Feldar is a handsome man.'

'My husband's Steward?' She considered, turning and looking over her shoulder to admire her back. 'Yes, he's not bad looking but he lacks refinement.' And, she was thinking, he's too close to home. More than that, there were questions about his loyalty. He had taken Peglar's side the night Ragul had made his spectacular wager against him. In fact, he had been the only one in the room who had.

The eunuch reflected again. 'Has my lady considered Cestris?'

She knew Cestris slightly, but he too had favoured Peglar, acting as one of his seconds when he'd fought Ragul in the cage. But he was wonderfully handsome – smooth-skinned, tall, and athletic, a champion at the Seven Cities Games. She had indeed considered him. Some would say he was too young for her, but what of that?

'However,' the eunuch added, 'it is said that Cestris finds the company of boys more stimulating than that of women.'

Vancia laughed. 'It would be interesting to find out,' she said archly.

All this was idle talk, as both she and the eunuch knew. It was a game they often played. Vancia was now close to the pinnacle of the power for which she had so long schemed. She had plotted, and manoeuvred, and intrigued, and even killed to reach the point at which she now stood. She had no intention of ruining it all by taking a lover. Blind as her husband might be and appealing though the lusty body of Cestris might seem, she would not risk everything by embarking on a frivolous excursion. She had done that once, more than seventeen years ago. It had been a brief affair, wild and indulgent, and had resulted in the birth of her daughter Malina. Through a combination of lies, careful planning and good fortune Karkis had never found out and had accepted Malina as his own. But it had been a trying time. Even though Vancia had swiftly ended the illicit liaison, she had endured a period of acute anxiety lest an enemy, and she had many, discovered her secret and made it known. No one had, and Malina had grown up

3

as a princess, cosseted in the luxury of the Palace. She was now ready for an advantageous pairing, one which would not only result in a handsome sum of Bride Gold for the ever-demanding family treasury but also would cement and strengthen her mother's prestige.

Vancia clapped her hands and the waiting women returned. They bore potions and lotions, and while one of them spread towels on a low bench another knelt and began to massage her limbs and body, working the oils gently into her skin. When they had done, they wrapped her in a loose chemise and a third woman brushed her hair and fashioned it into braids. The eunuch resumed his playing.

When she indicated that she was sufficiently perfumed and preened, the women drew back and the eunuch bowed and left. Vancia rose and crossed the chamber to a long couch at the far end, where she spent some time arranging her posture, curling her legs beneath her and draping one arm along its back. With her other hand, she adjusted her garment to best display her cleavage. She eased the material a little lower and finally was satisfied.

'Admit him,' she said.

One of the women departed and the others moved to the end of her couch. Vancia irritably waved them away. 'No,' she said. 'All of you go. Go.'

For a few moments, she was alone. The room was silent. The candles flickered on the cream marble, and the scented vapour from the water hung in the air. Then she heard a stirring and a panting which preceded the arrival of a short, fat man. He was wrapped in a heavy cloak and his bald head and brow were greasy with perspiration.

'Madam, you sent for me,' he puffed as he approached her.

Vancia smiled, thinly. 'Lord Sainter,' she said. 'Indeed I did send for you. Be seated.'

She patted the couch beside her. Sainter hesitated and then took a spot at its far end, as remote from her as he could manage. He avoided looking directly at her and fussed with his garments, tucking his cloak around him. He was uncomfortable in the presence of women. The more powerful and more attractive the woman, the more awkward he felt. Vancia knew this and exploited it. It was one of the means she used to manage him.

She pouted, fluttered her eyelashes, and touched the neckline of her gown, enjoying Sainter's unease. When she felt he had suffered enough, she spoke.

'I hear we have the girl. Where is she?'

Sainter cleared his throat. 'She is to be taken to a fortified villa, in Verlam, My Lady.'

Vancia frowned. 'Verlam? Where's that? Why there?'

'Verlam is a mile from Maris Partem, a little way off the road between there and Semilvarga. It's tiny, not even a hamlet, just a couple of buildings and a few olive trees.'

Vancia bent her fingers and studied the nails. She didn't reply so Sainter felt he should say more.

'Some traffickers seized the girl in Semilvarga and they put her up for auction at the slave market in Murgo. Verron, who is one of your son's men, keeps an eye on such things. He was on the lookout for slave women when he came across this girl. He realised who she was and bought her.'

Vancia straightened up. 'Bought her? Moon and

5

stars, why didn't he simply take her? How much did she cost?'

'The price paid was twenty golds, My Lady.'

Vancia visibly relaxed. 'Is that all? A trifle. And does this whore of Peglar's have a name?'

'She is called Yalka, My Lady,' said Sainter.

Vancia winced. 'How common. How vulgar. A peasant name. I'm not surprised. It's no more than Peglar deserves. Is there any news of him?'

'I'm afraid not. As My Lady knows, he got away from Maris Partem on a ship, The Morning Glory. Its captain became aware of who he was and was planning to hold him on board until the vessel returned to port, but they were waylaid by pirates. We thought that Peglar, too, had been taken as a slave, but it seems not.'

'So where is he?'

Sainter wriggled. The bathing chamber was intolerably hot. His clothing was sticking to him and he was sweating profusely, but nevertheless he kept his cloak wrapped tightly around him. He was still avoiding looking directly at Vancia.

'No one knows, My Lady. The names of all the crew – the ones that survived, that is – are on bills for the sale of slaves, but Peglar's is not amongst them.'

Vancia beamed. 'So perhaps he died at the hands of the pirates. Perhaps he never made it to shore.' She clasped her hands. 'Please let that be.'

'That would indeed have been an ideal outcome, My Lady, but I am told that Peglar was seen ashore, and even in Murgo.'

'In Murgo? The same place that this Yalka creature was sold? And they never met?'

'Apparently not, My Lady.'

'And now he has vanished.'

'Indeed so.'

'Mm.' Vancia was irritated. This was most unsatisfactory. 'So, what now?'

Sainter leant forward in the closest he ever came to eagerness. It was a sign to Vancia that he had a scheme in hand, and she knew there was nothing he enjoyed more. 'I think that we can work this situation to our advantage. It would seem that your stepson is quite attached to Yalka.'

Vancia raised her eyes and shook her head. 'I am perplexed. Attached? To a whore from the slums? Don't you find that despicable, even for Peglar?' Her disgust was intense. 'Nauseating!'

'Indeed, My Lady. However, we can make use of Peglar's obsession with the girl. Verron is making it known that she is being held in Verlam. He is spreading the word in taverns and inns in and around Maris Partem, and in all the towns and villages across the plain. He is confident that this will flush Peglar out. He will hear that she is captive, and where, and he will attempt to rescue her. The villa is discretely guarded, and when he tries to free her he will be caught.'

Vancia looked at Sainter for a long time before she spoke. He glanced up at her, accidentally met her eye and swiftly looked away.

'This had better work,' she said.

Sainter swallowed. 'Yes, My Lady.'

She raised her hand to him in a gesture of dismissal, and he started the process of levering his bulk from the low couch. Once upright he made to leave but Vancia raised a finger to stay him.

7

'Not yet,' she said. 'I instructed you to bring me news of Chalia.'

'Ah, yes, my lady. I spoke with Physician Narvil. He can do nothing for her and is of the opinion that she will not last much longer. A day or two, perhaps. A week at the most.'

'How sad. And so young, too.' Vancia's smooth words oozed insincerity. What Sainter told her was exactly what she had hoped to hear.

Vancia watched him waddle out. How he disgusted her, but there was no denying that he was useful. He was so obsessed with impressing her that he would do anything she told him. And sometimes no instruction was necessary, the merest hint would do, which was useful because then she could always deny any responsibility. Yes, he was useful, but she would dispense with him as soon as her plans were concluded.

She clapped her hands and two of her women hurried in with a selection of gowns. She chose one, slipped off her chemise and let it fall to the floor. The women began to dress her. The eunuch returned with his baglama and worked deftly on the strings, playing a gentle, undulating melody.

'What is that you're playing?'

'It's a composition of my own, My Lady. I call it "Salute to the Moon".'

'Charming. Quite charming.'

The eunuch bowed low. 'My Lady is very gracious. With My Lady's permission, I would like to dedicate it to her.'

Vancia turned to look through the window to where the full moon had just risen. It was large and red. She

8

had always thought that she and the moon had something in common.

'I accept the dedication,' she said.

She was content. Chalia, Peglar's mother and her rival, was history, or she soon would be. Karkis, her husband, was no longer capable of carrying out his duties as Master of the City and Ragul had been named as his Regent. Her daughter, Malina, was being pursued as a bride by all the high families and would make an advantageous pairing.

She was in control.

IN ANOTHER PART of the Palace, Karkis was in his study. He was seated with his back curved and his palms on his desk. He looked straight ahead but saw little. He could make out the wall of shelves only a few paces away, but he could not see the books on them. Instead, he saw a dark cloud, with a little light around its edge. For months now the cloud had been getting bigger and darker, and as it did so the light that surrounded it became fainter.

Although the day was warm there was a fire in the grate, which smoked and filled the room with a pungent haze. Karkis was acutely sensitive to cold and didn't mind the stuffiness the fire created. He was trying to remember when he had last felt well, and what it was like to be happy. He was thinking about his wives and his children, and how it was that he and they had arrived at the point where they now were. He was still Master of the City, but in name only. He could no longer read documents, concentrate during meetings, or process information. He had lost the ability to judge the relative importance of different matters, and the countless items that clamoured for his attention all seemed to be of equal worth. The last few times he had addressed the City Assembly he had lost the thread of what he had been saying, and his poor eyesight meant that his notes had been of no help. At Vancia's suggestion, he had declared Ragul his Regent, and that meant there was no longer anything for him to do. Sometimes he thought about his other son, Peglar, and wondered how it was that he had turned out to be so great a disappointment. He blamed the boy's sickly mother for that and refused to see her, even when Feldar reported to him how ill she was.

He felt for the flask which he knew was on his desk, and when he found it he withdrew the cork. It was a tonic which Vancia daily prepared for him. Because nowadays his hands trembled constantly he didn't trust himself to pour its contents into the glass beside it, so he lifted the flask to his lips and sipped. The liquid was bitter but he drank it all because if he did not Vancia would be hurt and angry. He had already had one dose that morning, and there would be another at bedtime. He popped into his mouth some of the raisins that he kept by him to mask the vile taste of the brew.

He rested the empty container on the desk and absently wiped a slick of drool from the corner of his mouth. He was old, his body ground down by the relentless wheels of time. He was tired.

2

MISSING

This was without doubt the worst time of Meshi's young life. It was worse by far than when he had been potboy at The Quiet Woman, bullied by the landlord, squashed by his pair, and tormented by drunken customers. It was worse even than the days after he'd defended Yalka from Big Ears by striking him over the head with a lump of wood. The man's thuggy friends had hunted him all over Maris Partem and it had been a relief when he'd gone with Syramos and Yalka to Semilvarga. And now this had happened.

When he returned to the rooms where they were staying he found Syramos playing a solitary game of Sentinel. It was a pastime the old man enjoyed and was good at, and as the boy came in carrying the two bags of provisions that Yalka had bought on the market he looked up, hoping he might get a game.

'Ah, Meshi. I was wondering where you'd got to.' Meshi didn't reply so Syramos continued, 'Isn't Yalka with you?'

Meshi shook his head.

'Did she say how long she'd be?'

'No.' Meshi frowned. He was sure that she hadn't, but perhaps she had. Sometimes he missed things, and sometimes he caught them at the time but then forgot them. He thought again. No, he was sure she'd told him to go ahead with the bags of shopping and she would follow him. 'I left her sitting by the fountain. I think she just wanted to be on her own for a bit. I expect she'll be along soon.'

But she wasn't, and they waited. As the afternoon wore on they both became concerned and it was harder to settle into doing anything. Meshi couldn't concentrate, and Syramos had abandoned his game and sat in his chair with a worried expression on his face. Eventually they heard a distant clock chiming the fifth afternoon bell.

'Shall I go look for her?' said Meshi.

'That would be a good idea,' said Syramos.

It was a relief to be doing something but Meshi had no idea where to begin the search. The obvious place to start was where he'd seen her last, Fountain Square. She had told him to meet her there, and he'd waited until he saw her coming towards him, carrying two bags. They seemed heavy and she'd looked relieved when he took them from her. She sat on a stone bench beside the fountain.

'Do you want me to take the bags?' he said.

She nodded. 'That would be great.'

She smiled and tucked back her hair in a gesture that always made Meshi go weak. He picked up the bags but had only gone a few steps when he realised that Yalka wasn't following him. He stopped and turned towards her. She was sitting on the stone rim of the fountain.

'Aren't you coming?' he asked.

'No, not yet,' she said. 'I just want to get my breath back. I'll hang out here for a bit. You go on. Tell Granddad I'll be back in soon to get dinner ready.'

'Right,' said Meshi.

He picked up the bags and set off across the square. He was disappointed that Yalka wasn't going with him. He liked her being beside him. He liked the idea of being seen with her and people thinking that they were together, that she was maybe his girlfriend. But he'd walked away, and that was the last time he'd seen her.

He half expected her to still be at the fountain, sitting on the stone parapet and trailing her fingers in the water. On the other hand, several hours had gone by so he wasn't surprised that she was not. The square was much quieter than it had been when they'd parted. Then it had been bustling, with the shops and drinking houses around the edge busy. Now they were empty. The market at the bottom end of the square was over, the stallholders packed up and departed.

Meshi looked around helplessly. Perhaps she had gone into one of the cafés for refreshment. He knew that was unlikely, but he worked his way around the square calling in each of them to see if she was there. She was not. He asked the few people who were around if they had seen a girl sitting by the fountain. Most of them shook their heads and moved on. Then one man said that he had.

'Yes, there was a girl there. She was talking to a small boy, a street kid. Then she ran off after him. She was shouting. I think he'd nicked her bag.'

'Did she have blonde hair?'

'Yes.'

'And a mark on her cheek?'

'I didn't see. I wasn't that close.'

'Did anyone follow her?'

The man looked at Meshi as if he was an idiot. 'Of course not. It happens all the time. Some little scab gets somebody talking, and then they snatch what they can and run off. Usually they work in twos or threes but this one was on his own. There's no point going after them. They're as fast as a fox and you can never catch 'em.'

'Did you see where she went?'

'Yes. He ran down that alley over there and she chased after him.' The man pointed towards an opening at the top end of the square.

'Did you see her come out again?'

A look of pain crossed the man's face. 'Of course. I've got nothing better to do than stand and stare at an alleyway to see if somebody who's gone in there comes out. What do you think?'

Meshi went to where the man had pointed and found that it was the entrance to a narrow lane lined with small buildings. They all looked the same, drab, anonymous and in poor repair. All the doors were closed and none looked as though they'd been used in a while. Most of the windows were covered with boards or sacking, and those that weren't were so grimy that he couldn't see through them. He knocked on the first few doors but without any hope. It was obvious that this was a dead place and few people came there. He walked the length of the lane to where it gave onto a wide street but it was empty. A man driving a donkey cart passed slowly by. That was all. No sign of Yalka, or any indication of where she might have gone when – if – she reached the street.

Disappointed, he went back to the square and asked a few more people if they had seen a young woman sitting beside the fountain. Some tried to be helpful, others did not.

'Lots of people sit there,' one man said. 'How am I supposed to know if any of the ones I've seen are who you want?'

'Stood you up, did she?' said another. 'I can't say I blame her.'

A woman was more helpful. 'I think I did see someone, a girl chasing a small boy, but I was a long way off. I can't say if it was the one you're looking for.'

That at least agreed with what the first witness had told him.

'When you find her, tan her arse,' said the man with her. 'Running off like that? She needs to be taught.'

'And what do you know about it?' the woman said sharply. Then to Meshi, soothingly, 'I should go home, my dear. You'll probably find she's gone back there and she's waiting for you.'

That cheered Meshi up. Of course. All this time he'd been looking for Yalka she could have been at home anyway. She could be preparing Syramos's dinner even as he was standing there asking about her.

'Thank you,' he said, feeling relieved, and he hurried back to their rooms.

The woman was wrong. Syramos was in the chair exactly where Meshi had left him, and the boy saw at once from the old man's expectant expression as he came in that Yalka hadn't returned.

'What do we do now?' said Meshi.

Syramos had no answer and Meshi sat down. There was silence, neither of them speaking, as they settled into an uneasy wait. Meshi couldn't take his eyes off the door, hoping every minute that it would burst open and Yalka would rush in with her hair blown, a smile on her face, and an explanation for what she'd been doing and where she'd been. But it didn't happen. Evening came, Yalka did not.

Over the following days, Meshi felt a pain that grew more intense with every passing hour. Always before when he'd been upset or worried about something, time passing had made things easier, but not this. This was different, and gradually an empty dread settled itself in his belly and he found himself haunted by horrors of what could have happened. Had Big Ears caught up with her at last? Or had somebody else just as evil? Was she even now lying somewhere bloody and broken, desperate for help?

The next day Syramos joined in the hunt. Meshi hoped that the direct involvement of a rhymer might make a difference but it didn't. They tramped the streets until their legs were weary and their feet sore, returning no wiser to empty rooms and the ache of Yalka's absence. Meshi went back again and again to the square as if with each visit he would get a different outcome. He widened the search, radiating from the square street by street until he had covered almost the whole of the city. Nobody had seen Yalka; no one knew anything.

Syramos went to the Guardians but they were no use. An unknown teenager with no money or influence was of zero interest to them, and they even found it hard to treat the old man's enquiry seriously.

'I should try the garrison,' said one of them.

'The garrison?' said Syramos. 'Why?'

'Well, you say she's got a mark on her face,' said the other one. 'That sounds like what I'd call a whore mark, so I bet that's where she'll be, off whoring.'

'That's right, try the garrison,' said the first one, grinning.

'And if you find her, send her round here,' said his companion. Both men laughed.

Syramos turned away from the insult but fury rose in Meshi. He wanted to take the two of them by their throats. Syramos, sensing his anger, put a hand on his arm.

'Come away,' he said. 'These men know nothing and if you react badly you'll be in trouble.'

Meshi had to admit that he was right. The two Guardians were big and he expected there'd be more of them nearby to join in if he started anything. He allowed Syramos to lead him away.

'What's a garrison?' he said.

'It's a group of soldiers stationed to guard a place. This one will be troops from Chamaris sent here to keep the Semilvargans down and make sure that they pay the tribute money.'

They walked on a little way in silence and then Syramos added, as if reflecting to himself. 'It was the soldiers in the garrison here that hung the parents of Yalka's friend, Eylese.'

Meshi was startled. Is that what a garrison did? 'Why?'

'Because her mother and father thought that the tribute Chamaris had imposed was unfair. People couldn't afford it so they organised a strike and nobody paid.'

'And they hanged them? For that?'

'They did,' said Syramos. 'They could have been punished in some other way but that wouldn't have been enough for the man in charge of the garrison. And do you know who that was?' Meshi didn't. 'It was Peglar's half-brother, Ragul.'

3

THE WAY OF A RHYMER

Meshi was finding it hard to concentrate. It was never easy for him, but since Yalka had vanished it had become particularly difficult. He missed her so much – the tumble of yellow hair, the lapis eyes, the cheeky expression. His hopes that he would find her, and she would laugh at him for being what she called a fussbucket, shrivelled and died. He'd looked everywhere. It wasn't simply a matter of her getting lost; she had been taken. If she could have got in touch with them she would, so either she was locked in somewhere, or worse. He blamed himself for leaving her alone, his only comfort being that Syramos was sure she was alive.

'I would know if she were dead,' he said.

Meshi wanted to believe that. 'How?' he said.

'I'm a rhymer. Rhymers know these things.'

Meshi hesitated for a moment, and then asked the question that had been on his mind from the moment he'd realised that Yalka had vanished. 'Why don't you use your rhyming to find her?'

The old man shook his head. 'Rhyming doesn't work

like that. The nature of rhyming is to foresee the future, not to illuminate the here and now.'

'But if you know she's alive can't you tell where she is? Sort of, like, talk to her in your head?'

'Rhyming isn't mind reading. I know she's not dead because I can feel a future in which she is a presence.'

'Oh.' Meshi wasn't sure he understood. 'In this future that you feel, is she all right?'

'She is there. And so is Peglar. There is little more that I can tell.'

And people pay for this? thought Meshi. People go to Syramos and other rhymers to ask them what's going to happen but if it's all like this, then why? It was so vague. There'd been people in The Quiet Woman who'd said it was all a load of rubbish, but there must be something to it because a lot of other people believe in it. Perhaps if Syramos could feel Yalka, it would work in the other direction. She might be able to locate him.

'Can Yalka rhyme?' he said.

Syramos paused for a moment before he answered. 'Yes. She can rhyme now and she will get better at it, but the way of a rhymer is not easy. It is a long journey from showing the first promise to achieving accomplishment. Her mother was adept as a rhymer, and that will be a help.'

'How do you do it?' he asked.

Syramos shook his head wearily. 'Rhyming is not something that can be taught. It's a gift.'

'Yes, but how do you find out if you've got the gift?'

Syramos frowned. 'I think that if you have it, you know it. The best way to be certain would be to go into a trance and find out what you see. If anything.'

'And how do you do that, how do you go into a trance?'

'Many questions,' said Syramos wearily, 'many, many questions. Very well, I can see you are curious, and in a young person curiosity is an excellent thing. A trance is a state of abstraction, and entering into one is a knack. Rhymers vary. There are no formal instructions and there are many different approaches. Some people chew or smoke armanca. I use it myself sometimes but it dulls the senses and fogs the vision, so it is better to will oneself into the trance if you can. Armanca also blurs one's speech, so when I use it I like to have someone there who can interpret my rhymes. Yalka is good at that.'

Meshi was thinking hard. Surely there must be some way to use such an amazing facility in their search. 'So what is it you see when you're in a trance?'

'It's hard to explain. Imagine you're looking at a lake. A breeze causes small ripples on the water. You are facing the sun. Because of these things, the sunshine and the ripples, you can't see what's in the lake. All you can see is the light on the water, the flecks of golden sunlight on the ripples. You can see nothing of what's under it. Now imagine a cloud momentarily hides the sun and the wind drops. The golden freckles disappear, the surface is flat, and you find you can now discern rocks, plants, and the creatures that make up what is in the lake.'

Meshi was puzzled.

'The lake is the future,' Syramos continued. 'The sunlight on the water is what conceals it from us. That is all that most people see. The cloud that hides the sun is the rhymer's trance, enabling him or her to still the ripples of time and look into what the lake contains. But it's not as simple as I make it sound. Sometimes however deep the trance, the sun continues to shine. The golden freckles stay and they continue to hide everything. And sometimes what is in there can be seen but cannot be explained.'

Meshi leant forward eagerly. 'But when the sun does go in and the water's clear, is it there? Is the whole of the future there, spread out for you to look at?'

'No,' said Syramos, and Meshi's face fell. 'The future isn't like that. Think about it. What the future contains depends on what happens in the present. What is done today determines what will occur tomorrow.' Meshi looked troubled again. 'Some events can't be changed and their effects are fixed. For example, if I chop down that tree over there, it stays chopped down. It can't be unchopped, restored to how it was. If I squash that lizard,' he pointed to a large, green one scuttling over the ground, 'it ceases to exist. The future continues without it. The plants and the insects it would have eaten are spared, or they're consumed by something else. Do you understand?'

Meshi shook his head.

'Well, a simple illustration is that if you were to fall out with a friend there would be a range of possible outcomes. You might stop speaking to each other. You might shake hands and continue as before. Or you might remain friends but with the nature of your friendship altered. Because people change all the time it's unlikely that any of these states would be permanent. They would evolve, one flowing into another. What I'm saying is that the circumstances at one point in time will be different from those at another. When I see into the future it's like that. I don't see final solutions, I see part of an ongoing story.'

'You mean, what you see in the future depends on when you look at it?'

Syramos had always thought that Meshi was rather dull, but perhaps he'd misjudged the boy. Why hadn't he put it like that? 'Yes, that is exactly what I mean.'

'Then how do you know what to say to people?' Meshi asked.

'Often I don't. Some rhymers get into trouble because they say things as they see them and people make decisions based on that, only to find that situations don't work out as they'd expected. It's one of the things that gets rhymers a bad name.'

'What can you do about it?'

'The best course is to be vague. I don't make specific predictions, rather I rely on possibilities. So, for example, if a mother-to-be asks me if her unborn baby will have a good life I make a reply which is positive and encouraging, but with the inference that it depends on what she and her partner provide for the child. Similarly, if a merchant asks me to foretell the prospects for the success of a trading voyage he is planning I trim my answer with references to the weather, pirates, the market, and his own record of success.'

'Isn't that cheating?'

'No. I tell people what I can from the incomplete picture before me.'

There was silence while the huge question marks floated around the room.

'So you can't tell where Yalka is,' said Meshi.

'No,' said Syramos, and Meshi had never seen him so dejected.

'But you can tell where she will be, although not when.'

'Yes,' said Syramos. 'That is possible.'

'Then do it,' said Meshi. 'Please.'

Syramos didn't respond.

'Do it, please,' Meshi persisted.

Syramos sighed. 'Whatever happens, while I am in the trance you must not touch me,' he said. 'You must promise me that.'

Meshi nodded, and Syramos took from his pocket the small wooden box that Meshi knew contained his armanca. He extracted from it a small stub of the dried root and studied it. To Meshi it looked like a pellet of horse dung. Syramos lay back in his chair, placed it on his tongue, closed his eyes, and began to chew slowly. His breathing slowed and deepened, and Meshi thought he had fallen asleep. Then the old man started to tremble. It began slowly at first, in his hands. Then it spread along his arms, through his shoulders and into his chest. Now his legs were trembling too, and soon his whole body was shaking. The chair was shaking. Meshi was alarmed. Was he ill? He reached forward, worried that Syramos might shake himself out of the chair and onto the floor, but then he remembered the instruction not to touch.

Suddenly the spasm stopped and the old man went rigid, with the muscles in his face and neck like cords and his knuckles white, as his hands gripped the chair. He wasn't breathing. Meshi was on the verge of panic, ready to break his promise, desperate to do anything that would end what he thought must be a fit.

And abruptly it was over. Syramos collapsed like an unstrung puppet and he flopped back. For a moment he remained like that, and then slowly he looked up. He seemed exhausted and he regarded Meshi as if he were a stranger.

'Are you all right?' the boy asked anxiously. 'Can I get you anything?'

'Water,' Syramos said in a hoarse voice.

Meshi filled a glass from the jug on the table and Syramos sipped, a little at first and then great gulps, draining it all.

'Did you see something?' Meshi asked, anxiously.

'Yes. No. I am not sure. The lake is murky. I did not see Yalka but I felt a dreadful movement, as if the whole of the living world, nature, the cosmos, was going through some sort of struggle.'

Meshi was horrified. 'What does it mean?'

'It means that there is to be a violent upheaval and a reckoning. It will involve you, me, Yalka, Peglar, all of the people we know. Its epicentre will be the City of Chamaris.'

Meshi was fearful. 'What does it mean?''

'It means that we must ready ourselves. We must leave here. We must go to a place near the city where we can wait and prepare.'

Meshi was horrified. 'We can't leave. We haven't found Yalka. Suppose she comes back and we're not here.'

'She will not. She has gone. I do not know where she is now, but I know where she will be. We must go to Maris Partem.'

4

BAIT

Yalka felt… she was…

In truth, she didn't know how or what she was feeling. When the urchin had snatched her bag in Fountain Square she had been irate at the snivelling little runt who had tricked her. Then she'd been consumed by vengeance. She'd get her bag back and smack the ignorant little turd who'd grabbed it around the ears.

And so she'd chased him, and when she realised he'd given her the slip the previous emotions gave way to frustration. Then there was the shock of her capture, followed by fear. Next came the embarrassment of being displayed like a piece of meat in front of a row of ogling men, only slightly eased by the satisfaction that her sale price had been higher than that paid for any of the other women. That was followed by curiosity: who had bought her? why? Finally came the icy dread when she discovered the answers to those questions.

Big Ears, or Verron to give the man his proper name, greeted her with a sneer. He was the last man in the world she wanted to see. The night he'd followed her home from The Quiet Woman would be always with her. She was fit and strong and a good fighter, and she might have got away from him, but she'd been drunk and Big Ears had been heavy on top of her. His foul breath was in her face. His disgusting hands pulled at her clothing as he tried to get into her. Then she'd been aware of an impact and he'd slumped like a butchered ox, the fight knocked out of him. It was Meshi, who had turned up, seen what was happening, picked up a lump of wood and smacked Big Ears on the head. Yalka knew that without Meshi's intervention her attacker would have done what he wanted with her. She would have been left, broken and bleeding, to survive or not. And now here he was again, ready to finish off what he'd started on that night. This time there would be no Meshi to step in. This time she really was on her own. This time she would not get away.

Yalka's usual responses to danger or menace were defiance and anger, but this time it had been different. This time she felt as though her insides had been torn out. Her legs threatened to give way and it was only by an act of sheer will that she managed to avoid falling in a faint. Instead, she gritted her teeth and faced her persecutor.

All right, let's get it over with, she thought. 'What do you want from me?' she growled. And then she got another shock.

'I don't want anything from you, blondie.' Big Ears was leering at her in that creepy way he had. 'You just have to come with me, that's all.'

'What do I have to do?' She had been afraid that she could guess the answer, but it wasn't what she expected.

'Do? You will do absolutely nothing. You'll just wait.'

'Wait? What for? Where?'

Then he explained the plan, Ragul's plan, the reason why Verron had been instructed to outbid all the other buyers, no matter how many crowns it took.

'We'll take you away, blondie, and put you in a house. It will be a nice house, and comfortable. And you'll be looked after. But you'll have to stay there.'

It was bewildering. What was this imprisonment for? Was it some sort of punishment?

'For how long?'

'That depends on how long it takes your boyfriend to find you. We'll spread it around that Lord Ragul has captured you, and we'll make it known where you've been taken. Then we'll simply wait for that little shit to come creeping out of hiding to rescue you, and when he does, we'll have him.'

She was bait; it was as crude as that. Peglar was her friend and she did not doubt that if he learnt what had happened to her he would seek her out. Wherever he was and whatever he was doing, he would drop everything and come to help her. She had no way of warning him. She was being set up to lure him into a trap, and she was powerless to prevent it.

'Follow me.' Big Ears went ahead into a shed beside the barn that had been used for the sale. There was another man behind her to prevent her from running away.

It was an office of sorts, a very untidy one. There were heaps of papers on every surface, and boxes piled higgledy-piggledy on shelves and chairs. Outside the door at the other end of the room was the biggest dog Yalka had ever seen.

'That's Safren,' said Big Ears. 'Best avoided if you

want to keep those nice legs of yours.' He pointed to a bowl on the table, with a hunk of bread beside it. 'Eat,' he said. 'It's a long journey and you'll need your strength.' He went out, slamming the door.

Yalka didn't think she could face food, but she hadn't eaten since the previous day so she made herself taste what was in the bowl. It was soup, and better than anything she'd had since she'd been snatched. She broke off some of the bread. It was crusty and fresh. She ate, drinking from the bowl and wiping it with the bread.

She'd almost finished when Verron came back, carrying a bundle of clothes.

'Here you are, blondie,' he said, dropping them on the floor beside her. 'Not high fashion, I know, but you're not going out anywhere or seeing anybody so it don't matter what you look like. Pick something, get out of them rags, and put it on. And don't hang about, we're leaving.'

She wouldn't have been surprised if Verron had remained in the room to watch her dress, and she was relieved when he left her alone. The clothes were of a better quality and fit than she'd expected. She told herself that things didn't seem to be going too badly. It seemed true that at the moment Verron wanted nothing from her, although who knew how long that might last. But over everything hung the threat to Peglar. She had to find a way to broadcast some sort of warning.

She'd chosen what to wear and put it on, and was retying her hair when Verron came back with another man.

'You ready, blondie?' he said, and then, looking her up and down, 'Ah, don't you look sweet. Doesn't she look a picture?' he said, turning to his companion.

The other man made a noise that indicated appreciation and agreement.

Yalka looked down at her bare feet. 'I've got no shoes.'

'No shoes,' said Verron. 'Now there's a thing.' He nodded to the other man. 'Should we give her some, do you think?'

The man looked at her feet and pretended to consider. 'If she's got no shoes it makes it harder for her to run away, don't it? So I say no.'

'I like your logic,' said Verron. 'What's more, she doesn't need 'em because she doesn't have to walk.'

'Don't I?' Yalka was relieved. Walking or running weren't problems for her. She enjoyed both, but the thought of trudging along between these two men was demoralising,

'No, my lady,' said Verron. 'You have a carriage, a very special one.'

He made a low, mocking bow and the other man laughed. When they led her outside she saw why. The "carriage" was no more than a large metal box on wheels. The two shafts sticking out from the front of it looked as though they'd been lashed on by a monkey, and between them was a large horse. The box had a door but no windows. Verron opened it and she peered inside. There was a wooden bench that looked extremely uncomfortable and a grubby-looking rug, but the worst things by far were the heat and the smell. The sun had turned the box into an oven, and as she leant in to inspect it she was hit by a stifling, stinking blast. It smelt as though a past user had both vomited in there and used it as a lavatory.

'You want me to get in that? Really?'

'My my, blondie, you are quick,' said Verron. 'Yes, I want you to get in that.'

'I can't. It's disgusting.'

'Yes, you can. And if you have a problem, me and my friend here will help you. Now shift your pretty arse.'

Verron's accomplice moved towards her, rubbing his hands and grinning. It seemed that yet again she had no choice.

'Where are we going?' she said.

'Verlam,' Verron said.

'Where's Verlam?' Yalka had heard the name but she couldn't place where it was. She hoped it wasn't far because a long journey in the foul box would be unbearable.

'It's off the road to Maris Partem, a few miles from Chamaris.'

She was incredulous. 'A few miles from Chamaris? It will take ages to get there.'

'A couple of days, maybe,' Verron agreed.

The idea was impossible. 'But I can't spend two days in that thing,' she said, banging the metal side of the box. It clanged like a bin.

'Oh, I think you can,' said Verron. 'It's amazing what people can do when they set their minds to it.'

'I'll suffocate. I'll be cooked. Why can't I go on a cart? Or ride the horse? Or at least be in something with windows?'

Veron stood back and folded his arms. 'Well I'm sorry the transport isn't up to your ladyship's high standards,' he said, 'but it's what there is. We need to get you to Verlam so we can tell the world where you are. But you mustn't be seen on the way.'

'Whyever not?'

'Because if Peglar were to find out he might be tempted to try to rescue you while you were on the road, before we were ready for him, and that wouldn't do.'

'Your fancy plan won't work if I'm stifled in that box. Peglar won't come looking for me if I'm dead.'

Verron gave her his thin-lipped smile. He was enjoying this. How she detested him!

'He won't know, will he? You see, when you come to think about it we don't really need you at all. So long as we spread the rumour that you're in Verlam you could be anywhere. Or nowhere. If it were up to me I'd just get rid of you, but Lord Ragul wants you there in person, so...' He shrugged. Then he must have noted her stricken face and felt a little compassion because he said, 'We'll make sure you've got enough water, and we'll pull off the road for a couple of hours in the hottest part of the day and park in the shade so you can cool off a bit. That do for you, blondie?'

It had to. At least he was making some concessions. She took a deep breath and climbed into the airless coffin. A water skin was thrown in after her, and the door banged shut. She sat on the bench, leant back and closed her eyes.

The stench was awful and it took her a few minutes to overcome a strong urge to throw up. She was in the dark, although not quite. There were a few chinks of light where the metal had been damaged, and in one corner a small patch had rusted through. The box seemed to have been a container of some sort because beneath the general stench of vomit it had a chemical odour. The slatted bench was only a narrow shelf, and extremely uncomfortable. She couldn't sit on it without banging her head on the roof so she moved to the floor and tried to settle herself there.

Then she heard a shout, there was a sudden jerk, and the contraption lurched forward.

It was worse than she'd imagined. The thing had no springing at all, and every bump, rock, and hole in the road produced a bone-jarring jolt. All Yalka could do to stop herself from being batted about like butter in a churn was to hold on tight to the bench and try to use the rug as a cushion. The effort of that, and the heat, which had started to build as soon as the door was shut, meant that she was soon dripping with sweat. The water skin was useless because she didn't have a free hand to grasp it, and if she had the box was lurching about too much for her to hold it to her mouth.

The horse's hooves clattered, the wheels rumbled, and the box clanged and swung. The heat built, and soon her head was throbbing. After what seemed an eternity they stopped, the door opened, and she was let out. Her legs were weak and she could hardly stand. Her ribs were battered and bruised from repeated collisions with the bench, and she had an agonising thirst. She leant on one of the wheels of the cart and fished out the water skin. The water was warm and tasted foul, but she drank until her dizziness improved.

When she looked around she expected to see buildings but there were none. It was dusk, and in the far, far distance she could see the lights of what must be Chamaris, twinkling faintly. It was still a long way away. Could she survive in the box for the hours it would take to cover that distance?

'That's it for today, blondie,' Verron said. 'The horse

34

needs a rest, so does the driver, and so do I. My arse is raw from sitting on top of that thing.'

And what about me? thought Yalka, who'd had it worse than either of the men.

'Where will we stay?' she said.

'Why here, of course,' said Verron.

She looked around helplessly. There was nothing.

'Get that rug out and put it down over there,' said Verron, indicating a brown patch of sandy earth. 'If you get cold you can snuggle up to me and I'll warm you.' He let out a lewd guffaw, an irritating, humourless sound.

His companion was giving the horse some water, and Verron squatted and opened a wicker container. 'There's some bread here, and some cheese,' he said.

She ignored it. The stink of the box was in her system and the very idea of food made her gag. She dragged out the rug, threw it on the ground and painfully lowered herself onto it. She was asleep in a moment, but her rest didn't last long. The ground was hard and she ached so much that she couldn't find any comfortable position. And there were the mosquitoes. The place was alive with them. Normally they didn't trouble her, but this particular batch seemed fascinated by her and soon she was itching from where they'd feasted.

Verron and his associate lay a few paces away. They were both snoring and they seemed sound asleep. That set her wondering. Could she escape? Could she get up and run away? No, not run, she couldn't do that in her present state but she could walk. But where would she go? There were no signs of life near. It would be worth a try, though, and better than more hours in the tin box. If she could get away and hide, the plot to snare Peglar would collapse. She'd wait a few more minutes, then go. She lay on one side, using the rug to try to shield herself from the biting insects.

The next thing she knew Verron was standing over her banging two tin mugs together. It was dawn but not yet fully light.

'Breakfast is served,' he said.

He pointed to a loaf of bread on top of the wicker box. She was hungry and so she broke some off. It was coarse and hard.

'The facilities for females are over there,' said Verron, pointing to a bush a few yards off the road. 'We won't look.' He winked, and again treated her to his obnoxious weasellish laugh.

Yalka had no use for the bush. Her body felt like a dried husk and she didn't think she could wring any moisture from it.

'When will we be there?' she said,

The other man looked in the direction of Chamaris. 'By tonight, all being well. So long as we don't stop in the middle of the day.'

'Two hours off in the worst of the heat, or keep going and sweat it out. It makes no odds to us, blondie, so it's your shout,' said Verron.

'Let's keep going,' she said.

RYKER'S OFFICE

P eglar was at the desk in what Ryker called 'the office.' In reality, it was little more than a lean-to built against the wall of the barn where the slave auctions were held. He supposed he was lucky. The pirates who'd captured The Morning Glory hadn't known who he was, and so they hadn't killed him, or worse, taken him to Chamaris to hand him over to Ragul. Then, instead of being sold for slavery the slave dealer, Ryker, had seen that he was different from the others and could be useful. He kept him, and set him to make sense of the chaos of paperwork that choked the tiny space.

The job was simple enough to explain but almost impossible to accomplish: he was to go through the papers and put them in an order which would enable Ryker to retrieve any he might need. This was the same Ryker who appeared to have difficulty reading even the simplest material. However, daunting though the task might be, it did give him access to the record of the sales of slaves, and he hoped that would enable him to learn who had bought the friends he'd made on The Morning Glory and where they'd been taken. Even more important to him was that he might find the record relating to the sale of a female slave that these same friends had told him of. A female whose description, incredible as it may seem, resembled Yalka; the girl he'd lost, the girl he thought he might never see again.

He'd been working for several days but seemed to have made no progress in locating what he was looking for. Ryker's method of storing the documents was simply to chuck them all in together – receipts, bills of sale, letters, statements, notes, all sorts of jumbled fragments – and whenever he looked for one his haphazard searching overthrew any previous order. The effect of this was that although it was logical to expect the most recent items to be nearest the top of the heap, that wasn't the case.

Now he was looking forlornly at a clutch of papers. Some were torn, some crumpled, and some had rings from the bottoms of glasses and mugs. The only thing that seemed to be in any sort of order was a big ledger. It was worn and many of the pages were loose but it noted some of the sales. The slaves weren't named but they were described. It was easy to find his shipmates from The Morning Glory – Allendur, Reddall and Beldrom: 'Three males, white, in sound health, about twenty-five to forty.' There was also the name of their buyer and details of where they'd been taken. Peglar recognised the name of the place and he had a feeling that it was one of the farms owned by his father, over in the direction of Rasturoth.

He turned the page, and there she was. 'Female, white, blonde, good shape, about seventeen.' That would have been enough, but what came at the end hit him like a thunderbolt. 'Egg-shaped birthmark on left cheek.' It had to be Yalka, there was no one else it could be. He'd seen a few other women with facial marks but they were usually on their foreheads. And the age: seventeen. And the hair: blonde. It must be her. Now where was she?

The name of her buyer was given as Verron, and the destination was listed as Verlam. He knew where that was, near Maris Partem. She'd be going almost back home. It was obvious that Allendur and the others had been bought to work on the land. When Peglar considered why this Verron individual might have bought Yalka the possibilities made him sick. He had to find her, he had to get her away from him.

He knew it wouldn't be easy. He couldn't go after her alone. That would most likely result in him being caught and then neither of them would be free. He needed to get help. Alendur, Redall and Beldrom were a very useful trio and the obvious – in truth the only – option. Find them, free them, enlist their help. Simple.

But first, he must get out of there himself, and he had no idea how to do that. Ryker was a relaxed jailer, but a jailer he was and his regime was tight enough to make escape difficult. Peglar spent his waking hours working in the office/hut. He had a sleeping space in a stuffy alcove behind the shelves. He was allowed out only three times a day. First thing in the morning he would empty his chamber pot and wash in a tub of greenish rainwater in the yard. In the middle of the day, he would get ten minutes for what Ryker called 'a leg stretcher'. And at the eighth bell, when his work was done, he was permitted to go to a hut at the end of the yard that contained a foul, stinking closet. None of these excursions offered any possibility of escape. The yard was bounded by a high fence, but the main problem was that he was under the unwavering scrutiny of a creature. It was probably a dog but it was the size of a bear, and it certainly growled like one. Its name, he was told, was Safren.

Safren was huge, and a dark, gingery brown. Its hair was thick, like fur. It had heavy jowls, a slobbering maw, and nasty-looking yellow teeth. It watched Peglar whenever he left the office, and when he was inside it the animal guarded the door. It punctuated his day with low growls and snarls, continually reminding him of the impossibility of running away.

'I need this lot all sorted,' Ryker had said when he introduced him to the mountain of papers, 'so I can find things. My old woman used to do it but her eyes have been going and they're so bad now that she can't manage. She gets tired and her head aches.'

It took less than an hour for Peglar to see why it gave Ryker's "old woman" a headache. It gave him one, too. The obvious thing to do was to put the documents in date order, but there were no dates on many of them. Instead, they were numbered, but there were different numbering systems – 1, 2, 3; A, B, C; I, II, III; Aa, Ab, Ac. and so on – with no way of telling their significance or which system succeeded another. By the end of day three he'd sorted all the documents according to the type of number system they showed. There were nine heaps covering the desk, some of them staggering and threatening to fall, and he stared at them morosely, his dejection deepening by the hour. What would be Ryker's reaction when he discovered that he was unable to do what was wanted? Most probably he'd put him back into the slave market and get rid of him.

Then he had an idea.

The eighth bell had long sounded when Ryker came into the office, grumbling about some merchant he thought was trying to diddle him. Peglar listened patiently and made sympathetic noises. Then he said, 'You told me your wife used to manage your paperwork.'

'You mean my Berissa. Yes, she did, till her eyes got bad. She had everything ship-shape, all in proper order.'

Given the way things were now, Peglar doubted that, but he had to choose his words carefully. He must convey that he needed help without giving the idea that the job was impossible.

'Your wife has used her own scheme to number the papers. I can see that it's very carefully worked out and it does a great job, but there are a couple of things about it that I don't understand. Would it be possible for me to meet her so she can explain it to me? I don't want to risk putting things in the wrong place, where you might not be able to find them later. And it could save me time.'

Ryker laughed. 'But time is the one thing that you've got plenty of.' Peglar waited. This wasn't the answer he wanted. 'I'll see,' Ryker said at last. 'It won't do no good, though. Berissa won't be able to help you. She's blind as a bat.'

He went, leaving Peglar to spend another night in the cramped alcove. His bedding was smelly but there had been no suggestion from Ryker about any sort of replacement. How long could he stand the boring days and disagreeable nights? He'd been trying to maintain any fitness that he might still retain by doing some of the exercises that Cestris had shown him, but there was no room to move properly and he felt sluggish from his sedentary life. On top of that, his poor diet had clogged up his insides. It was worse than being on The Morning Glory. But what were his options? With Safren outside the door there was no chance of escape. He thought about starting a blaze and setting fire to the papers. That would get rid of his job. The problem was that it might also get rid of him.

He was considering this when the door opened and Ryker came in, leading a woman by the hand. She was cloaked and bent, and she felt ahead of her with a cane, tapping on the floor.

'This is my old woman,' Ryker said. 'Berissa.' He turned to the woman. 'This here is Peglar,' he said, bending to face her and raising his voice. 'He's making sense of the papers and he needs you to tell him what you were doing.' He looked back to Peglar. 'She won't be able to see nothing but she might manage to give you a pointer or two.'

'Thank you,' said Peglar. Then, raising his voice too, 'I'm pleased to meet you, Madam Berissa. I need your help.'

Berissa looked vaguely in his direction but not directly at him.

'See what I told you?' Ryker said to her, shouting again. 'This one's a classy act. He's too good to sell. When he's done here we might keep him.'

Berissa didn't reply.

'Well, I'll leave you to it,' said Ryker. Peglar was aware that the door wasn't locked this time, which was a surprise. More surprising still was the change that came over Berissa as soon as Ryker left. She straightened her back, lay down her cane, and pushed back her hood. Peglar saw at once that she was nowhere near as old as she'd looked when she came in. In fact, Ryker's 'old woman' must have been some years younger than Ryker himself. He got another shock when her eyes fully opened, she looked at the heaps of papers and then at Peglar.

'So he's got you on this, has he?' She let out a cackle that would not have disgraced a witch. 'You poor boy.'

Peglar was astounded. This was not the blind old woman Ryker had led him to expect. He had no words.

Berissa cackled again. 'Your face! Not what you thought, eh?' She waved towards the table. 'He used to have me on this. Day after day. It drove me crazy. I could see these stinking papers in my sleep. And it's not as if he needs them. He hardly ever looks at them, and when he does he can't properly read them so if you do sort them out he simply mixes them up again. He just piles everything up. Bills too. He leaves those until the people he owes get mad enough to send somebody to collect their money, and then he pays whatever they ask. Some of them have got wise to that now and they ask for more than they're owed.'

Peglar could make no sense of what he was hearing and seeing. 'But your husband told me you were blind,' he said loudly.

The woman winced. 'There's no need to shout. Ryker shouts at me because he thinks being blind is the same as being deaf.'

Peglar was lost. 'You're not blind.'

There was the cackle again, this time accompanied by a snort. 'No, I'm not. I can see as well as you can but I just had to get away from this cell and all Ryker's

43

rubbish. So I thought, I'll pretend my eyes are failing, and that's what I did. Of course, I had to make it seem convincing. I couldn't just wake up one morning and tell him I couldn't see, so I pretended over the weeks that my sight was getting worse, so he would agree there was no point having me here.'

'And it worked.'

'Like a dream. Naturally, I have to act up a bit when he's at home, and when I'm out with him. You know, walk into things, drop stuff. But when he's not there, and that's most of the time, I can just be normal.' She smiled at him. It was friendly and warm. 'So, young man, that's my story. Now what's yours? And in particular, what's your plan for getting out of this shithole.'

Peglar was dumb. He was astounded Berissa should say that. Was she implying she would help him?

'You don't have a plan, do you,' she said. 'Well, you'd better get one. His nibs' idea to keep you is a non-starter. He'll have to sell you because he'll need the money. A fine young man like you with lots of work in him will fetch a good price and Ryker's near skint. So what are you going to do?'

Peglar felt hopeless. 'I don't know.'

Berissa looked at the door. 'Does he lock that at night?'

'Yes.'

'I thought so.' She slid from the chair and knelt on the floor. There was a narrow gap under the bottom shelf and she extended her hand into it and fumbled around. At first she didn't seem able to locate what she wanted, but then she did and withdrew her hand. She wiped away the dust and cobwebs she'd collected on her arm and sleeve and held something out towards Peglar. 'You'll need this.' And when Peglar didn't take it, 'It's a key. To the door. Take it, hide it, and when you get the chance, get out and get the fuck away.' Still Peglar didn't react. 'What's the matter with you?'

'Thank you. But I can't. Getting through the door's one thing, but then there's the dog.'

'You mean Safren?' Berissa's cackle seemed somehow mocking. She stood up. 'Here,' she said, 'come with me.'

Berissa went through the door and Peglar heard the rattle of the chain and a low growl as the big dog stood up.

'Come on,' she said, looking back over her shoulder.

Peglar eased himself through the door, wary and ready to dash back inside. Berissa was standing beside Safren. The beast looked monstrous. Its head came well above her waist. Its eyes were glassy and it was drooling, and making a low rumbling sound deep in its throat. She rubbed its head, on top, between its ears and its tail wagged, hammering a tattoo against the wooden wall. She reached into a pocket in her cloak, pulled something out, and slipped it into the animal's mouth.

'Meet Safren,' she said. 'The noisiest guard dog in all the seven cities, but also the daftest.'

Peglar wasn't persuaded. 'But the size of it. And those teeth. And he growls all the time.'

'He? He?' said Berissa. 'Well, you'd better get that right for a start. Just take a look at the underparts. This here is a lady dog. And she's a sweetie. She loves having her head scratched, and she'll do anything for food. Give her some treats. Get to know her.'

'But the growling.'

'All show. A nervous twitch.' Peglar didn't move. 'Come on, she won't bite.'

That was exactly what Peglar was afraid she would do, but he edged forward.

'Here, make friends.' Berissa reached out, took his hand and placed it on Safren's head. She stooped and looked into the creature's face. 'This here is a friend,' she said to it. Then to Peglar, 'Scratch her head, just there.' She guided Peglar's hand to the spot and he rubbed. 'See? She likes it.'

Peglar continued rubbing and moved closer. Safren began to make a noise like a cat's purr but in a far deeper register. She leant against him and her weight made Peglar step back.

'You've got the key and you've got Safren. All you have to do is make sure that every meal you get you save her a little something. She's particularly partial to sausage.'

There was a sound at the end of the barn. They both knew what it was and hurried through the door. Berissa pulled her hood back, grabbed her cane, and resumed her stoop. Peglar scrambled behind the desk. They were only just in time.

'So how are you two wise owls getting on?' said Ryker as he came through the door. He looked at Peglar. 'Has my old lady been useful? Have you got everything sorted?'

'Oh yes,' said Peglar. 'It's been very useful. I have everything I need.'

6

ON THE ROAD

The preparations for leaving Semilvarga took time. Meshi's distraction meant that he was unfocused and kept starting jobs but not finishing them, and Syramos seemed increasingly infirm, often losing the thread of a conversation and failing to complete a statement or instruction.

The priority was to get hold of some form of transport. Syramos insisted that he could walk, but it was a long way from Semilvarga to Maris Partem and while Meshi could manage it the distance was much too great for the old man. When they'd arrived in Semilvarga a few weeks ago Syramos had sold the horse and the carriage that they'd used to get there. He'd said they wouldn't need them any more, and now they did. Couldn't a rhymer see that? It was another example of what Meshi thought was the unreliability of rhyming, and he was coming to the conclusion that the whole business was very hit-and-miss, with quite a lot of miss.

Syramos gave Meshi some money and he went to look for something that would take them to Maris

Partem, a cart or a carriage and a horse or mule. All the carriages he could find were falling apart or cost more than he had. It seemed that something with wheels was out of the question and they would have to make do with just a horse. He found one that looked sturdy but it had a problem with one of its feet. The seller assured him it was nothing to worry about, merely a slight strain caused by a bad landing from a jump a couple of days before, and promised Meshi that it would soon be gone. The boy believed him and handed over the cash.

Most of what Syramos had owned had been destroyed in the fire that burnt his home along with the rest of the River Settlements, and Meshi had almost nothing, so they had little to pack. They stowed what they had in a pair of leather bags and Meshi slung one on each side of the horse's saddle. He stroked the animal's nose and walked around it. It seemed good-tempered and willing. He just hoped that the injured foot wouldn't turn out to be a problem. Would it make sense to wait a few days to give it more time to heal? Probably, but Syramos was impatient and said they should go to Maris Partem without delay. So they left, with Syramos mounted on the horse and Meshi leading it by a rope.

At the beginning of their journey the road was busy, with people from nearby farms and villages coming into Semilvarga with produce to sell, but as they got farther from the city it quietened and the road emptied. The horse plodded on and Syramos seemed to be dozing. Meshi looked at the flat road stretching before them across the dusty plain. It appeared endless, and he realised what a long and boring way it was going to be. The horse's limp was getting worse, and he wondered if there was the possibility of swapping the animal for another at one of the farms on the way. He halted and looked up to Syramos on the saddle.

'The horse has got a problem,' he said. 'I think its foot is worse than the seller let on. I think we're going to have to stop and get it looked at. What about there?' Meshi pointed to a group of buildings in the middle distance, a mile or so off the main road. 'Might there be a horse healer in that village, do you think? We could turn off and see.'

'That's Murgo,' said Syramos.

'Oh,' said Meshi. Should that mean something to him? It didn't.

Syramos spoke with fierce distaste. 'Murgo is a viper's den, a snake's pit. It's nothing but gambling houses, drug marts, brothels, and inns. There's a slave market too. There will not be a horse healer in that hole. There will be nothing of any benefit to man or beast. We will not be going there.'

'Right,' said Meshi, surprised at the intensity of this attack. Surely it was worth a try. Nevertheless, he led the horse past the turning and continued down the road. It was clear that they would not be going to Murgo, but regardless of that, the animal needed help.

The morning wore on, the sun climbed higher, and the heat built. When it was at its hottest Syramos gestured towards a clump of trees near the edge of the road.

'Let us stop there and rest for a while until the sun is past its peak.'

Meshi led the horse into the clearing, where all three of them could enjoy the cool canopy, and helped Syramos down. There was a small, ramshackle kiosk sharing the shade, and while Syramos hobbled over to investigate it Meshi examined the horse's foot. The animal was patient, as if it knew that he was trying to help it, but it winced when he touched the hoof. Would it be able to walk to Maris Partem? Meshi was doubtful.

Syramos came back from the kiosk with two wooden bowls and held one out to Meshi.

'What is it?'

'Kurds and honey. Try it.'

Meshi filled his spoon and took a mouthful. The texture was unusual, slimy and flakey at the same time, but the taste wasn't bad. You might even say it was nice, although there was a bitter layer underlying the sweetness. Still, it was welcome. Meshi was hungry and he ate it all and licked out his bowl. Syramos finished most of his and Meshi returned the bowls and spoons to the kiosk.

He was turning away from the counter when he heard a noise in the distance. It was like somebody running wild in a blacksmith's forge, a clattering, clanging racket of metal sheets being banged together. He looked along the road and saw something approaching rapidly, coming from Semilvarga and heading the way they were going. The cloud of dust it was raising at first masked what it was, but as it came nearer he could see it was a horse pulling a metal tank on wheels. The contraption bounced and lurched on the ruts and gulleys, and that was what was making the din. There were two men on top of it, one of them driving, both of them hanging on tight.

Instinctively Meshi stepped back, away from the road and under the trees. The thing was nearer, upon them, and then with a boneshaking din, it was past.

'Blood and bones, what was that?' said the woman in the kiosk as the contrivance vanished down the road.

'Some kind of tin coffin on wheels,' said her partner. They all looked to where it was receding.

'What a racket. And did you see the speed it was going? And bouncing around like that.'

Meshi was speechless. It wasn't just the careering box and the sweating horse, it was one of the men on top of it, the companion to the driver. He would have known him anywhere. For some minutes he couldn't speak. His heart raced and his legs were leaden.

Syramos could see that something was wrong. He put a hand on Meshi's shoulder. 'My boy, you've gone white. What is the matter?'

Meshi found his voice. 'That man, on that tank thing, the man with the driver. He was the one who attacked Yalka. The one I brained and who was looking for me.'

'Are you sure?' said Syramos.

'Yes. I'd know him anywhere. He's got great big ears and a mean face. If he saw me I'm in trouble.'

'He won't have seen you,' said Syramos. 'You were tucked well into the shade and that thing they were on was past us in no time. Besides, bouncing around like that he would have a problem picking out his own mother.'

'They were going like there was a herd of bulls after them,' said the kiosk woman. 'Anyway, what do you think can have been in that box?'

'I don't know,' said her partner, 'but I hope it wasn't anything fragile.'

Syramos was looking thoughtful. 'I've never before seen anything like that tin cart and I get an uneasy feeling from it, auras of pain, fear, and evil. The men were heading in the direction of Maris Partem,' he said. 'We must keep a sharp lookout for them and be on our guard.'

Meshi was on edge. Suppose Big Ears had seen him but had been in too much of a hurry to stop then, and now he was waiting farther along the road to ambush them. Suppose Big Ears and his companion weren't going to Maris Partem but were taking their ramshackle box somewhere else and now, having dropped it off, they were on their way back and any minute they would appear, coming along the road towards them. Fortunately, the road was dead straight so he could see from a long way off if anything was approaching.

It took them three more days to get to Maris Partem, and every minute of that time Meshi was on tenterhooks. The good thing was that their horse's leg improved. Meshi had thought that the animal would never last and they'd be forced to find a replacement, but the woman in the kiosk had come to their rescue.

'Your horse has got a bad leg,' her partner said to Meshi.

'I know,' said the boy. 'It's been like that since we got her, and it's getting worse. I've looked to see if there's a stone in her hoof but I can't see anything. The man who sold her to us said it was because she landed badly from a jump.'

'Have you checked for blotches on the sole? That would show if it's bruised.'

'It's not that,' the woman interrupted. She sounded exasperated. 'It's a tendon.' She searched under the counter and brought out a small pot which she held out to Meshi. 'Here, rub this on it twice a day.'

'What is it?' He opened the lid and took a sniff. It smelt foul and he recoiled.

'It's a concoction I've devised. It's pounded tripe and pig fat, but the important ingredient is my own secret collection of herbs.' She placed her forefinger along her nose and winked. 'Rub it in well and it will be better in no time.'

The smell of the stuff was almost enough to turn Meshi's stomach, but he took a deep breath, loaded some onto his finger and smeared it on the horse's fetlock and pastern, rubbing it in as he'd been told.

To say it was an instant cure would be exaggerating, but it was remarkably effective. Within a couple of hours the limp was improving and after two more applications, that evening and the following morning, the horse was not only walking almost normally but it seemed quite lively. Syramos invited Meshi to climb onto her back behind him, but the boy didn't want to push the animal too hard so he continued to walk, although he would have liked to ride because his legs were tired and his feet hurt.

With the horse cured they made better progress and soon Meshi could see Maris Partem in the far distance. The closer they got the more fearful he felt. Finally, and too soon for him, they were entering the streets on the western edge of the town.

'Where are we going?' he said. He was anxious not to go near The Quiet Woman, the tavern where he'd worked and which had been, and perhaps still was, a favourite haunt of Big Ears.

'Help me down,' said Syramos. Off the horse, the old man found it hard to stand upright. 'I don't know when I last spent so long in a saddle,' he said, trying to straighten up. Then he hobbled away. 'This way,' he said.

He stopped a short way along the street at a door that looked stouter than the others, reinforced with metal bands and heavily studded. Syramos pulled on a handle jutting from the doorframe and deep inside the building a bell jangled.

'Who lives here?' Meshi said.

'A woman called Acosra Flynt, and her pair, Myander. She is my conserver. She looks after my money.'

Meshi was surprised. His idea of a conserver was an elderly man sitting at a table piled high with bags full of golds and guarded by fierce attendants brandishing zircas. 'I didn't know a woman could do a job like that,' he said.

Syramos looked at him and shook his head. 'Oh, you will be surprised what a woman can achieve once she has set her mind to something.'

There was the sound of a heavy bolt being drawn back and the door opened.

7

VANCIA VIEWS VERLAM

'Point out Verlam.'

Vancia was on the balcony outside her room and she scanned the view. Far away was a line of low hills. On the left, where they met the sea, was Semilvarga, although it was much too far away to be seen clearly. Between her and the hills was a vast plain, divided by the river that snaked to the estuary at Maris Partem. She knew that many of the estates and farms that dotted the countryside belonged to the House of the Leopard. It was that rather than the majesty of the landscape that made her feel that the view was highly satisfactory.

Sainter stood behind her, lingering on the edge of the room and not venturing onto the balcony. Vancia knew he didn't like heights and that standing on the balcony made him anxious. That was why she enjoyed luring him out.

'Come closer, Lord Sainter,' she cooed, turning to him. 'Stand here beside me and point it out. I want to know exactly where Verlam is and where this wretched girl that Peglar is so smitten by is going to be lodged.'

Sainter edged out and tried to avoid looking down, but it was hard because that was exactly what he'd been asked to do.

'Verlam is near Maris Partem,' he said shakily. 'It's a little way off the road that runs from there to Semilvarga. You see that tall building in a grove of olive trees, the one with the tower? That's it.'

'Ah, yes,' said Vancia. 'Pass me that gadget.' The gadget was a telescope. It had once belonged to Peglar and she'd come across it when she'd supervised the clearing out of his quarters. 'Hold it for me.'

Sainter took the telescope and tried to direct it towards the tower.

'Moon and stars, man, hold it still,' Vancia said irritably.

Sainter rested it on his shoulder. He was so close that Vancia could smell him. It was a highly perfumed, oily aroma that didn't quite mask his body odour. It was yet another thing that made him unpleasant to work with but, Vancia told herself, he was loyal, sly, well-informed, and as committed to the destruction of Peglar as she was.

The telescope still wavered slightly but she could see the dusty road, quiet at this time of day, and not far from it a grove of olive trees surrounding what must be the tower he'd pointed out. It looked to have three floors and a low spire. Beside the tower and on the edge of the grove was a long hut. As she watched, two figures in military uniform came out and stood talking in the sunshine. One turned in her direction and she could see the golden leopard on his chest.

'Our men are there,' she said.

'Yes, madam. Lord Ragul ordered a detachment of the Household Guard to await the delivery of the girl. She should be on her way from Murgo even as we speak.'

Vancia turned from the view and let go of the telescope. Sainter scrambled and only just managed to prevent it falling from the balcony. Keeping him on his toes like this was another thing that she liked to do.

'Thank you, Lord Sainter,' she said. 'You may go.'

She waved a hand dismissively and Sainter bowed and hurried off. Vancia noted how he always seemed relieved to get away from her.

She looked back to the plain. Had Peglar heard about the girl yet? For reasons she was unable to understand he seemed to be popular among some people in the city, and beyond. Getting rid of him and his influence was a high priority. She'd removed his mother and the boy would be next. With Peglar gone there would be nothing to interfere with the smooth succession of Ragul to the Mastership of the City.

That was an event which she reasoned could not be far off. The speed of her husband's decline was astonishing. It seemed it was only a few months ago when he had been a charismatic and decisive leader, in total control. Then he'd started having problems with his eyesight. It had seemed trivial at first, no more than an irritation, but it quickly got worse. For some time he'd been able to carry on, and she'd eased herself into a position where she could help him with the administration. Over the weeks he involved her more and more. Others could have done what she did, most obviously Feldar, the Steward, but she didn't trust him, and taking on the role herself had a huge bonus: she could influence events. She realised that as her husband's sight deteriorated he was no longer able to see what he was initiating, assenting to or approving. She soon saw that this offered opportunities that she was able to turn to her advantage. Now almost everything that came from the Master's office passed through her. With Ragul in place, that would continue.

Her thoughts were interrupted by one of her waiting women.

'Madam, your next visitor is here. Chancellor Crestyn is in the ante-room.'

'Show him in.'

She came in from the balcony and advanced with her hand outstretched and her sweetest smile. She was fairly sure that the man neither liked nor entirely trusted her, so she was at pains to charm him.

'Lord Crestyn, what a pleasure it is to see you. Do sit down. Will you take tea? Or,' with a conspiratorial twinkle, 'something a little more bracing?'

'Thank you, My Lady, but no,' said Crestyn. He took the seat she'd offered.

She settled herself opposite. 'Thank you for coming, Chancellor. Now, tell me of your meeting with Lord Lembick. I'm eager to know how it went.'

Crestyn seemed to hesitate before answering. 'Lord Lembick sends his compliments. He wishes it to be clear that he has the utmost respect for the House of the Leopard, and he is truly dazzled by the qualities of your daughter, Lady Malina. Her beauty, her elegance, her charm, her wit, her...'

'Yes, of course,' Vancia interrupted. 'I'm well aware

of Malina's merits, but what does he think of our pairing proposal?'

Crestyn looked uncomfortable. 'Lord Lembick has given it a great deal of consideration, but he regrets that he cannot agree to the Bride Gold required for the hand of your daughter. He feels it is, er, a little on the high side even, and these are his words, for such a jewel.'

Vancia was surprised. 'On the high side? Five hundred golds on the high side? I thought we were being restrained.'

Crestyn looked puzzled. 'With respect, ma'am, five hundred golds was not the sum that I was instructed to ask of Lord Lembick.'

'Instructed by whom?'

'By Lord Ragul, ma'am. He told me to set the sum at one thousand.'

Vancia's jaw actually dropped, she couldn't prevent it. 'One thousand golds? Is he mad? I have never heard of any Bride Gold payment coming anywhere near that.'

'I agree entirely, ma'am, and I am relieved to hear that. Lady Malina is without doubt the most eligible young woman in this or any other city and her worth is incalculable, but such a request is enormous.'

Vancia was stupified. Her own Bride Gold had been six hundred golds, the highest sum ever paid for a pairing, and she had deliberately set her daughter's price lower. She loved Malina dearly, but not enough to accept that she was worth more as a marriage partner. And here was Ragul doubling it.

'What on earth can my son have been thinking of?'

Crestyn coughed delicately. 'I believe his decision is based on the House's current financial position and the problems we are experiencing.'

'This is making no sense to me,' she said. 'Problems of a financial nature? We are the wealthiest family in the wealthiest city on the plain. How can there be problems?'

'Sadly, ma'am, there are. For some time I have been warning that the position of the Household Treasury is not what it used to be. There have been extraordinary expenses and the reserves are being consumed at an unsustainable rate. I have been in regular discussions about the situation with Your Ladyship's husband, and more recently with Lord Ragul. I am sorry that it appears you have not been informed.'

'How can this have come about?' Vancia asked weakly. She felt lost. She had seen nothing of this in Karkis' papers, and Ragul had never mentioned it.

'There are several reasons. Some time ago Lord Karkis ordered that the Household Guard should be expanded. He was troubled by reports of unrest in the tribute cities over the amounts being demanded of them, and he was concerned about keeping the Palace safe. The strength of the Guard was almost doubled. Then there was the fire in the River Settlements. Lord Ragul admitted responsibility for this. A lawsuit was brought against him which was expensive to settle.'

'But my son took that back. He denied he'd been involved.'

Crestyn looked uncomfortable. 'Unfortunately, My Lady, the court did not believe him. They awarded a substantial sum in compensation.'

'Compensation for the Settlement dwellers?'

'Most of the money was taken in legal fees, but some did reach the Settlers.'

Vancia was seething. The notion of money from the

Household Treasury going to people like the little slut that Peglar had taken up with was intolerable.

'Then there are the harvests,' Crestyn continued. 'There have been several bad summers and yields from the farms have been low. It means that the dues paid by our tenants have been much lower than normal. Finally, there have been losses at sea. Piracy is rife. In the past year alone, four of our ships have been taken, and to make things worse another one went down in a storm and an extremely valuable cargo was lost. We could perhaps have absorbed that but the cargo wasn't ours and its owners demanded full compensation.'

Vancia's mouth was set in a firm line. How could all this have escaped her? 'How long has this been going on?' she said.

'There has been a gradual deterioration over a number of years, but several problems have come together at the same time.'

'That,' said Vancia, 'is unfortunate.'

'It is, ma'am.' Crestyn shuffled and looked uncomfortable. 'And we must not forget Lord Ragul,' he said.

'What do you mean? What about my son?'

'Well, and it pains me to say this, ma'am, but he has had our financial situation explained to him on many occasions but he either ignores what is said to him, or he is unable to grasp its relevance to him. His expenses are large and continue to grow.'

It didn't look as though it pained him to say it, Vancia thought. Rather the Chancellor seemed pleased. 'What expenses?' she snapped. 'Surely they are no more than those of any young man.'

'Sadly they are. Although he no longer rides, Lord

Ragul maintains several strings of horses. He has a vast number of personal staff. He throws large parties. He supports several spongers and hangers-on. His gambling debts are considerable. He shows no sign of attempting to bring any of this under control. When I point these matters out to him he simply says that he has to maintain the lifestyle expected of the Master's Regent.'

Vancia rarely felt out of control but she did now. She looked around her room at the opulent furnishings, at the trinkets and vases, at her extensive collection of jewellery, and at the cluster of serving women who stood in a group in the ante-room, doing nothing, simply awaiting her pleasure. That the House of the Leopard should be running out of money was unthinkable.

'I knew nothing of what you have just described. Please be straight with me, Chancellor. How serious is our position?'

'Very serious,' said Crestyn. 'The House has borrowed from several of your conservers and is in debt to some of the other houses.'

'Which?'

'Chiefly the House of the Raven and the House of the Heron. Lesser sums from a few others. I do not need to remind you, ma'am, that when there is a debt it is not just money that is owed. There are other obligations too.'

The implication of those words stayed with Vancia for some time after Crestyn had gone. The loss of financial independence would mean she would be unable to manage events in the way that she wanted. Why had she heard nothing of this from Feldar? Why had it not been mentioned in any of her husband's papers? Why had Ragul not told her? The situation must be taken in hand. She sent one of her women to summon Ragul.

His reply was both annoying and disquieting. 'Lord Ragul sends My Lady his compliments,' the woman said, 'but his knee is troubling him today. He therefore suggests that you go to him.'

Vancia thought the woman smirked as she gave this message. It was the last straw. That her son should fail to answer a summons from his mother was insufferable.

She was still angry when she arrived at his rooms. It was an awkward encounter, even though Ragul greeted her with his usual affability.

'Mummy!' he held out both hands but did not attempt to get up. 'I was just saying to Buri here how much I was looking forward to seeing you.' Burian made a bow that might have been sardonic, it was hard to say. 'Do sit down, Mummy. Your woman said that there is something you want to discuss with me.'

'There is,' said Vancia, settling herself. 'I have just been with Chancellor Crestyn. He has been updating me on the state of the Household Treasury.'

Ragul pulled a face. 'Crestyn, pah. He and Feldar are two of a kind. They have no fun themselves and they don't want anyone else to have any, either.'

'Do you know the situation?'

Ragul looked sulky. 'I might have heard something about it.' Then, like flicking a lever, his mood changed. 'But don't you worry about that, Mummy. We men will deal with that and the ladies can enjoy themselves.'

'But you're not dealing with it.'

The sulkiness returned.

Burian chipped in. 'My Lord was telling me that he

has plans. He intends to request a larger allocation from the City Assembly.'

'Yes,' Ragul agreed. 'Being the Master's Regent is an expensive business. They must realise that.'

'They will not agree.'

'Then we'll put up the rents on our estates.'

'The farmers don't have the money to pay.'

'Then I'll think of something else.'

8

SAFREN

Peglar was still wary of Safren. It was all right for Berissa to say that the growling was nothing to worry about and for her to tell Safren that Peglar was a friend, but did the animal understand that? More important, did it agree? Berissa might think that the creature was soft and sweet, and perhaps it was with her, but what was the point of having a guard dog if it didn't guard?

The main problem was that Safren gave conflicting signals. The response to any approach or unexpected movement would be a menacing snarl, resonating low in the throat. It was the sort of sound that told you that its originator not only objected to the situation but was capable of doing something about it, so you'd better watch out. It was accompanied by the baring of teeth. However, at the same time she would be wagging her tail, so which end was to be believed? Then there were the eyes. They were severely crossed, producing a manic stare that made her look completely crazy and not to be trusted.

The key that Berissa had found for him was safely tucked away under a pile of papers, and Peglar was confident that there was no chance of Ryker finding it there. So in theory he could unlock the door and walk out at any time. There was a narrow path, with a tall wooden fence on one side, the shed wall on the other, and a gate to the yard at the end. And there was the problem. To get from the shed door to the yard gate he would have to pass close to Safren. Very close. Too close, Peglar thought. He wasn't good with dogs and he wasn't prepared to take any chances. So he was in a kind of limbo. But one thing was clear. The opportunity for getting away would shrink every day he remained there. He had to act now.

Berissa had told him that the path to Safren's heart was by way of treats. 'Spoil her and she'll follow you anywhere,' she'd said. Peglar didn't want to be followed by Safren, he just wanted to get past her, but accepting Berissa's guidance was his only choice. He resolved to embark on a charm offensive. It would mean some sacrifices on his part, but if it worked it would be worth it.

Treats as such were impossible to come by, so the only route open to him was to divert some of the food that was given to him in the direction of the dog. Berissa had said that Safren was partial to sausages, and these were a staple item on the menu that Ryker provided. In fact, it seemed to Peglar that they were the only item, and he'd reached the conclusion that whoever prepared his evening meal didn't know how to cook anything else.

At the next mealtime, Ryker brought in a plate as usual, and with a flourish that would not have been out of place in the Great Hall of the Palace, he placed it in front of Peglar. On it were three curving, orangy-brown tubes lying in a shallow puddle of amber liquid.

'Ah, sausages again,' Peglar said, inspecting the plate and sniffing appreciatively. 'That's great.'

'I'm glad you like 'em.' Ryker sounded relieved. 'I wondered if you might be getting a tad fed up of them.'

'No, never,' said Peglar, putting on what he hoped was a convincing show of enthusiasm. 'They're my favourite.'

'Mine too,' said Ryker. 'There's nothing like a well-stuffed sausage.' Then, with the air of somebody welcoming a new member to an exclusive club. 'I get them from this chap on the market. He makes them himself, right here in Murgo.'

Peglar restrained himself from asking what the chap on the market put into them, he didn't think he wanted to know. When Ryker turned his attention to the collection of papers that Peglar had that day been organising, he slid two of the sausages off his plate and hid them under the table.

'Finished already,' Ryker said, looking back. He smiled with approval. 'Scoffed them quick, didn't you? Same again tomorrow? The man I get 'em from does a spicier version if you like.'

Peglar thought it best to stick with the standard fare rather than test Safren's palate with something exotic, so he said, 'These are delicious, thanks. I'll look forward to them.' He wiped his mouth and forced a burp of approval.

Ryker stayed a little longer, talking to Peglar about how sorting out the paperwork was progressing. It was obvious that he had no idea about how the records needed to be ordered, or any understanding of the progress Peglar had made. The important thing for Ryker was that something was being done, it didn't seem to matter what. He was so preoccupied that he didn't notice when he took Peglar's plate that the fork was missing.

Peglar waited for some time after Ryker had left. It was not unknown for his keeper to spend some time in the evening on odd jobs in the yard, and on one occasion he'd come back to the office after Peglar thought he had gone to tell him something he'd forgotten to mention earlier.

When Peglar thought a reasonable interval had elapsed he put his ear to the door. He could hear nothing apart from Safren's wheezy breathing. Right, he said to himself, if I'm ever going to get out of here I've got to deal with that dog.

He went to the pile of papers where he thought he'd stowed Berissa's key, panicked because it wasn't there, realised he'd gone to the wrong pile, dug under the one beside it, and found it. Then he located the two sausages he'd hidden beneath the table and speared one on the fork. The other he put in a pocket. He slid the key into the door lock and turned it, as quietly as he could.

He knew Safren had sharp ears, and the warning murmur that came as he eased the door open wasn't a surprise. Nevertheless, he froze. If she became agitated she might bark, and that would be a problem. He waited while the grumbling died down, and then cautiously he stepped over the threshold.

Safren was chained at the end of the passage. Peglar was relieved to see that the chain was short enough to stop her from reaching the doorway; that meant that so long as he didn't come forward he was safe. But if he was to deliver the sausage treats, go forward he must. He took a deep breath and edged a few steps into the passage, holding out the fork and ready to dash back inside and slam the door at any sign of trouble.

The chain rattled as the big dog stood. There was the usual growl and she regarded him with her huge, yellow eyes; much, Peglar thought, as she might eye a tasty titbit. She didn't try to come towards him but watched and waited, motionless and suspicious. The crossed eyes made it hard to interpret her mood, she just looked mad. The last thing he wanted to deal with was a dog that was mad.

He crept closer still and stretched out the hand holding the fork with the sausage at its tip. Safren strained against her chain. Her nose twitched and a ribbon of drool swung from the corner of her mouth. Peglar ventured another step. He was closer now. The sausage was within reach, and so too was his hand. Safren looked at him with her head on one side, as if she was not sure what to make of this strange behaviour. Then she sniffed the sausage, licked it, rolled her eyes, and with bewildering speed whipped it off the fork with her tongue and in one gulp swallowed it, as far as Peglar could see without chewing.

Safren licked her lips. 'Down without touching the sides, eh?' Peglar said, in a tone he thought was calm, although that was not what he felt.

Safren growled. Despite the gruff noise she appeared to like the offering and Peglar was relieved. He took sausage number two from his pocket and speared it on the fork. Again he held it out to Safren. Her response was the same.

Berissa had told him that the dog had to get used to him and he should talk to her. He had scant experience with animals. When he was a boy there had been a small, yellow monkey that had lived in a cage in the kitchen garden of the Palace, and he had sometimes petted that. And he had ridden horses, but he didn't like them.

What do you say to a dog? 'There, do you like that?' he tried. Safren looked at him as though she could understand human language perfectly well, but not the one he was speaking. He tried again. 'Good Safren, nice Safren. I'll bring you more tomorrow.'

He reached towards Safren thinking he might pat her head, but her upper lip curled and showed her big, yellow teeth so he withdrew, cautiously backing away and watching all the time. She watched him right back. When he got to the door she lay down, put her chin on her paws and closed her eyes. She knew he wouldn't be going anywhere.

Back in the shed Peglar hid the fork under his mattress and sat on his bed. He was relieved that the experiment seemed to have gone satisfactorily. He wouldn't go as far as to say that he had made friends with the dog, but he had made an overture and her reaction had been, if not wholly enthusiastic at least tolerant. He concluded that the sausages were acceptable and that further donations would be accepted. And he was grateful that he still had all his fingers.

Then came a problem. The key had seemed stiff when he'd unlocked the door. Now the whole mechanism had jammed and it wouldn't turn at all. He adjusted it and wiggled it but it made no difference. The door wouldn't lock. He tried for a long time and eventually gave up. The door would have to remain unlocked. There was no choice, but what would be Ryker's reaction?

It turned out to be better than Peglar could have hoped. He was awake early, trying to come up with some explanation for the state of the door, but it wasn't needed. He heard Ryker arrive, heard the rattle of Safren's chain and some words from man to dog, and then the key being inserted into the lock. This is it, Peglar thought.

There was some muttering, and rattling, and then the door opened and Ryker came in, with Safren padding behind him and sniffing everything in her path.

'Moon and stars, would you believe it?' said Ryker laughing. 'You won't credit what I did last night. Or didn't do, more like. I can't have locked the door. I must have forgotten. You weren't locked in.' It was clear that he thought this was very funny. 'What a lummock I am! You could have walked out and made a break for it. But then, you'd have had to get past my doggy here.' He turned and rubbed Safren's ears, and obligingly she growled. And wagged her tail.

Breakfast was bread and cheese, and as usual Ryker sat on the other side of the table from Peglar and talked to him while he ate. What he said was much like the news he gave every morning. He was going to look at some barley he might buy. One of his horses needed shoeing. The pirates had some more slaves to sell but they wanted too much for them. Berissa was insisting on him repainting their main room, and he couldn't imagine why because being blind like she was she couldn't see it now so why go to all the trouble and expense of making it different? That sort of thing. Peglar listened, nodded now and again, and murmured to indicate interest or agreement – or simply to show that he was still conscious.

Safren was lying between them. Occasionally she glanced at Peglar, and when her master was distracted he slipped her some of his cheese. The pieces vanished in an instant, and Safren swabbed his fingers with her rough tongue. Peglar found gifting the cheese painful because he'd lost most of last night's supper and he was hungry, but he told himself that if his plan worked the sacrifice would be worth it. It was clear now that Safren was receptive to bribery, and if that meant him going short of food for a time, then so be it.

The day passed slowly, with Peglar drinking a lot of water to try to satisfy his empty stomach. When evening came and Ryker brought in the food, Peglar saw that his captor had honoured the promise he'd made the night before; once again the dish of the day was sausages. While Peglar pretended to eat, Ryker rummaged through some of the papers that Peglar had carefully filed on the shelves. He was disarranging records that had already been sorted, but Peglar didn't mind. If everything went to plan he'd soon be well away from the filing drudgery and then Ryker could shove his papers.

While Ryker was occupied with this, Peglar managed to secrete all three sausages in the hiding place under the table.

'Hungry again, weren't you,' said Ryker.

'I must have been,' said Peglar.

'Well, I like to see good food appreciated. Same again tomorrow, I take it?'

72

'Mm, please,' said Peglar, trying to sound keen.

'It shall be.'

Ryker went to the door and started to lock it but then abandoned the process. 'Doesn't seem worth shutting you in,' he said. 'Where would you go? Anyway, Safren's as good as any door lock. I'll lengthen her chain a bit so she can keep an eye on you.'

Peglar peered through the doorway and along the passage at the dog.

'Stay put and sleep tight,' said Ryker.

Safren looked at Peglar and growled, and her tail wagged.

9
_____

SETTLING IN

Yalka lay on the ground and tried to focus. Verron/Big Ears stood over her.

'Is she all right?' said his companion. 'She looks half dead.'

'She'll be fine,' said Verron. 'She doesn't have to be on top form. Just alive enough for that slimy turd of a boyfriend to come out from under his stone to find her.'

Yalka's head throbbed with an excruciating beat. In the end she'd passed out in the box, and when the metal oven was eventually opened she'd tumbled out onto the ground. She lay now where she'd fallen. She groaned and rolled over, got to her knees and struggled upright. It was hard to stand, but she wouldn't give either of those two vermin the satisfaction of thinking they'd got her down.

'So, blondie,' said Verron, 'this is your new abode. What do you think?'

She forced her eyes to focus on the scene before her. It didn't look too bad. In fact, in different circumstances she might have liked what she saw. It was a square tower set in a grove of ancient olive trees, calm and picturesque. It had a ground floor entered through a gracefully arched doorway and there were another two floors above. Topping these was a stumpy spire, and it looked as though there was a walkway between that and the battlements that rimmed the wall. The building was high and from there you would be able to see a long way across the plain, perhaps even as far as Semilvarga. And of course, the reverse was true. It could be seen from a long way off, which she realised was the point of bringing her there.

The tower looked old, and in a better frame of mind she would have thought it romantic. It reminded her of a story that Peglar had once told her about a girl from a rich family who loved a low-born youth, a bit like her and Peglar but the other way round. The girl's father disapproved, and when he heard that the couple were planning to run away together he locked his daughter in a tower. It was on the edge of an inlet called Lovers' Creek, and one of the tests Peglar had faced before his initiation had been to swim it. He'd done it, although it had been hard.

'The bottom floor is a kitchen and storeroom,' said Verron. 'You won't go in there, it's for the maids. The top two are yours. The only way to get to them is up the stairs inside. There's a door at the top of the first flight and it will be kept locked. Follow me.' Verron marched towards the tower.

Yalka didn't want to move. She was battered and sweaty, and her head was throbbing. Her ribs were sore from being shaken against the wooden seat and she had a huge bruise swelling on her thigh. The clothes she had put on at the start of the journey were ruined. She probably stank.

'Come on,' Verron said. 'Shift your arse.'

He strode ahead of her towards the tower and she forced herself to go after him. His pal walked behind, as usual. Closer to the building she could see that the place wasn't in as good condition as she'd at first thought. One of the ground floor windows was broken, its frame holding a few jagged shards of glass, and the paint on the door was peeling. Verron pushed it open and went in. Yalka and the other man followed into a dingy hallway. It was narrow with a room on each side, and between them a flight of stairs with a sturdy-looking door at the top.

'Kitchen here,' Verron said, pointing to one of the doors. 'Laundry and other stuff opposite. You won't be using either of them, they're for the maids.' Verron must have noted her surprise. 'Yes, blondie, maids. You're going to be living like a lady. There'll be a new one every two or three days. We don't want you getting to know any of 'em in case you try to make friends and lean on her to help you. So they'll be changed, regular. There's another woman and she'll be in charge and see to all that.' He started up the stairs. 'You'll be up here.' Then, when she hesitated, 'Come on, I've not got all day.'

His companion pushed her in the back, so hard that she almost fell up the first couple of steps. At the top Verron brought out a key and unlocked the door. She followed him in and he stood back.

'Your palace, my lady,' he said.

The room was not unpleasant. It was bright, although a bit dusty. There was a table in the middle, and a couple of chairs and a comfortable-looking couch. There were bookshelves but there was nothing on them.

'The windows don't open,' said Verron, going to one and tapping it. 'We don't want you trying to escape that way, or throwing yourself out and topping yourself just so your precious boyfriend loses his reason for coming here. It's the sort of daft thing you young folks do.'

It wasn't. There was no way that Yalka would kill herself, not while there were people like Verron and Ragul around to be hated and destroyed.

'Over there,' said Verron, pointing through another of the windows, 'is a hut the guards use. They'll stay clear and keep their heads down so they don't scare young Lord Turdface away. Then when he turns up they'll have his nuggets.' Verron thrust his hips forward and clutched his groin to emphasise what he meant. There was a repulsive relish in the way did it and he looked hard at Yalka, enjoying himself by trying to make her feel uncomfortable. 'The steps over there in the corner go up to your bedroom and washroom,' he said. 'You can explore them yourself.' Verron looked about him with the air of someone who'd just shown a choice property to a potential purchaser. 'So there you are, blondie. You won't see me again until it's all over. Then it will be just the two of us.'

He leant forward and kissed her, suddenly and roughly, on the mouth. She was too startled and tired to be quick enough to push him away, and by the time she reacted he'd retreated and was out of range.

'I'll be back,' he said, and winked. Then he turned to his companion and said casually, as if she wasn't there, 'Pity about that whore mark. She'd be a proper dish if it wasn't for that.'

'Gives you a good idea of what she's about, though,' said the other.

The two of them laughed and walked to the door. Verron slammed it behind him and she heard the key turn. She went to it to check, but it was locked and felt very firm. She crossed to the window and watched the two men emerge, climb onto the tin torture chamber, and drive away.

She was on her own. It was blissfully quiet. For the past two days there'd been deafening din, and the hollow bang and boom of the box was still in her head. In between there'd been Verron's harsh and grating orders, and his comments heavy with innuendo. Now there was silence.

She was very tired. She went to the corner and climbed the stairs to what Verron said was her bedroom. It wasn't bad. There were windows all around this room too. She tried a couple of them but Verron was right, they were nailed shut. They gave a good view of the road from Semilvarga to Maris Partem. She would be able to see Peglar if he came that way. How could she warn him that the tower was a trap?

She went to the bed and felt the mattress. It was thin but she'd slept on worse. There was a closet with a few clothes, not many but enough. She picked up a couple of the garments. They weren't new but they felt to be of good quality. She went through another door to a tiny washroom where she found a blotchy mirror, a basin, a jug and a tin bath. She would love to be able to bathe but she doubted that the maids would be willing to carry enough water for that up two flights of stairs. There was also a roll of muslin. She could guess what it was for, but there was nothing she could use to cut it to make pads. She went back into the bedroom.

There was a curtain across one corner. Verron hadn't said anything about that. What was behind it? She drew it aside carefully, just in case it was hiding something unpleasant. All it concealed was a ladder, bolted to the wall, with a trapdoor at the top. She stared at it for a moment, then curiosity overcame weariness and she hauled herself up the rungs. She expected the trapdoor to be locked but it wasn't. However, it seemed as though it hadn't been opened for some time because it was stiff, and when it did yield dust and debris fell on her head and into her eyes. She shook herself clear and climbed into the fresh air.

She was on the roof, on a narrow walkway between the spire and the battlements. She couldn't believe that they would have gone to the trouble of sealing all the windows but left this open. Not that it was any help as far as escape was concerned. The battlements were low and it would be easy to get over them, but there was nothing to hold onto to climb down, and she'd break her neck if she jumped or fell.

Still, the roof was a welcome amenity. She took a deep breath. The air was wonderful. There was a fine view over the flat plain towards Chamaris and back to Semilvarga. She thought wistfully about her Grandfather. He wouldn't know what had happened to her or where she was. Was he still in Semilvarga? And what about Meshi? She had been with him and had sent him away just before the event that led to her capture. If she hadn't done that she might not have been caught. Meshi would have had no problem sorting out the little brat who had taken her purse. Although if he had, he might be the one who had been sold as a slave. She went to where she could see the soldiers' hut. The door was closed. There were a couple of horses grazing among the trees nearby, but no other signs of life.

She climbed back down the ladder and went to the washroom. She felt hot and sticky. There was water in the jug, so she stripped, wet a cloth and wiped herself all over. The cold water made her feel better and she didn't bother to dry but stood with her eyes closed while she cooled. Back in the bedroom, she put on a loose tunic from the stock in the closet.

She was startled by a sound from below. Someone had come into the house. She went quickly down to the living room below. There were noises of movement from below, and the sound of a chair being scraped across the flagstones. Then she heard footsteps on the stairs and a key turning in the doorlock. It opened and a woman was there. She was well-built, severe-looking, and dressed all in black. She held something in her hand.

'Yes, it's a weapon,' she said.

Yalka looked more closely. It was a long kitchen knife that the woman held at her side.

'It's very sharp,' she said, 'and I won't hold back from using it. I am in charge.'

Not an encouraging start, thought Yalka, but she would try to be friendly.

'My name is Yalka.'

The woman sniffed. 'I know who you are. I shall call you girl.'

'What's your name?'

'We don't use names here. You may call me madam.'

Yalka knew that if this person had a right side it would be sensible to get on it. She was also aware that her spirit of rebellion had got her into trouble before, but she couldn't stop herself from saying, 'If you're going to call me girl I shall call you woman.'

The woman sniffed again. 'Verron said you might be trouble. We shall have to see about that.' She twirled the knife in her fingers. 'There will be a maid here shortly. You won't be told her name either. Every morning she will fetch you water for washing, empty your chamber pot, and prepare your food. There will be a different maid every few days. You are responsible for your own cleaning, and to do that you will be provided twice a week with dusters, a mop and a bucket.'

Woman paused. To see if there were any questions? To make sure that what she said had sunk in? Yalka wasn't sure, but if she was going to get out of there she had to take some action. The woman still blocked the door. Yalka did not doubt that she was fitter and faster than her jailer, but the knife was a problem. If she was to be on equal terms she had to get hold of a weapon of her own.

'There's a roll of material in the closet that I assume is to make pads. I'll need something to cut it with.'

Woman smiled thinly as if to say, 'Nice try'. What she actually said was. 'Tell me when it's needed and the material will be made ready for you. The maid will be here throughout the day, from around the sixth morning bell until the evening. I shall be here most mornings and some afternoons.'

Yalka deduced that she would be left on her own the rest of the time. That would be when she would have to make her escape. But how?

Woman closed the door and Yalka heard the key turn. She was alone again, and although this

82

accommodation was much better than the cell where she'd been held before she was sold, she was still a prisoner.

She went to the row of windows overlooking the grove and the road that snaked along the coast towards Semilvarga. It was met by at least a dozen other tracks that came from the settlements and farms that dotted the plain. Peglar could come along any of those. How could she possibly get a warning to him? A message scrawled on a sheet draped from the battlements? Even if it wasn't spotted by Woman or the men in the guard house, by the time Peglar was close enough to see it, it would be too late.

10

ESCAPE 1

It took several sausage suppers before Peglar felt ready to risk trying to escape. He knew there would be only one chance. If he was prevented, either by being stopped by Safren or caught by a human, that would be it. He would have lost the trust he had slowly gained from Ryker and his future treatment would reflect that. But the longer he stayed the harder it would be for him to get away. He must make his plans and go, and that depended on wooing Safren.

Often Ryker didn't leave the yard immediately after supper and there would be footsteps, noises of things being moved about outside, grunting and muttering that sometimes went on for a long time. Peglar had no idea what these were about but they sounded serious. He would wait until they were over, and then he'd wait a bit longer, just in case, before easing the door ajar. The first time he did this he saw that Safren was in her usual place at the end of the passage beside the gate, lying on the heap of flattened rags that served as her bed. He also saw, to his alarm, that she wasn't chained. Ryker must have left her like that because he was now leaving the door unlocked.

She looked at Peglar with suspicion and made a noise that sounded to him like large stones being rolled around in a drum. She stood up, bared her teeth, and stared at him with her long tongue hanging out. Then she must have seen or smelt the sausage that he was holding out on the fork. Her tongue wiped across her muzzle, she got to her feet, stretched, and ambled towards him. She stopped a pace away and faced him, her lip curled and warning in her crossed eyes. Then she leant forward and sniffed the sausage Peglar was holding out towards her. She put her head on one side, looked at Peglar, and inhaled the offering, just like before. Then she did the same with the other two. She looked as though she could manage more of them but Peglar had none, so he closed the door and retreated into the shed. He was relieved to get back into safety, and he listened to the quiet keening from Safren when she realised that the feast was over.

The next night was the same, except this time after the last sausage Peglar ventured to rub the dog's head and ears. Her coat was as thick as a bear's, but it was rough and coarse, not soft and smooth. It was hair, not fur. She seemed to like the attention for a few seconds but then became bored, gave him a hard look, and went away.

And so on and so on. On the fourth night Peglar opened the door to find Safren already waiting for him. It was an unnerving experience because he had stooped to look through a crack in the door, and when he opened it he found Safren's wet nose level with his face and only a couple of inches away. He decided that it was time to try to establish some control and demonstrate that he was in charge, so he gave Safren the first sausage but kept the other two concealed. She expected more than one because she waited, making a little whimpering sound that was surprising coming from such an enormous creature. Peglar rubbed her head and then gave her sausage number two. This time he overcame his fear of her teeth and offered it from his fingers rather than the fork. To his relief, she took it gently. Again he waited, and this time Safren did something extraordinary: she sat down. There was no sound from her but she regarded him stolidly, making it clear that she wasn't going anywhere yet. After a few moments he gave her the third sausage, which she took. Then she turned away and went back to her bed.

Peglar reflected on this. Because of her ambiguous response to him, simultaneously growling and wagging her tail, he had assumed that Safren was at least confused and most probably fairly dim. However, perhaps she was brighter than he thought. That was because it seemed that she could count, at least she could manage up to number three. He'd treated the dog as a problem to be overcome, but perhaps that was a wrong assumption. She might be an asset. Perhaps he could make use of her.

Ryker must have been impressed by Peglar's appetite for sausages, because now he provided four each evening rather than the usual three. Peglar was tempted to eat the fourth one, maybe even eat two of them and trim Safren's ration, but he restrained himself to just potato and gravy and kept all four sausages aside. It will be worth it in the end, he told himself when his rumbling stomach kept him awake in the night.

The pattern became established. When Peglar opened the door he would find Safren ready and waiting. The relationship had moved on. Now there would be no growling, no curled lip. There was no tail wagging either, but Peglar was happy to sacrifice that. He would release the sausages one at a time, with an increasing interval between them, and each time the dog would wait patiently, watching him closely. After every sausage Peglar would rub her head and ears. When sausage number three was done she would go back to her heap of rags and lie down again. Safren didn't get the fourth sausage. Peglar kept that and added it to the reserve that he was starting to build up.

Peglar felt no urgency to escape, and he had only the most general idea of what he would do if and when he did. Rescue his friends from the farm and then locate Yalka, but he had no plan for how he would do these things, or any notion of how his life might move on after he'd accomplished them. Besides, the daytime routine wasn't unpleasant. The work was what he made it and it was far from being arduous. He spent his time sitting at the table, pushing papers around and pretending to organise them. Luckily, on the couple of occasions that Ryker had come in to retrieve something that he needed Peglar had been able to remember the required document and recall where he had put it. So Ryker was satisfied, life was reasonably comfortable, and he would have been adequately fed if he had eaten all of what was provided.

Ryker himself was easygoing and that was becoming a problem, because he had started to spend an increasing amount of time in the shed, talking to Peglar while he worked, ate, or in the evenings after supper. At

88

these times he would deliver monologues about Berissa, her difficulties and demands, his home life, trade, the price of slaves, and issues with the pirates who supplied them. Almost all these troubles were financial, and they confirmed what Peglar could see from the records: Ryker was on a slow but seemingly irreversible slide towards insolvency.

The conversations with Ryker – although they could hardly be called that as Peglar said very little – were tedious but probably not enough of a reason to get away. However, there were others, more pressing. As the summer approached its peak the shed became more oppressive, stifling during the day and stuffy by night. He slept badly and he was sluggish. Cestrris had shown him some exercises when he'd been training for the Challenges and he did what he could but the space was cramped, and his sedentary lifestyle began to tell on him. Along with – maybe because of – this, what might be happening in Chamaris increasingly nagged him and filled more and more of his thoughts. His mother was gone. He was miserable that he hadn't been able to prevent that, and he was sure that Vancia had played a part in it because he had with his own eyes seen her visit an apothecary and buy poison. Then there was his father. He knew before he'd been exiled that his health was declining, and with him weakened there would be no one to keep Ragul or his scheming mother in check. If those two took control the impact it would have on the city and beyond was horrific. And of course, there was Ragul himself; his self-centred, insensitive, emotionally castrated half-brother. There was certainly unfinished business there.

Most important of all, however, was Yalka. He knew

who had bought her and the record of the sale gave the name of the place she'd been taken. Was she still there? Was she being treated well? She was a slave, so what was she being required to do? He thought about her most of the time, and the more he did the more he missed her. He remembered the times they had sat together on the Great Stone in the Citadel, talking while they looked down on the city, and beyond that on the River Settlements which had once been her home. He remembered her quickness, her sharp humour, and her sense of right and wrong, as solid and dependable as lodestone. He remembered her startling eyes, her delicate features, and her amazing hair. He remembered how, the last few times they had been together, he had noticed how her body was taking on the shape of a woman, and the effect that had had on him. He remembered the mark on her cheek that some people disparaged but that he wanted to kiss. He could wait no longer; he had to find her.

Beyond laying by a stock of sausages, there was little preparation to be done for his escape. He had no personal possessions apart from two sets of clothing, the coarse workwear of a slave. From time to time Ryker would allow him out into the yard to wash these, and to do that he would have to pass Safren.

'She seems to have taken a fancy to you,' Ryker said, when instead of growling at him the dog looked up with large moist eyes and her hot tongue hanging out. Peglar was concerned that Ryker would think this suspicious but the man went on to say, 'She's a quiet one now, but you just try to get past her without me here and she'll have your leg for her supper.'

Peglar would have to risk that, but he was confident

that he'd managed to bond with Safren, even if it was a relationship that relied on tubes of minced meat. He pushed aside thoughts of what might happen if or when they ran out. Would Safren's view of him change from being a provider of treats to that of an escapee, and therefore game?

So there was only his clothing, the fork, which he thought might at some stage be useful, and the sausages. The latter posed a problem. He had to be sure there were enough, but he also needed to guard against them going bad in the heat. Fortunately, although the weather was warm it was dry, so they were unlikely to grow mould. Still, it made sense to use up the oldest first, but as the reserves grew he knew that he couldn't continue what he was doing any longer. There weren't enough sausages to keep Safren going for long but they would have to do, and after they were gone they'd have to rely on what they could find. There was no point hanging about. He resolved to go the next day.

The evening before he decided that it was important to ensure he had enough energy for what might be a strenuous journey, so he ate all four of the sausages that Ryker provided, and he even licked the plate. The experience was unusual because this time Ryker sat with him while he dined. He hadn't done that for some time, and Peglar was thankful for it, otherwise his scheme for setting aside food for Safren would never have got going.

That night Ryker stayed longer than usual, until Peglar thought that he must have somehow got wind of what Peglar was planning and was setting out to thwart him. He gave a long account of an interminable row with Berissa about the repainting of their home. He'd refused, she'd insisted, he'd given in, and now he felt intense resentment that he had been forced to accept defeat. He was also wondering if she could see more than she let on. Peglar had no experience of interpersonal relationships of this sort and he could offer no advice. Luckily it seemed that none was required and all Ryker wanted was a sympathetic ear, so Peglar sat with him and put up with it, all the time willing him to go.

At last he did, and as usual Peglar waited and listened for the usual sounds from the yard. This time there were few, and it seemed that Ryker, having stayed longer than before, must have gone straight home. It was time to make a move. Peglar opened the door, quietly and slowly, glad that the sausage gravy he'd had the presence of mind to apply to the hinges a couple of days before had silenced their squeaking. All seemed clear, and he crept out.

Safren was already waiting for him, her tongue hanging out expectantly. She licked her muzzle and stood so close he got the full benefit of her breath. He gave her the usual three sausages. However, this time she didn't go back to her bed after the third one but instead stood waiting. Could it be a slip-up in her counting? Or could she smell the reserves that he'd wrapped in his spare tunic? He hoped not, because if she could they wouldn't be reserves for long.

He moved towards the gate that led out of the passage and into the yard. Safren came with him. What would she do when he opened it? There was a stout cord with a metal clip hanging from a hook high on the wall. The clip would fit the loop on Safren's collar, but she was strong and it was obvious to Peglar that if she took it into her head to go somewhere he wouldn't be able to stop her. However, he took the cord anyway. A piece of rope might come in useful for all sorts of things, apart from restraining a dog. He rubbed her ears and she wagged her tail. She also growled. Which of these responses was he to believe? And what would she do when he tried to leave through the gate?

The answer was simple: nothing. Peglar slowly undid the bolt and cautiously pulled the gate open. It made a noise that in the silence of the night he was sure could be heard right across the plain, but there didn't seem to be any reaction from anywhere. Tentatively, he crept through the gap, bracing himself for the dog's dissent, but there was none; Safren followed him. The next thing was, would she let him leave the yard? She did, and she came too.

Peglar was so relieved he had to wait a moment to get his breath and for his racing heart to slow down. When he felt calmer he headed for the road, where he took a moment to get his bearings. A full moon was rising, low and red. Peglar worked out what he judged to be the direction of Rasturoth and the location of the farm to which Alendur, Reddall and Beldrom would have been taken. He set out, and Safren loped along beside him.

11

DAMAGE REPAIR

'A chariot race?!' It was unthinkable, and for Vancia another indication that her only son was losing his grip on reason. 'A chariot race?! Who came up with such an absurd notion?'

'It was Sainter, Mummy.'

Vancia sighed. Most of Sainter's schemes were effective, but sometimes he went to extremes and lost his connection with reality. This seemed to be one of them. She snapped her fingers at a servant. 'Find Lord Sainter and tell him I want to see him at once. Here, in my Audience Chamber.'

"Audience Chamber" was a grand term for the room they were in. It was in fact rather small, barely larger than her bedchamber, but it did at least have a dais and something that looked like a throne, and that was where Vancia sat. Two of the chairs below the dais were occupied: one by Ragul and, just behind him, by his companion, Burian.

While they waited for Sainter to arrive Vancia reviewed what she had just heard. Ragul had told her that he and Burian proposed a chariot tournament. There would be several races and the climax would be a very special event, a race in which they would be the only competitors. There was nothing extraordinary about that. The size and shape of the Arena dictated that only two chariots could race at a time, and athletic young men from noble families would often challenge each other, with heavy betting on the outcome. What seemed to Vancia totally bizarre was that since Ragul's knee had been broken in the combat with Peglar he had been scarcely able to walk, let alone drive a racing chariot. Sainter's schemes were usually well thought-out, but this time he seemed to have lost his grip.

Sainter's arrival was, as usual, accompanied by a great deal of panting and puffing. His scholar's robes were draped over a formal gown so that he appeared swaddled and swamped, and he was in his usual red-faced lather. Vancia wondered, as she had many times before, why on a warm day in a hot country a fat little man should insist on covering himself in so much clothing.

Sainter bowed. 'My Lady,' he gasped.

There was a moment while Vancia indicated that he should sit, and he settled himself on one of the chairs before her and tried to calm his breathing.

'Lord Sainter,' she said with an icy smile when he seemed at last composed. 'My son and Lord Burian have just presented to me an idea which I consider to be extraordinary. It is that they intend to race, in chariots, around the Arena, in public. They say the suggestion came from you.'

'Yes, My Lady.' Sainter didn't go on, having long ago concluded that in the House of Karkis it was best to provide information only when doing so could no longer be avoided.

'Well?' Vancia waited for him to elaborate.

'It was indeed my proposal,' Sainter said. 'It came about after a conversation with the Palace Steward, Feldar. As you know, he makes it his business to keep in touch with what people in and around the city are saying.'

Vancia did know. Sainter was referring to the network of observers and informers who reported regularly to the Steward. The existence of this web was one of the things that made the removal of Feldar so difficult, even though it was an outcome she very much desired.

Sainter didn't elaborate and Vancia had to push him again. 'So what did Steward Feldar tell you?'

Sainter wriggled uncomfortably in his chair and looked nervously at Ragul. 'Apparently, My Lady, people are saying, and I stress that this is only hearsay and I am sure cannot be a correct interpretation of the public mood...' Vancia sighed and Sainter hurried on. 'The impression from the information gathered by Feldar's agents, and I repeat that it is only an impression...'

Vancia's impatience and exasperation exploded. 'Oh, by the stars, man, get on with it.'

'Yes, My Lady, of course.' Sainter looked chastened. 'Steward Feldar reports, or rather his agents do, that across the city Lord Ragul is, I am afraid... no longer as well-liked as he was.' There was a sound somewhere between a grunt and a growl from Ragul. Sainter concluded that his boats were well and truly burned so he went on. 'When Lord Ragul was serving in the army he was popular and had a reputation for bravery which was admired by all. But following his return there were suggestions from rivals that some of the accounts of his courage were exaggerated, and there were rumours of prisoners in Semilvarga being treated badly, on his orders, when the uprising was put down.'

Ragul had gone puce and looked ready to erupt. Vancia thought he might strike Sainter and held up her hand to restrain him.

'The Semilvargans who suffered were rebels and enemies of the city,' she said. 'These rumours of which you speak were probably started by them in order to discredit Lord Ragul. It cannot be only that.'

'No, ma'am,' said Sainter, and shook his head sadly. 'It is also Peglar.'

Vancia and Ragul both spoke at once. 'Peglar?'

'Yes, Peglar. His popularity with the people is growing.'

'How can that be?' said Vancia. 'Peglar is disgraced and has been exiled.'

'Ah, well that's it,' said Sainter. 'Some individuals, and I'm sure it's only a small number but they do exist, believe that your stepson has been hard done by. He was hailed as a hero at the time of the burning of the River Settlements because he saved lives and ended up in the Sanitarium for his trouble. He was scarcely out when he was accused of assaulting Lady Malina, and people find it hard to understand how this might happen, two contradictory events so close together.'

'Kindly do not refer to Peglar as my stepson,' said Vancia. 'He is nothing to do with me, and I have severed any ties I may have had to him. Anyway, there was undeniable proof of his guilt.'

Ragul was angry. 'You yourself witnessed Peglar attacking Malina. You said so, before my father and Uncle Mostani, and others too.'

Sainter looked extremely uncomfortable. 'Well yes, My Lord. I did recount what I thought I had seen but as I think I said at the time, it could be no more than an impression. It was difficult to see clearly what was taking place because I was at the far end of the room where it happened and it was dimly lit. It was hard to hear because I was behind a curtain. In retrospect, I am perhaps not now as sure of the exact nature of the events that took place, or as secure in my interpretation of them, as I was then.'

Ragul was struggling to try to get to his feet. 'Blood and bones, man, what are you saying?'

Sainter was cowering and looked like a frightened rabbit. 'Nothing, My Lord. It's merely my recollection. I am sure that it all happened exactly as Lady Malina said. But rumours spread, and Lady Malina has herself modified her account, and now a few people are speculating that the whole accusation is false.' Sainter glanced at Ragul and cringed.

'Is that all?' said Vancia. 'We can easily deal with that. Malina will issue a sworn statement confirming what she said originally.'

'Sadly, ma'am, there is more,' said Sainter. He looked so wretched that Vancia almost pitied him.

'What more? Let's have it, man. All of it. Now.'

Sainter took a deep breath and mopped his brow. 'It's the combat. Lord Ragul was declared the victor. In my own view that was a correct decision,' he added hurriedly, 'but there are those who say, wrongly I believe, but they are saying it, that the contest was very close and a few even hold that Peglar won.'

There was a long silence.

'Finally,' Sainter said, 'there are some who feel that the sentence of permanent banishment from the city on pain of death was too severe.'

He looked at the three pairs of hostile eyes fixed on him, and at the staff that Ragul held threateningly. In her mind's eye, Vancia had an image of Sainter scurrying from the room with Ragul after him. The picture was so comical that she almost laughed. But the situation wasn't funny. If these views were gaining traction, that was serious. The Master of the City was no longer elected by the Assembly, but without its support it would be hard to wield any authority. The Assembly would be swayed by the wealthy families, and ultimately they would follow the wishes of the citizens. The gossip must be stopped. Moreover, the sources of the stories must be identified and dealt with.

'This is complete nonsense,' she said. 'It's mere tittle-tattle, put about by troublemakers and rebels.'

Sainter flapped his hand in a gesture of helplessness. 'My Lady, My Lords,' he fluttered, 'I do not myself believe any of this. It's simply what Steward Feldar tells me he has heard.'

'I shouldn't wonder if Feldar has spread some of this rubbish himself,' Ragul growled. He had abandoned his attempt to get up from his chair. 'It's that queer-boy Cestris and his faggot friends that are behind this. I should never have let Peglar get away. I should have had him killed before he left the city.'

'Well you didn't,' said Vancia, 'so what is to be done now?'

'Ah,' said Sainter, 'that, My Lady, is what lies behind my suggestion of a chariot race.'

'How could a chariot race possibly help?'

'It will provide My Lord with an opportunity to show off his prowess as a hero. I am confident that will do a great deal to re-establish his popularity.'

Vancia was finding the conversation simultaneously irritating and wearisome. 'That may be true if my son were well, but with his knee in the state that it is there is no way he could handle a racing chariot, let alone win a head-to-head in one.'

Sainter was looking more at ease, and even pleased with himself. 'That is part of it,' he said. 'Lord Burian will have the traditional racing chariot with two horses and Lord Ragul will have a carrus with three. Three horses are harder to control than two, and a carrus has a seat which makes it bigger and heavier, so it's slower than a two-wheeled chariot.'

Vancia felt that she was being dragged into a world of fantasy. She was incredulous. 'So there will be a race, and my son will have the slower chariot, and therefore he will lose, and that will show him as a hero?'

Sainter sat back on his chair with a satisfied smile. 'Ah, but My Lady, Lord Ragul will win.'

'How can that be?'

'Because Lord Burian will ensure that it happens.'

Vancia was now convinced that she had somehow stumbled into the land of the insane. 'That is the silliest thing I have ever heard. People will see through it at once. My son will be a laughing stock.'

'Forgive me, My Lady, but not if the proceedings are carefully managed. The task for Lord Burian will be to give the appearance of putting his all into the race, while at the same time conveying the impression that he is unable to prevail against the superior technique of his master. I am sure that he possesses the skill to do that.'

There was a pause while Vancia thought. She studied Ragul and Burian. The idea seemed to appeal to Ragul, and his anger had ebbed. Burian looked calm, possibly even smug.

'I am confident that if it is properly done, winning the race will restore Lord Ragul's stature in the public eye,' said Sainter.

'I suppose that could happen,' said Vancia. She was not yet convinced. The success of Sainter's plan would depend on Burian. If he was capable of carrying it off, it might work.

'There is another benefit,' said Sainter.

'Which is?'

'The event that I propose has the potential to make you a great deal of money.'

Vancia was interested. 'Explain.'

'It is like this, ma'am,' Sainter said. 'There is no doubt that, given the faster chariot and Lord Ragul's lingering injury, Lord Burian will be expected to win. Therefore the odds offered for bets on the outcome will be weighted in his favour and against Lord Ragul. If, My Lady, you were to wager heavily on the success of your son, when he does win the payout will be substantial.'

Sainter's proposal was tempting. Restoring Ragul's reputation would be a boon, but if the same event could also generate some much-needed funds for the House, it could be a triumph.

'Can you do this, Burian?' she said. 'Can you lose the race while still making it seem as though you are trying your very best to win it?'

Burian grinned, an expression that Vancia had always thought made him look like an incontinent ape.

'Yes, My Lady. I can,' he said.

'It is, of course, essential that we exercise the utmost discretion,' said Sainter. 'If our little scheme were to become known, all would be lost. Indeed, the situation would be worsened rather than improved.'

Vancia looked around anxiously. No one else was in the room but there were always servants close at hand. Might they have overheard the conversation? It was remarkable how even the most confidential matters that were discussed in the most secret places in the Palace quickly became known and spread around the city. 'The walls have ears,' Karkis sometimes said.

'How long will it take to arrange this contest?' she asked Sainter.

'To allow time for the news to get around and for the proper build-up of excitement, to prepare the vehicles and horses, to set up the betting arrangements,' he pondered for a moment. 'I think it could be done in a week.'

'Very good,' said Vancia. 'Set about it.'

12

UNEXPECTED

News of the race spread quickly and interest swelled. There was endless talk about it in the taverns and coffee houses. No one could see any possibility of Ragul winning. The gossip was that it was he who had made the challenge and many concluded that he was out of his mind. There were lengthy queues outside the premises of the bookmakers and conservers. Even those who rarely laid a wager saw this as an opportunity to make money. Burian was the clear favourite and the odds on him shortened daily, while those on Ragul grew to absurd heights.

The buzz was something that the city had not known for many months. Vancia realised that since her husband's withdrawal from the public eye, the atmosphere in Chamaris had been flat. Ragul no longer enjoyed appearing in public and declined or avoided ceremonial occasions. The Seven Cities Games were not due to take place for another year. Musical and dramatic performances had dried up. All this meant that apart from an occasional rhyming, there had been little to interest the people of the city, nothing to celebrate and nothing to look forward to. So the chariot race filled a vacuum and it was on everyone's lips. Even the servants were gossiping about it, and Vancia's informants told her that it was a hot topic at social events and gatherings of all sorts. She was even becoming excited about it herself.

She placed a large number of bets. A few of them she handled personally because it was only to be expected that a mother would support her son, however misguided others might think it to be. However, to avoid arousing suspicion most of the wagers were handled by other people acting for her. Crestyn had been unhappy about releasing the amount of money required for the stakes but she had insisted. However, she had to admit, if only to herself, that the Chancellor had a point; it was a risk. There were any number of reasons why the race might not work out as intended. One of Ragul's horses could go lame. He might lose his reins, lose a wheel, or become ill. The rainy season was approaching and the event might be washed out. And there was one more worry; Burian might after all win. If he did, her losses would be phenomenal.

She slept little at the best of times, but as the day of the race approached she hardly rested at all. On the evening before she sent for Burian. She gave the instruction that he was to come on his own, without Ragul.

'You understand what you must do?' she asked him.

'I do, My Lady.'

'And you can do it? You can lose the race while appearing to be trying your very best to win it?'

'Without doubt, My Lady.'

'You are sure of this?'

'Yes, My Lady.'

'Very well then. I am depending on you. We all are.'

'Of course, My Lady.'

Burian bowed and left. There was no more that she could do.

The event was scheduled for the afternoon, and when Vancia arrived at the Arena it was packed, with more people outside unable to find a place within. There were to be three races before the final one, the one that would feature Ragul and Burian. In the first two, a pair of charioteers were to race each other, and in the third the two winners would compete.

All the charioteers were highly trained athletes and as the races progressed excitement built. The gaming tables were busy as spectators queued to bet. The final race finished, the winner was crowned, and it was time for the climax, the contest that most of the people had come to see.

There was loud applause for Burian as he entered the Arena and did a circuit of the track, waving. Vancia had to admit that he looked magnificent, bronzed, fit, and strong. His chariot was the latest racing design, stripped down to the bare minimum. It consisted of little more than a board for the rider to stand on, held in the lightest of frames between the two wheels. The pair of black horses that pulled it were lively and spirited, and they shone as though they'd been polished.

Ragul's appearance got a different reception. There was some applause but it was tempered by jeers. The carrus looked heavy and cumbersome, more suited to work on a farm than racing around the Arena. In contrast to Burian, Ragul was fully clothed, but his robes couldn't hide the fact that he was overweight and out of shape. The three horses which pulled him were a motley bunch, one brown, one dappled and one a sandy colour. Burian's rig looked to be a winning combination; Ragul's did not. The queues at the gaming tables swelled.

Vancia looked up as Sainter took a place beside her. She rarely felt emotions of any sort and couldn't remember when she had last known the butterflies she was experiencing now. 'Is this going to work?' she said.

'Oh certainly, My Lady.'

'Well, it had better.'

'The arrangements have all gone extremely well, My Lady, and the outcome is in no doubt.'

And at first, it wasn't. The track consisted of two long, parallel straights linked by short curved ends. The arrangement of the track made it difficult to pass a skilled charioteer once they were ahead. Overtaking on the ends was virtually impossible, so in order to win, the technique was to get ahead on the first straight and hold on to this advantage.

Ragul and Burian lined up their rigs. Burian's horses were eager to go, while Ragul's looked as though they'd rather be at pasture and might not last half the race, let alone the full ten laps. Because of the difference between the rigs, the Judge allowed Ragul a start of 100 paces, and this had to be measured out and agreed. That done, the two contestants took up positions on their separate lines. The Starter raised his whip, and the crowd quietened in anticipation. The atmosphere was tense enough to slice. Then the whip was cracked, and they were off.

Although his getaway was slower, Ragul had a clear

lead at the first bend. This was partly due to the staggered start favouring him, but it was mainly because Burian fumbled a rein. This trouble seemed to be an ongoing problem because although he kept close to Ragul down the next straight he didn't seem to have enough control over his horses to challenge him. They completed the first lap, then the second, and the next, and still Burian couldn't find an opportunity on any of the straights to get his chariot past the carrus. It should have been easy, especially now he'd regained control of his horses, but he didn't seem able to manage it. Some in the crowd started booing, and as the race continued more joined in.

The jeering was directed at Burian, but there were cheers for Ragul.

'You hear them, My Lady?' said Sainter, who was smiling broadly. 'People are supporting your son because he's holding his own against the formidable odds. What price Peglar's popularity now?'

Vancia nodded. She scanned the crowd. Many looked distraught and she guessed that most of them had put money on Burian. Then, as she watched, the mood abruptly changed and spectators leapt up, whooping and waving. It lasted only a second or two and then there was a collective gasp and hands went to mouths. Vancia's attention flicked back to the track.

Ragul and Burian were at the final bend and the race was nearly done but Burian seemed to have torn up the script. As the two chariots careered out of the corner they were close, and on the straight leading to the winning line Burian pulled out to overtake. The crowd was wild, the noise deafening. His chariot drew level, and then there was disaster.

Vancia saw what happened as if it was in slow motion. As the chariot went to pass him, Ragul yanked his reins so that his carrus swerved sharply. It clipped Burian's wheel and the lightweight chariot tipped onto its side and its driver was flung out. Burian's foot caught in the reins and he was dragged along the track until his head smacked into the stone edging and the rein snapped. He was left there, limbs impossibly twisted, skin scraped raw, while his horses galloped on. Ragul brought his own rig under control and trotted sedately over the finishing line. He was the winner. Burian lay inert.

There was uproar. Some of the crowd jumped the parapet and Guardians struggled to keep them away from the motionless Burian. Others ran across with a stretcher. Two men in the scarlet robes of physicians appeared.

Vancia watched this for a moment and then turned away. There was no way that Burian could have survived what had happened to him. Ragul had won the race, she had gained a great deal of money, and Burian was dead. And she had seen what she had seen. What did it all mean? She watched the commotion for a few moments, then turned to Sainter and told him to take her to the Palace.

They hardly spoke on the way but that had nothing to do with grief or shock, at least not on Vancia's part. She felt nothing for Burian. She had never liked him and she had often wondered why Karkis – or most probably Feldar – had ever put him forward as a companion for her son. She'd always found him weak, shallow, stupid, and vain. He'd been a bad influence, and she was pleased that she would no longer have to put up with him.

A little later Ragul came to her quarters.

'Buri's gone, Mummy,' said Ragul.

'You mean gone to the Sanitorium?'

Ragul laughed. 'No point in that. That crack he got on the head just about knocked his brains out.'

Vancia looked at her son. He seemed unconcerned, cheerful even. That was not what she had expected. The young man who had been with him since the day of his initiation was no more. He and Burian had been inseparable, always in each other's company. Some people had even speculated that they were lovers. She'd expected him to be at least sad, if not actually grieving.

'Your friend is dead,' she said. 'Do you not feel anything?'

Ragul frowned. 'But he broke our agreement, Mummy. He was trying to get ahead of me. You have always told me that I should do whatever it takes to win. That's what I did.'

It was true. That was something she had often said. She had drummed it into both Ragul and Malina when they were little, and repeated it to them when Malina had misgivings about her role in Vancia's plot for Peglar's disgrace. She was gratified that the lesson had been learnt.

'Besides, Mummy,' said Ragul, 'he'd served his purpose.'

Vancia felt the closest she ever came to joy. She held out her arms to Ragul and embraced him. Perhaps there was hope for the House of the Leopard after all.

13

THE FARM

The farm wasn't hard to find. It was exactly where Peglar thought it would be, about ten miles in the direction of Rasturoth, and it was the only settlement of any size on that part of the plain. It was surrounded by scrubland and low rocks, so it was easy to approach it without being seen.

'Farm' was a grand term for the haphazard collection of dilapidated buildings he found. The house was small and seemed in reasonable order, but a long outbuilding and several sheds looked on the verge of collapse. He assumed that was where Alendur and the others would be. Between the buildings was a yard where a few chickens were clucking and pottering. In one corner of the yard was a well and in another a fire pit, with a cooking pot hanging from a trestle.

Peglar had left Murgo and its slave market under a full moon. It started red and enormous and shrank and yellowed as it climbed. He kept walking until it set in the early hours of the morning. Safren had ambled along beside him, occasionally making a detour to investigate an interesting find in the undergrowth. A few times she'd growled, he guessed at something she could smell or see but he could not, and once she'd crouched and barked, but the rest of the journey had been uneventful.

Once he'd stopped walking Peglar found the night to be chilly, and he was glad of Safren's company. She radiated warmth and he rested against her coarse coat, but he was unable to get much sleep. Dawn couldn't come soon enough. It seemed to him to be an age between noticing the first faint light of the new day and finally seeing the golden rim of the sun creep up from the sea beyond Maris Partem. Maris Partem, where he assumed Yalka was. It was the last place he had seen her, but was she still there? Or had she and her Grandfather gone to make a new life somewhere else? Did she think of him as often and as much as he thought of her? He was determined that he would find her again, but when would that be?

As soon as the sun was up he resumed his journey, with Safren at his heel, and it didn't take him long to reach the farm. All that was in Peglar's plan was to find the place; he had no idea what to do when he got there. The first thing would be to confirm that he'd got the right spot and it really was where Alendur and the others had been taken. But after that, what?

He stopped a little way off and hid behind one of the low rocky outcrops that were a feature of the landscape around there. He tugged Safren's collar to pull her in beside him and she licked his hand. She made a gentle groaning sound deep in her throat and he guessed that she was thinking about sausages. She'd long ago consumed virtually all of the stock he'd got together for the journey. Suggesting to her that she should put up with the hunger pangs was not an option. He reached into his pocket for the last one and gave it to her. It seemed to do for now, and she lay down beside him. He licked the greasy residue off his fingers. He seemed to have been hungry for days, and he felt it was affecting his energy levels and his ability to think. He could do with breakfast, and a single sausage wouldn't keep Safren satisfied for long.

The farm looked deserted. Every farm he'd seen in the past had had its own dog, often more than one, and he was wondering what the reaction might be if he came out from behind the rocks with Safren when a man emerged from the house. It was hard at that range to tell how old he was, but he was a man, not a youth, and he looked broad and strong. He turned his back on the yard, faced the wall of the building, pulled down his baggy pants, and took a long piss. Then he turned around, stretched, readjusted his clothing, and looked up at the sky. He had a proprietorial air and Peglar guessed he must be the head of the place, the farmer. He crossed the yard to one of the sheds. There was a chain on the door and he removed it and went inside. The door swung shut.

For some time nothing happened, and then the farmer came out. Now he was carrying a hefty-looking axe and two men trailed behind him. They were chained together and looked so different from when Peglar had last seen them that it took him a moment to realise who they were, and when he did it was a shock. One of the men was Alendur and the other was Beldrom. They were without doubt the men he knew, but they were stooped and cowed. He expected a third but the farmer, who he assumed was the same man who had bought them at the slave market, the man whose name was on Ryker's bill of sale, pushed the shed door closed behind them. Only two, so where was Reddall? He watched while Alendur and Beldrom collected a shovel each from an untidy heap of tools piled against the wall and followed the farmer along a track that led around the back of the shed.

All was quiet for a few minutes while Peglar waited to see if the farmer came back. If he did he would go and look for where Alendur and Beldrom had been taken to work and see if he could get those chains off them. His attention went back to the farm building, where the door opened again and a young woman, no more than a girl, emerged with a basket of clothes. She put it down in the yard, picked the contents up one at a time, shook them out, and hung them on a line. Peglar couldn't see her well but she looked almost as downtrodden as his two friends, a little mouse of a girl with a skinny frame and wispy hair. Then the farmer did come back. He said something to the girl, who winced as if expecting a blow and followed him inside.

Peglar was troubled. The way Alendur and Beldrom looked had been a shock. Only weeks ago they'd been stoking the boilers on The Morning Glory. They'd still looked fit in Murgo when they'd been sold. But they had gone downhill since then. What had been done to them? His problem was how to free them. The farmer had left them to work somewhere but they might not be alone. They might have been handed over to be supervised by someone else. Trying to get near them so he could find out more could be risky. Away from the rocks there was little cover, and it would be difficult to stay unseen. And there was Safren. She was hardly inconspicuous. There was nowhere he could leave her, and she'd stick out like a great brown bear if he came out into the open with her.

Still, he couldn't stay there, he had to do something. Safren was still lying beside him and he bent and clipped the rope to her collar. She looked at him as if he was mad – which he probably was because if she took it into her head to go somewhere there was no chance of him stopping her – but she gave a resigned sigh and put up with it. He shook the rope and she stood up and stretched, and he led her out from behind the rocks and headed towards the farmhouse.

He was twenty paces away when the door opened and the farmer came out. He stood watching Peglar, and he didn't look welcoming. The axe he was still holding glinted in the morning sun.

'You stop right there, my friend,' he said. His tone was anything but friendly, it was hard and sharp as his axe, and Peglar did as he was told. 'And who might you be?'

'I'm looking for work,' Peglar said.

'You've got a dog,' the man said. It was an accusation and a warning. 'Don't think you can try anything. If that thing comes near me I'll chop its fucking head off.' He raised the axe just to show that he meant it.

A low growl rumbled in Safren's throat, and Peglar rested his hand on her head in a way he meant to be reassuring. He hoped the man would see the wagging tail and ignore the growl. 'She's good-natured,' he said. 'I don't want any trouble. I'm looking for work, that's all.'

'It doesn't look good-natured to me,' said the man, but he lowered the axe. 'What's your name?'

'Pe… Pender.' Peglar mentally kicked himself for almost giving his real name.

'Pe… Pender, are you? Well, there's a name for you. Looking for work, you say. You don't look up to much to me. Farm work is hard. What can you do?'

Peglar knew he wasn't at his best. He'd been fit when he was captured by the pirates but his time shut up in Ryker's shed combined with the poor diet meant he'd lost some of his bulk. 'I'm stronger than I look,' he said. 'I used to be at sea, a stoker.'

The farmer looked sceptical. 'A stoker?'

'Actually, I was a trimmer.'

'And what's a trimmer do?'

'It's the trimmer that gets the coal from the bunkers and takes it to the stokers so they can feed the fire. It's heavy work and I was good at it.'

'Were you now? That may be, but I don't have any vacancies at the moment. I don't need anybody.'

While he'd been speaking a woman had come out of the house. It wasn't the girl who'd put out the washing but someone much older. Peglar guessed she was the farmer's pair, and probably the washing girl's mother. She looked Peglar up and down. She didn't appear to be kindly disposed but she wasn't as hostile as the man.

'That's not right,' the woman said. 'One of those slaves you bought can't work. any more. That leg of his is going to take a long time to get well, if it ever does. The two of them that are left can't do it all on their own. We need another pair of hands.'

The farmer looked annoyed at the woman's interruption but it was plain that he was used to doing what she told him. He looked back to Peglar.

'I don't pay,' he said. 'You get your bed and board,

that's all.' He seemed to think for a moment, then added, 'Am I supposed to feed your fucking dog too?'

'She comes with me,' said Peglar. 'She's a good guard dog. She'll keep your place safe.'

'This keeps my place safe,' said the man, twirling his axe. He thought some more. 'All right then, I'll give you a try. You can fill in for the slave who's sick. Just till he gets better, mind. After that, we'll see. And if it turns out you're a slacker or not up to it, you're out on your arse.'

'Thank you,' said Peglar. 'I'll work hard for you, you'll see.'

'Mm, you'd better,' said the farmer. 'This way, then.' He moved towards the shed where Alendur and Beldrom had been, and made a motion to Peglar to follow.

'No, not there,' said the woman, and she reached to take Peglar's hand. 'You can sleep in the house. You can have the back bedroom.'

The farmer looked cross. 'What?'

The woman gave him a hard look until he stepped back. Peglar followed the woman into the house. He was relieved. It would be better not to be in the barn with Alendur and Beldrom and, he assumed, the sick Reddall. He wanted to link up with his two friends and it sounded as though Reddall needed help, but being separate from them would give him a better chance of managing how he approached that. And the farmer's woman didn't look like someone you argued with.

14

RUMOURS

Syramos and Flynt were in the parlour, playing Sentinel on a large circular board on the table by the window. Eylese was watching them. Syramos had been teaching her the game but it was tricky. However, she knew enough to see that Flynt was overstretched and had left one of her lancers exposed. She had seen the danger too late and was wondering how to counteract it. She still had a dragon in reserve, but Eylese thought the best move would be for her to use her wizard. She was itching to suggest this to her but she knew it would be wrong to interfere.

Suddenly the door burst open and Meshi rushed in. He was red in the face and even more flustered than usual.

'Whatever's the matter?' said Myander, dropping the embroidery she was working on.

'It's Verron,' said Meshi, panting. 'You know, Verron, the man they call Big Ears, the bastard who attacked Yalka, the guy I clubbed.'

'Yes, what about him?'

'He says he's got her.'

'Got who?'

'Yalka.'

There was a second's silence, and then Eylese, Flynt and Myander all spoke at once.

'Where?'

'When?'

'What do you mean, "got"?'

'How do you know?'

Meshi was bewildered. His mouth hung open and his head snapped from one to another as he tried to decide which question to answer first.

'Here, sit down,' said Flynt, pulling out a chair. 'Take a deep breath, and tell us all about it from the beginning.'

'Begin by saying where you were when you heard it,' said Syramos.

'Right,' Meshi said, settling himself. 'Well, it was like this. I went to the market like you told me, to get the things you said, and I was there, and everybody was talking about it. They were saying how Verron's been mouthing off in The Quiet Woman about having got hold of the mardy mare who used to work there, and he's locked her up to teach her a lesson.'

'Did anybody mention Yalka by name? Did anyone say it was her?' said Syramos.

'No,' said Meshi, 'but it must be. There were only four of us at The Quiet Woman. Just me, Yalka, the landlord, and his wife. It can't be her, so it must be Yalka.'

'It sounds like it,' Eylese agreed. 'Do you know how he got hold of her? Or where he's keeping her?'

'They were saying that he found her somewhere near Semilvarga,' said Meshi.

'Semilvarga,' Syramos repeated. 'That was where she vanished. In my rhyming I saw her here in Maris Partem, with Peglar. That's why I decided to come back, why I insisted that we leave as soon as possible. But she must have been in Semilvarga all along. Perhaps all the time we were looking for her she wasn't far from us. Perhaps she came home and we weren't there,' he added, sadly.

The old man sounded so glum that Flynt put her hand on his arm. 'No one knows that. You did what your rhyming told you to do.'

Eylese turned to Meshi. 'Did you hear where Verron is keeping her?'

'Yes,' said Meshi. 'There's a place called Verlam. I know it. It's just off the main road to Semilvarga. It's tiny. There's nothing there, just an old tower and a couple of ruined farm buildings. That's where they say she is. Locked in the tower.'

'I know the place too,' said Flynt, 'but I don't think anybody lives there any more. How can we be sure that these rumours are true? Perhaps it's just something that this Verron creature has been boasting about.'

They all turned to Syramos, who looked stricken. 'Can you tell if it's true, Rhymer? Can you see if Verron really has got Yalka?'

Syramos sighed. 'I've explained before, I am not a fortune teller. A rhymer can see the general direction in which a life is heading and can identify some of the milestones and signposts on the way, but I can't pick up fine detail or specific times. No rhymer can.' He looked at the faces around him. 'Since Yalka was lost I have gone into trances and focused on her, and on Peglar. I've been able to see some things clearly. There will be huge upheaval in Chamaris. Peglar and Yalka will both be there, and after that they'll be here in Maris Partem, but not necessarily together. Beyond that I am unable to go. I cannot say how they'll get here, or when, or where either of them is now.'

Eylese was concerned but she was also comforted. If Syramos could see Yalka and Peglar together in the future, it meant that in the end they would both survive. Didn't it?

'Very well. Let's suppose it's true that Verron really does have Yalka locked up in the tower,' said Flynt, 'and now he's spreading the news that he's got her. It would make sense.'

'Sense?' said Myander. 'Isn't he just trying to finish off what he started that night Meshi clobbered him?'

Flynt shook her head. 'No,' she said. 'I mean, it might be that in the long run, but it's more complicated than that. It's a plan, and I think a fairly canny one. Question: who does Verron work for? Answer: Ragul. Question: what does Ragul want? Answer: Peglar. If Peglar hears that Yalka is a prisoner in this tower the most likely thing is that he'll go rushing there to rescue her. Verron will have set people up to lie in wait for him, and when he turns up they'll grab him.'

'And Verron will get the five hundred golds reward,' said Eylese.

'No doubt.'

'But nobody knows where Peglar is,' said Myander.

'Exactly,' said Flynt. 'It's designed to lure him out of hiding.'

There was silence while they all digested this.

'We must help him,' said Myander. 'What can we do?'

'The first thing we must do,' said Syramos, 'is to find out if these rumours are true and if my Granddaughter really is in the tower in Verlam.'

'I'll go there,' said Meshi, jumping up. 'I'll go and see.'

'No, it can't be you,' said Syramos. 'It's too dangerous. Verron knows you and he wants your blood for what you did to him. He'll have his thugs there and he might even be there himself, and that would turn out badly for you.'

For Eylese there was nothing to discuss. Her friend was in trouble so she must be the one to help her. 'I'll go,' she said.

Flynt looked scornful. 'And walk into a bunch of bored guards?' she said. 'Not a good idea.'

'It should be me,' said Syramos. 'I am her blood.'

Eylese wondered what Syramos would be able to achieve if he did go there, but what she said was, 'If she sees you she might call out, and that would be a problem.'

'I'll pass myself off as an old man of the road,' Syramos persisted. 'I'll dress in a shabby cloak and keep my face hidden.'

Eylese was firm. 'No,' she said, 'it really does have to be me. Verron doesn't know me and neither do any of his lot. I'll put on an overall and I'll pretend I've gone there to clean.'

'But there probably already is a cleaner,' Flynt warned.

'Then I'll say I'm another one, sent there to help out. I'll think of something.'

'And if she is there, what will you do then?' Myander said.

'I'll find a way. We have to get her out,' said Eylese. 'If we can do that we'll be saving both her and Peglar.'

'If the tower's being guarded, getting her out will not be easy,' said Flynt.

'I'll find a way,' Eylese repeated. She had no idea what that way night be or what it might involve, but she knew she had to try.

15

VERLAM

I t had seemed so simple when they'd been talking in Flynt and Myander's parlour. Go to the tower, see if Yalka's there, and if she is help her to escape. Eylese had been confident she could do that. Now she was anything but, and she became increasingly edgy as she made her way towards Verlam.

The place wasn't hard to find. Everybody knew Verlam tower. It was a local landmark and she'd seen it before from the road, but she'd never been close. As she got nearer she thought it looked creepy. She certainly wouldn't want to be shut up in it, and she hoped that her friend wasn't. On the other hand, she hoped that she was, because if she wasn't there, where was she?

The building sat in a grove of ancient olive trees which were as gnarled and twisted as old witches. It looked a bit like a castle. It was high, with a stumpy steeple on top and battlements around the roof. She guessed it had been built originally as some sort of defence, a fortress to control the road.

She was surprised at the number of people she

passed on the way. They were mostly men, and they were not travellers. They just seemed to be hanging at and around the roadside. She thought about asking what was going on but none of them looked friendly.

When she got closer to the tower there was no one, but the building seemed to be deserted. She approached through the trees and she was on the lookout for soldiers, servants, or any sign of life. There was none, although there was an outbuilding quite close which had smoke idly curling from the chimney. It was mid-afternoon, and Eylese guessed that if it was a guard house, and that seemed possible, the occupants would be enjoying their siestas.

She was wondering what to do and whether she could get any closer without being seen when a woman came out of the building and, unnervingly, looked straight at her. She was mean and severe, not young but not old either. She scowled at Eylese.

'You're the relief, I suppose,' the woman said, walking briskly towards her. 'Well, you've certainly taken your time getting here.'

Eylese glanced behind her to see if the woman was talking to someone else. She wasn't, Eylese was the only one there. She thought quickly. It could be a trap, or it could be an opening. She took a deep breath and trusted her luck. She stepped forward, bowed her head, and dropped a curtsey.

It seemed it was the right thing to do because the woman's sour expression softened, but only a little. 'You're late,' she grumbled. 'Where have you been? No, don't bother answering. You lot are all the same. I've no idea where Verron finds you. Anyway, I've got things to do. Get yourself in there and start by washing all those pots that the other one left. Then you can warm up the dinner. It's broth. It's in the pantry but don't serve all of it. That girl's got an appetite like a horse and she'll eat everything if she gets a chance.'

The woman hurried away, leaving Eylese looking after her and wondering what was going on. It seemed that she'd been mistaken for someone else. Who? And was 'that girl' Yalka?

She looked back to the tower. It seemed deserted but even so she was cautious as she moved towards the door. It was ajar, disconcertingly inviting. She gave it a gentle push, still with the idea that she might be walking into a trap. Verron was slimy and cunning, and she wouldn't put anything past him.

She stepped through the doorway into a narrow hall with a flagstone floor and a room on each side. The door of the nearest one was open and she could see that it was a kitchen because there was a collection of plates, pots, and vessels of various sorts on a table beside a sink. Those must be the things she'd been told to wash.

She stood still. The place was silent. 'Hello,' she called softly. 'Is anybody there?'

There was a staircase ahead and she could see at the top a small landing and a door. The stairs looked rickety but the door appeared to be very solid, bound top and bottom with metal bars. If Yalka was being kept in the tower, that's where she would most likely be.

Eylese started up the stairs, climbing slowly. The treads were worn and their creaking sounded deafening in the quiet of the afternoon. When she reached the top she stopped, took a deep breath, and tapped quietly on the door.

'Hello. Is anyone there?' she whispered. She was

trembling, half expecting the door to be wrenched back and to reveal… she couldn't imagine what. There was a moment's pause and then she heard a faint sound of movement on the other side. 'Yalka, are you there?'

Eylese could feel the hesitation. Then she heard someone say, 'Who's there?' It was a voice she knew, and her heart skipped a beat.

'Yalka? Is that you? It's me, Eylese.'

There was a moment's hesitation. 'Eylese? Eylese? Oh, my stars! What are you doing here? How did you get here? How did you find me?'

Eylese was tearful with joy. 'Yalka. I can't believe it's you. Are you all right?'

'I've been better,' came the muffled voice. 'They're keeping me shut in all the time and It's driving me crazy, but I'm okay. Look down. Can you see my fingers?'

The door was hefty but there was a wide gap under it, and four fingertips were protruding. Eylese knelt on the floor and stroked the fingers, and they responded. With her head on one side, she looked through the gap. She could just make out another eye looking back at her.

'Blood and bones, girlfriend, what are you doing here?' she heard Yalka say.

'Meshi heard a rumour. It's going round Maris Partem that a man they call Big Ears has been telling everybody he's keeping a girl locked up in a tower,' Eylese said. 'It sounded like it might be you and this is the only tower in the area, so I came to check. I can't believe it really is you. Your Granddad and Meshi told me you vanished in Semilvarga.'

'Granddad and Meshi? Are they here?'

'They're with Flynt and Myander in Maris Partem. But what happened to you? Where have you been?'

'It's a long story. Big Ears bought me.'

There had been a lot of surprises in Eylese's day but this was by far the biggest. 'Bought you? I mean, how? Why?' Then she had an awful thought. 'Are you... I mean,... has he?'

'No, I'm okay. It was a bit rough getting here, but he's not been near me since I arrived. I've not seen him, only a couple of maids and an older woman. I was set up. Somebody grabbed me in Semilvarga and they took me to a slave market in a place called Murgo.'

'Oh no! I've heard of Murgo. It's got an awful reputation.'

'Well, it's deserved. It's a dump. I was kept in a cell and then taken to an auction in this barn, along with a lot of other women. I was the last one up and Big Ears bought me. Twenty golds, I cost him. I thought he'd done it so he could fuck me and after that, I don't know, finish me off. Anyway, it wasn't for that, it wasn't for sex. Not yet, anyway. He said that he'd spread the word about where I was and then wait for Peglar to turn up to get me out. Then he'd grab him and take him to Ragul for the reward.'

Eylese was trying to process all this. Murgo was horrific, the slave market notorious, and to be sold there like a sack of potatoes didn't bear thinking about. 'How did Big Ears know you'd gone to Semilvarga?'

'He said he got it from you. You told him that me and Granddad had gone to Semilvarga.'

Eylese was bewildered. 'No. I never told him anything.'

'He said he'd tortured you till you told him.'

Eylese was horrified that her friend might think that she'd betrayed her. 'No. He never came near me. I've never even spoken to him.'

'I didn't believe him,' said Yalka, 'but he's such a louse that I couldn't get it out of my head that he might have hurt you.'

They touched fingers again. It was such a tiny contact but it meant so much.

'You've got to get a message to Peglar that whatever he hears about me, it's a trap,' said Yalka. 'You've got to stop him coming here.'

'We're already onto it,' said Eylese, 'but no one knows where he is. The best thing would be to get you out. Will this door open?'

'Do you think I'd be in here if it did? There's a woman in charge, a mean old cow. There's only one key and she keeps it.'

'I think I met her. She was just leaving as I got here.'

'Probably. She goes away in the afternoons. Then she comes back in the evening and opens the door so the maid can give me my dinner, and then she clears off again and doesn't come back till the morning.'

'She seemed to think I'd been sent to work here.'

'Did she? It's time for a new maid. They change them every couple of days. They say it's to stop me from getting to know any of them well enough to persuade them to help me. I expect she thinks you're the new one.'

'Is there no one else here?'

'There are a few guards. They live in a hut round the back but I don't see much of them. I think they spend all day lying around tossing each other off.'

'Might the real maid turn up?' said Eylese.

'I expect that's possible,' said Yalka. 'She'd normally

be here by now, but perhaps they've not managed to find a new one.'

There was another long pause while both girls thought about what they might do. It was hard talking under the door. Eylese was getting a crick in her neck and her back was aching. She climbed stiffly to her feet.

'I'm going to get you out,' she said.

'How?'

'I don't know yet, but I will.'

16

WORK

Peglar had assumed that he would be working with Alendur and Beldrom, and he had been thinking about what he would say to them and how he might set them free. However, it didn't turn out as he expected. He was taken straight away to a scrubby field. It was rough and uncultivated, and strewn with stones.

'See these?' said the farmer. 'I want 'em all picked up.'

Peglar's heart sank. There were thousands of stones there, so many that it would take weeks, months even, to make an impression. It would need maybe as much as a year to clear every one of them. 'What, the whole lot?'

The farmer sneered. 'Not what you were thinking of when you asked for a job, eh? All right, not every single one. Start with just them that are bigger than your fist. Collect 'em up and make a pile over there by the trees.' He pointed to the corner where a small pile had been started. 'A trimmer, were you? Well, let's see how you get on with real work.'

The farmer supervised Peglar for a few minutes, then

ambled off. Peglar watched him to see which direction he took and whether that might show where Alendur and Beldrom were, but he seemed to be bound for the farm. He'd hoped that there might be some food on offer but there was none. He had no water either and his throat was dry. Safren sniffed among the stones but decided there was nothing there for her, and went to lie in the shade, not too far away.

The job was back-breaking and the roughness of the stones soon made Peglar's hands raw. He started at the point nearest to where he'd been told to make the pile so he could throw what he'd picked up onto it, but when he got too far down the field to do that he had to carry them, and that took much longer.

He felt that he'd been working for many hours but it was probably only a couple when the farmer returned with a small cart and told Peglar to use that. He did and that helped things to progress more quickly, but he could only half fill the cart because if he loaded it to the top it became much too heavy to move over the rough ground.

The advantage of being left on his own for most of the time was that he could stop when he felt like it and stretch to ease his aching back. The sun arced overhead and the heat built. His thirst was intolerable and he was looking about to see if there was a pool or some other source of water anywhere when he saw someone approaching. It was the girl who had been hanging out the washing. She had a pitcher and a basket.

'Mother said I was to bring you these,' she said. She put what she was carrying on the ground and backed away. Her tone was sullen but her attitude was shy; it was an uneasy combination.

Peglar went for the pitcher, grabbed it and drank and drank and drank. The water was warmish but it tasted better than anything he'd ever had, even when he'd lived in the Palace. Safren, who'd stood to watch the approach of this stranger, concluded that she was neither interesting nor a threat and settled down again. Then she registered that there was water and came over. She was used to drinking from a bowl and the pitcher was a challenge, but Peglar tilted it for her and after a bit of experimentation she settled into long, slurping gulps. The girl watched, standing a little way off. When the pitcher was empty Peglar held it out towards her and she came forward cautiously and grabbed it, then hurried back to her previous spot.

Meanwhile, Safren had become very interested in the basket. It had a lid, and Peglar raised it to reveal food, and a lot of it. There was bread, eggs, hard cheese and olives. There were tomatoes and apples. There was nothing obviously intended for a dog but he doubted that Safren would turn down an invitation to share. She wolfed two eggs and some of the cheese, which seemed to satisfy her for now. Peglar ate what was left. He was ravenous and the temptation was to eat as fast as Safren, but he knew he would suffer if he did and he forced himself to slow down and chew every mouthful carefully. The girl observed him intently.

When he'd first seen her in the yard she'd reminded him of a mouse, and now she was closer that impression was even stronger. She was small and slight, with a pinched little face. Her lips were thin and her hair was a dry, brittle brown, held out of her eyes by a hairband embroidered with pink flowers. The headband was the only gesture towards femininity about her. Her smock was the drab dun of a peasant. Her fingers were stubby and her nails bitten. Peglar reckoned she couldn't have been more than twelve, and he had a sudden flashback to his half-sister Malina at that age, brushed, perfumed, and pampered by the Palace, already a lady. It reminded him of Yalka's rants about the morality of some people having so little while others had more than they would ever need. Where was she? When would he see her again?

Peglar turned back to the basket. There was nothing more in it that he could eat, so he replaced the cloth and closed the lid. 'Thank you for the food and the water.' He smiled at the girl, who looked swiftly away. 'What's your name?' he said.

'Wossly,' she said. Or that's what Peglar thought she said because his question threw her into confusion and she snatched the pitcher, took the basket, and almost ran away across the field.

Over the rest of that day and the following one he continued to work on the stones, and the next day too Wossly visited with a lunch basket and watched him while he ate. On the third day he invited her to join him in sampling what was in the basket, but she shook her head and retreated. Was it embarrassment? Or was it coyness? Peglar wasn't sure. The girl was certainly not confident around him, but he liked her. She was no beauty but she seemed thoughtful and kind.

The farmer, whose name he learnt was Jorian, came to examine his progress from time to time. He would point out some stones that Peglar had missed, stay for a few minutes, and then leave. Based on this evidence Peglar assumed that his work was satisfactory.

When he returned to the farm at the end of the third day he asked the farmer's wife about the sick slave.

'It was a scythe,' she said. 'It cut his leg wide open, down to the bone, and now it's gone bad.'

Peglar winced. The injury sounded nasty. 'How is he?'

'Poorly. It's not getting better.'

'I could look at it if you like,' said Peglar. 'I know a bit about treating wounds and I might be able to help him.'

Actually, Peglar knew very little about dealing with wounds, apart from what he'd picked up when he'd been in the Sanitorium after the fire in the River Settlements, but he was worried about Reddall and he wanted to see him. He also needed Alendur and Beldrom to know he was there. He hadn't found out where they went during the day and hadn't yet been able to contact them. If he could talk to Reddall they could begin to plan their escape, although if his leg was as bad as the woman said they might have to wait until he was fit enough to move.

The woman led him to the shed. Safren was going to come in with him but at the doorway she turned back and he soon realised why. The smell in the small space was appalling. It was the sour stench of something rotting, and it was enough to turn his stomach.

He found Reddall lying on his back on a low mattress. His eyes were closed and his breathing was irregular. His face was the colour of butter, and shiny with sweat. He showed no awareness of there being anyone there. A dressing on his leg covered the flesh just above his knee, and when Peglar knelt to examine it he could see that it was bloody and stained with puss.

'I'll need some hot water, some salt, and some vinegar,' he said to the woman. 'Oh, and some honey. And a spoon. And some rags, clean ones.'

As soon as the woman had gone, Peglar spoke, quietly and urgently. 'Reddall, how are you? Remember me? It's Peglar, from The Morning Glory. I found out who'd bought you and the others and I've come here to get you out.'

There was no response. He leant over his friend and the smell was appalling. He patted his cheek gently but without effect. Reddall's lips looked dry and Peglar searched around for water but there was none. He began to feel angry at such a lack of care for someone who was seriously injured.

He opened the shutters to let in air and light so he could study the wound. Cautiously he lifted the edge of the dressing. The leg was weeping and the fabric stuck to it. Peglar gently pulled it away and Reddall moaned, but he didn't come to. Beneath the covering, his wound looked awful. The cut was not clean, and probably the scythe blade had been filthy because what he saw was a zigzag gash with fluid oozing from it and the flesh around it swollen and inflamed. Despite the impression Peglar had tried to convey to the farmer's wife, he was way out of his depth. He'd heard of gangrene and knew that it was frighteningly serious and could be fatal. If that had set in there was nothing he could do.

The woman returned with the things he'd asked for, and this time the girl was with her. Peglar tipped the salt into the hot water and stirred until it dissolved. Then he poured in a generous slug of vinegar. He dampened one of the rags and delicately sponged the wound, working along its length to tease the filth out of it. Reddall moaned some more but he still didn't wake. Peglar hoped that was a good sign, although he feared it might not be. When he'd got the gash as clean as he could he poured some of the salt and vinegar mixture over it.

'It needs to be left uncovered for a while,' he said to the woman, 'to let it dry out. Then put some honey on one of these rags and wrap it around his leg. Don't make it too tight. Where are Jorion and the other two slaves?'

'They've gone to the next farm to get some goats. They'll be driving them back here soon.'

'Right. Wait until they get back, then put the honey on. It needs to be washed with salt and vinegar like I've just done and then have the honey poultice twice a day. He's in a bad way, so don't forget.'

He took a last, sorrowful look at the patient but there was no sign that Reddall had any idea that he'd been there, and he left the shed to go to the house. The woman and the girl walked beside him.

'This is Wossly,' the woman said, steering the girl towards him.

'I know. She's been bringing my food. Thank you.' He nodded to the girl and smiled.

The girl made a sound which was probably a giggle but sounded like a snort.

'Do you like her?' It was an unanswerable question. Peglar had only met her a couple of times and they'd hardly spoken. The woman didn't wait for an answer. 'She's a good girl.'

'I'm sure she is,' said Peglar.

'Clean, and a good cook. And she makes all her own clothes.'

'Good,' said Peglar. Where was this leading?

'Jorion and me were talking,' the woman said, 'and

we were wondering if you'd be interested in pairing with her.' She held up her hand to ward off Peglar's expression of astonishment. 'When she's old enough, we mean, she's not sixteen yet.'

Peglar was speechless. There were a thousand reasons why the idea was unthinkable. Top of the list was Yalka.

'We wouldn't want any Bride Gold for her,' the woman added hurriedly. 'Just for you to take her on and keep her. You seem to be a fine young man and we're sure you'd look after her.'

Peglar struggled for the right words, ones that would allow him to refuse without causing offence, or at the least to stall. 'It's good of you to think of me, but I've promised myself to someone else. I can't afford another pairing yet.'

'She wouldn't cost you much. She's got very simple tastes.'

There was a long pause. Peglar wanted to shout at the top of his voice that this was not only impossible but also stupid and unwelcome, yet if he rejected Wossly without appearing to think about it that would insult the woman and Jorian, and probably hurt the girl too. 'Thank you,' he said, 'and thank your man. Please leave me some time to consider if I can manage it.'

'You do that,' said the woman. 'It will be a good pairing. You won't regret it.'

The woman was talking as if Peglar had already agreed and he wanted to tell her that he hadn't, but he left it and she and her daughter went into the house. He needed space. He called to Safren, asleep in the yard, and she trotted over to him. He rubbed her head and ears. 'Well, what do we do about that?' he whispered to her. Safren looked at him with her crossed eyes and her tongue hanging out. She didn't appear to know.

Part way through the next day two men came to the farm. Peglar would have missed them if he'd been working in the field, but in moving one of the stones he'd gashed his hand on a shard of flint and he'd come back to the farm to clean it. Jorian had been angry to see him away from his work but Peglar had told him firmly that he didn't intend to get into the same state as the man in the barn and he insisted on treating the cut.

He was bathing it at the well when he heard a growl from Safren and a moment later he saw two riders approaching. As they drew close he could see that they wore the golden leopard crest of his father's House on their chests, and although he knew neither of the men he kept his head down and his face averted, just in case.

They dismounted and Jorion met them at the door to the house, where they talked. Peglar couldn't at first make out what was being said but he could tell from Jorion's tone that the visitors were not welcome. Then the voices were raised and he could hear.

'But that's impossible,' Jorion said. 'Where can I find that kind of money?'

'It's not our problem,' said one of the men. 'The rent is the rent, and that's what you owe the Estate for the next year.'

'But it went up last year, and now it's gone up again, this time by even more.' Jorion was almost whining.

'Don't blame us,' said the first man. 'It's the same for all the farmers on the estate. That's the sum we've been told you owe and that's what we're here to collect.'

'Blame your new landlord, Lord Ragul,' said the

second man. 'He's taken over from his father and it seems he needs more revenue than the old man.'

'So he takes it off us tenants,' Jorion complained. 'He's got no end of money and we've got nothing. How does he expect us to manage?'

'And what's he need it for?' said Jorion's wife, who had come out to join in the conversation.

'He's got lots of plans,' said the first man. 'Anyway, if you want money why don't you catch young Peglar, his half-brother. There's a big reward out for him. If you got that it would keep you on velvet for the rest of your lives.'

Peglar froze and a chill struck deep inside him. He turned so that his back was towards the men and he bowed his head. It was vital to get away without arousing any attention but he was desperate to hear what else might be said.

'What's he supposed to have done?' said Jorion's wife.

'Shagged his sister,' said the second man. 'Well, his half-sister, Lady Malina. And he didn't get as far as actually shagging her, but that's what he had in mind.'

'Yes,' said the first man, 'except some say it was a put-up job and he never touched her. Whatever, he was outlawed, and Lord Ragul's offered a reward of five hundred golds to anyone who brings him in.'

'Dead or alive,' added the other man.

Jorion whistled. 'Five hundred. That would do for me.'

'What's this Peglar like?' said Jorion's wife.

'What would he be now?' the second man asked his companion. 'Eighteen? Nineteen? Anyway, a young lad.

Tall, skinny, dark hair. You won't find him around here, though.'

'Why not?'

'He'll be in Verlam. They've got his girlfriend shut up in a tower and as soon as he hears about that he'll be there to rescue her faster than a buck in a warren. Verlam is where you'll find him.'

'Where is this place?' said Jorion.

'Down near Maris Partem, just off the Semilvarga road. If you go, though, you'll have to join the queue. When we came through there was no end of chancers hanging around, all hoping to be the first to spot Peglar and hand him over.'

Peglar left the well and went across the yard in the direction of the field, keeping his back to the group who were still talking. Safren padded along with him. His world had fallen in. How long would it be before Jorion and his woman put two and two together and guessed who he was? And how could it be that Yalka was imprisoned? Or was that just a story designed to draw him out of hiding? If it was true and she really was locked in somewhere she'd hate it. She so loved her freedom and the open air.

An hour ago he'd been wondering what to do. Now he knew. Alendur, Beldrom and Reddall might need him here, but Yalka needed him more. He must go to Verlam.

17

ESCAPE 2

Getting Yalka out of Verlam tower was a firm promise and Eylese was determined to keep it, but she had no idea how. She went slowly down the stairs and sat on the bottom step where she could think.

She considered the possibilities. The door to the room where Yalka was being kept looked and felt very solid. So did the lock. Were there any tools that she could use to force them? She went to the kitchen and examined what was in the cupboards. She found pots, dishes, a hefty-looking frying pan, and a rolling pin. The last two could be useful weapons but she doubted they would make much impression on the door. Was there another key? Possibly, but where might it be? A search of the drawers and hooks yielded nothing. She tried in the storeroom but found only old boxes and broken furniture. Her schemes grew wilder. Fetch Meshi and get him to shin up the outside of the building with a rope? Set the place on fire so that Yalka could be rescued in the confusion? On her way to the tower she'd seen people hanging around on the roadside. Could she get their help to raid the place? None of these haphazard schemes made sense; she had to be the one to do the job, and on her own.

Then she had an idea. It wasn't a complete thought, just a tiny spark on the very fringe of her thinking. She went back to the top of the stairs and knocked on the door.

'Yalka?'

There was a pause before she heard movement on the other side and a muffled answer.

'Yalka, I've got an idea. Tell me what happens here.'

'What do you mean, what happens here? Nothing. I'm locked in, I have nothing to do, I'm bored senseless, and it's driving me mad.'

'I know. I think we can get you out but I need to know the routine. Is every day the same? Who brings your food? When do they come? Start from the morning and go through the day.'

'All right. Well, I wake up early. Maybe as early as the fifth bell, but I've no way of telling the time so I don't know. Woman and the maid don't sleep here, so there's only me. I do some warm-ups, run on the spot, do sit-ups, press-ups, and a few more things. Then I wait. I hear a noise downstairs which I think must be Woman arriving, because she keeps all the keys. The maid must get here soon after because a bit later they both come up here together. Woman opens the door and stands just inside it. She's always got a knife with her, a big carving knife, and she stands and watches while the maid puts my breakfast on the table. The maid then goes downstairs to get water, and she carries it up to the washroom. She comes back down with the chamber pot and takes that below so she can empty it.'

'And does this person you call Woman stay with you while all this goes on?'

'Yes. Right by the door. With the bastard knife. She watches me all the time. It's creepy.'

'Then what?'

'The maid brings the chamber pot back, takes it upstairs, and collects my breakfast things.'

'Do you get a knife with your breakfast?'

'No, nothing like that. It's just finger food. You know, some cheese, bread, olives, maybe a tomato. The maid takes away anything that's left and they both go out. Woman locks the door, and that's it. I'm on my own again for the rest of the day. I think the maid stays in the house because I can sometimes hear noises from downstairs.'

'What sort of noises?'

'Things being moved about. Clattering from the kitchen.'

'Voices?'

'No. When the maid changes over and a new one comes they talk for a bit, but not for long. Woman doesn't stay here. She comes and goes because I see her from the window walking through the olive trees. She's away every afternoon and comes back when it's time for me to be fed in the evening. Then it's the same routine.'

'So Woman could come back here any time now.'

'Yes.'

'What does the maid bring you in the evening?'

'Broth. It's always the same. Sour and boring.'

'Good. Well, I have a plan. To start with, Woman thinks I'm the new maid, so that's what I'll be.'

'But what if the real one turns up?'

'Then I'll tell her there's been a mix-up and get her to send the other one away.'

'And what then?'

'We'll get away from here and hide you somewhere you can be safe. We'll have to be careful, though, because when I came along the road from Maris Partem there were a lot of people around.'

'Whatever for?'

'For Peglar. They're hoping he'll come along to find you and they'll be able to grab him and get the reward. There were loads of them, hiding in the scrub. I think some of them are sleeping there.'

'Bloodsuckers.' Yalka almost spat the word. 'I've got to get out of here before he learns where I am and comes to help me.'

'Yes.'

The plan was simple, although it did depend on everything working as predicted. It wasn't easy to explain it to Yalka through the door because all the time they were alert to the possibility of either Woman or the real maid turning up. And of course, there was always a chance that they might alert the guards, although Yalka said she rarely saw them. When they'd been over it a couple of times and were satisfied that they'd covered everything, Eylese went down to the kitchen to carry on with the jobs Woman had given her.

She worked first on the pile of dishes, pots and pans that were on the table. Food was caked on them and it didn't look as though they'd been touched for some time. Eylese wondered what the maids did if it wasn't washing up. It would need hot water to do a proper job but there was nowhere to heat any. She began to understand why the dirty dishes had been allowed to pile up.

She saw another door at the back of the kitchen and found it opened into a small scullery. In one corner was a built-in copper, with a fire underneath. Even though the fire had died down and was now only a few glowing embers the room was stiflingly hot. She lifted the lid off the copper and was pleased that the water felt warm. It was warm enough for now, but she would need it to be hotter later.

There was a pile of wood beside the fire and Eylese carefully arranged some sticks and blew on them until they began to blaze. She found a tub of what must be the broth that was served to Yalka and set it to heat up. It looked disgusting and smelt rank. She was thankful that Yalka wouldn't have to eat any of it. Then she filled a bucket with warm water and took it to the kitchen so she could finish washing up.

She was completing the job when the person who had greeted her when she arrived – presumably this was the one Yalka called Woman – came in. She had the same disapproving look as before, a fusion of frown and sneer, and Eylese assumed that this was her default expression. She picked up the items Eylese had cleaned one by one, clearly looking for faults. When she couldn't find any she looked even more displeased. She had a long knife in one hand, and over the next hour Eylese saw that while from time to time she might swap it from one hand to the other, she never put it down.

'Well, at least you're an improvement on the last girl,' Woman said. Then, in case Eylese might take this as approval, she added, 'But that's not saying much.' She transferred her attention to the scullery. 'I see you've put the broth on to warm up,' she said. 'How did you know to do that?'

'I asked the girl you're keeping upstairs what she had to eat in the evening. She told me broth.'

She was going to add that Woman had also told her about the broth when they first met, but she didn't get the chance. Woman pounced. At last she had found something to criticise and she could hardly contain her glee. 'You are not to talk to the prisoner. Didn't they tell you that when they took you on? I am the only one who speaks to that girl. No one else is permitted to say anything.' She sighed as if the whole of existence was in tatters and she was the only one holding it together. 'Anyway, make sure the broth is thoroughly heated. It's a few days old and I don't want her vomiting all over her rooms. And neither do you, because you would be the one who would have to clean it up.'

Woman almost smiled. Eylese presumed it was because she was relishing the prospect of seeing her on her knees mopping up the contents of Yalka's stomach.

Eylese quickly realised that Woman was one of those individuals who love to find jobs for other people, and if they can't find them they invent them. There was the table to be scrubbed, and then all the things that had been washed had to be stored away. Eylese did that while Woman sat on a chair in the middle of the kitchen directing where the various items were to go. When Eylese had finished that and thought she might get a break, she was sent to the scullery where there was a large basket containing towels, bedding, and a wide range of clothing. Some of it might have been things worn by Yalka but the rest were men's, and Eylese thought there was a possibility that Woman was being paid to take in washing that was actually being done by the maids. The succession of jobs was relentless, and although Eylese was used to housework because that was what she did for Flynt and Myander, by the time she'd finished the tasks that Woman set, her neck and shoulders were aching and her hands were red and sore.

At last Woman seemed satisfied and ready to move on, and it was a relief to Yalka when she said that it was time to collect the broth and take it up to 'her ladyship'.

'Remember what I told you about making sure it's good and hot,' she said.

'Yes,' said Eylese. She certainly would remember that. It would be as hot as she could possibly get it.

She decanted the broth into a heated earthenware bowl, put some bread on a plate, placed both on a wooden tray, and followed Woman, who still had the knife in her hand, up the stairs. At the top, Woman delved down the front of her gown and brought out a large key on a cord around her neck. She put the key in the lock, turned it, withdrew it and dropped it back into its hiding place.

She opened the door and Eylese looked through. It was the first time she'd seen the inside of the room that had been Yalka's prison. Yalka was standing at the far side, opposite the door. That was where she told Eylese she'd been ordered to wait when Woman and the maid came in.

'You first,' said Woman, and she stood back to allow Eylese to enter. When she'd done so she took up a position just inside the doorway and stood with the knife at her side, ready.

Eylese went to the table a few paces away and put down the bread and the broth. She was trying hard to look as though she was ignoring Yalka, who came forward and stood behind the table, ready to sit. Eylese had her back to Woman. She caught Yalka's eye and the girl gave an almost imperceptible nod.

'This bread's mouldy,' said Eylese, picking up the bread plate and walking towards Woman. 'I'll get some fresh.'

Woman was making to refuse, but the distraction was just enough for Yalka. With a shriek she hurled the bowl of broth at Woman, a couple of paces away. Although Woman dodged, the hot liquid splashed over her front and into her face. She put up a hand to protect her eyes and as she did so Eylese chopped the edge of the bread plate hard onto the wrist holding the knife. Woman gasped in pain, dropped the knife and Yalka seized it.

Eylese was now behind Woman and holding her around the chest, pinning her arms. Woman struggled and kicked, and although she was powerful Eylese was stronger and she held on. She manoeuvred her away from the door, hooked her foot in front of her, gave her a mighty push, and Woman fell forward. Eylese dived on top of her, kneeling on the small of her back and forcing her face down on the boards. She started to shout.

'Quick, the muslin,' Eylese gasped. 'Shut her up before the lookouts hear her.'

Yalka had the roll of muslin ready and started to circle it tight around Woman's head. Woman writhed and tried to bite but Eylese held her tight.

'Stop your racket or we'll smother you, you evil bitch,' Yalka growled.

Woman stilled and Yalka wrapped some more. Then she took the knife and cut the fabric. She sat on Woman's thighs and began to wind the roll around her calves. Then she worked her way up, both the girls lifting her to get the muslin under her body, round and around, and all the time pulling tight. When the trussing was done the girls got off Woman and stood over her.

'One squeak out of you and I'll cut your throat,' Yalka told her, and she poked the knife under Woman's chin. The fight seemed to have gone out of her.

'You're hurting me,' she mumbled.

'Good,' said Yalka. She found the key cord around Woman's neck, cut it and fished out the key.

Yalka and Eylese stood up and looked at the person on the floor. There was no trace of her former truculent self. She looked beaten and pathetic, bound like an inexpertly wrapped mummy. Eylese almost felt sorry for her. Almost, but not quite.

The two girls went to the door. 'Have a nice night,' said Yalka, as she closed it behind her and turned the key.

On the landing, they hugged.

'We've got to get past the guards,' said Yalka.

'And all the people on the road,' said Eylese. 'Thank the heroes it's dark.'

'Yes,' said Yalka. 'Then we've got to spread the news that I'm out, so Peglar doesn't come here looking for me. We'd better get going.'

They walked away from the tower and Yalka hurled the key to her prison door as far as she could into the olive grove.

18

A MOVEMENT

The messenger was fearful of giving the news. 'She's gone, ma'am.'

'Gone! Gone!! What do you mean, she's gone.' Vancia was livid. This was the latest in a whole pack of things that were going wrong. She picked up a vase and flung it, flowers and all, at the unfortunate go-between, who had to leap aside to dodge it. The vessel smashed on the marble floor and the broken blooms were scattered. 'Gone when? Gone where? How did she get out?'

The messenger was in a pickle. He couldn't avoid an answer but he was wary of saying something else that might not be welcome.

'On your mother's life, speak,' Vancia screeched, 'or I'll have you taken from here and flogged till you no longer can.'

The messenger cleared his throat. 'One of her friends got into the tower by masquerading as a maid,' he said. 'They must have come up with the plan between them, because when the housekeeper came back to take the girl her evening meal they both set on her and overcame her. Then they bound her, and got away.'

'Both of them?'

'Yes, ma'am.'

'And where are they now?'

The messenger glanced around anxiously to see if there were any more objects that could be thrown. 'Nobody knows, ma'am. They have not been seen.'

Vancia stared at him wearily. Her anger had drained away, replaced by an exhausted bewilderment. Here she and her son had at their disposal all the resources of the Palace, including the Household Guard, which Crestyn told her had been significantly augmented, and yet a boneheaded girl, a slut from the slums and her half-baked accomplice could outwit them. 'Send for Sainter,' she said. 'Get him at once.'

Sainter was a long time coming. He never seemed to hurry, but whenever he arrived he was invariably out of breath. He came in now, panting and perspiring. Vancia ordered him to sit and waited impatiently for him to recover.

'You've heard that this Yukka person has got away?'

'Yalka. Yes My Lady,' said Sainter. 'The news is all over the Palace.'

'And I suppose everyone thinks I'm a laughing stock.'

'No, no, My Lady, certainly not.'

Vancia snorted, remarking to herself again what a pathetic object Sainter was. Pathetic and prim. It was a pity he was so useful.

'Does my son know?' she said.

'I cannot say, ma'am, but I should think that by now he does.'

Throughout this exchange, Vancia had been pacing up and down in front of Sainter, who was on a low bench and still dabbing at his brow.

'She must be caught. There is no chance now of Verron's scheme working because if the news has spread as rapidly as you say, Peglar will certainly have heard it and he won't go anywhere near the wretched tower. But she must be caught. Caught and whipped. Flayed to within an inch of her worthless life. And the trollop that helped her.'

'Yes ma'am.'

Vancia halted her pacing and took a seat facing Sainter. 'And what are we going to do about him?' she said.

'About whom, My Lady?'

'About my son, Lord Ragul. My people tell me that the chariot race, far from increasing his popularity, has diminished it.'

'That is what I have heard too. Lord Burian was well-liked and few people believe that the collision was an accident.'

'Of course it wasn't an accident,' Vancia said crossly. 'I saw it happen and there's no doubt that it was intentional. The problem is that it was also clumsy. I approve of what my son did, but I am in despair that he couldn't manage to do it better.' Vancia waited but there was no reply from Sainter. 'Something must be done. We can't undo the "accident" or make my son go back and do it again properly, but people will remember it. Those who saw it will describe it in detail to those who did not. The day the Master of the City murdered his companion will be talked about for years. We must find some way to prevent that. We must take steps to repair my son's reputation.' And his sanity, she thought but didn't say.

'Yes, My Lady. Well, it just so happens that I have been giving some thought to exactly what you say and to ways in which Lord Ragul might be given a new place in the public's esteem.'

Vancia regarded him with interest, but also with caution. He was without doubt the most repulsive creature, but he was as cunning as a fox. 'Indeed? Do you have anything in mind? And I remind you that your last strategy for increasing my son's popularity was a complete failure.'

'I understand that, My Lady. It is unfortunate that the chariot race did not achieve the aim intended. It was a disaster on several counts, not only due to the death of Lord Burian but because in addition a lot of people lost money, some of them a great deal of it. They had placed bets on Lord Burian to win, and the collision cost them what they believe should have been their legitimate winnings. They blame Lord Ragul for their loss, and once an infection finds a seat, it grows. Other complaints and speculations are now surfacing. Specifically, whether the combat between Lord Ragul and Peglar was fair. They say that Marshal Thornal was wrong to declare Lord Ragul the winner, and point to the fact that since then your son has had difficulty walking, while on the night of his exile Peglar was able to leave the city on foot without difficulty.'

'Is that all?' said Vancia, sourly.

'There are other grumbles surfacing all the time. My Lady knows how once a cavity appears, vocal members of the public will pick at it for their own gain.'

Vancia did know this. There was kudos in being the

first to circulate a rumour, no matter how wild, particularly one that concerned a figure in the public eye, and some people appeared to compete to do this. Its effect was to make the gossip wilder and wilder.

'There is a hill to climb,' Sainter continued, 'and I fear that improving Lord Ragul's image throughout the city and beyond could take a long time.'

Vancia smiled grimly. She did not doubt that it would, and she pondered again on the insanity of a system that placed her dolt of a son in a position of power that was closed to her daughter Malina, who was both clever and beautiful. But things were as things were. In time the customs and practices of the city might be changed but that would take both the will to do it and skills of leadership, and she knew her son possessed neither.

Sainter broke into her thoughts. 'I suggest something different, ma'am, a new approach. What I think is needed,' he said, 'is not entertainment or the temptation to make money. We must offer the people a distraction, an interest that will divert them from Palace chatter.'

Vancia was immediately interested. 'Explain.'

'What I have in mind is the creation of a movement, something which would absorb people's attention, glorify the city, and to which Lord Ragul would be inextricably linked.'

'And what might that be?'

'I have recently been conducting research into the life of Farumon. You have heard of Farumon, ma'am?'

Vancia recalled that Farumon was one of the warriors of the Golden Age who was reputed to have served the city with glory. There were some stories about him but she couldn't remember any of them.

'Only the name,' she said. 'Wasn't he one of the ancient heroes?'

'He was indeed, ma'am. The story which concerns us here is of his death. It so happened that Chamaris was under attack, besieged by all the other cities of the plain, against whom there had been a long and arduous war. The siege continued for many weeks. Matters were desperate and the people were suffering. Farumon asked for fifty volunteers to fight with him to lift the blockade. They came forward, and under Farumon's orders they crept out of the city at night using a network of secret tunnels, which some say still exist. The tunnels enabled them to emerge onto the plain in secret. The interesting thing is that all of them were women. Farumon had ordered them to wear white, and when the enemy sentries saw them they took them to be ghosts and fled. Panic spread, and soon the whole of the enemy's forces were running away, stumbling over each other in the dark and leaving behind their equipment. Farumon's band burnt the enemy's encampments, stole their provisions, and drove off their horses. It was a triumph. However, there was a small pocket of resistance, and in challenging it Farumon himself was severely wounded. He was carried back to the city where he died. The legend goes that as he passed away he told those around him that he would not be dead, merely sleeping, and if ever there came a day when the people of Chamaris needed him they were to call on him and he would return.'

'Yes, I remember the story now,' said Vancia, 'but what use is it to us?'

'Its use would be if we are able to make a link between Lord Ragul and the glorious name of Farumon.

Let us put it about that Farumon came to Lord Ragul in a dream. He told him that his golden sword was buried in the Citadel, and instructed him to retrieve it and build a shrine in which to treasure it. And so that his promise to the city might never be forgotten, there is to be a regular ritual where the sword is shown to the people and they are reminded of Farumon's pledge.'

'What sort of ritual?'

'A parade. A procession, in which Lord Ragul figures prominently, preferably bearing the sword. People would be encouraged to beg the spirit of Farumon for blessings and favours. They would also be asked to make contributions to the upkeep of the shrine and the maintenance of those ministering there. It would be implied that those who contributed most would have the best chance of their petitions to Farumon being heard. This could bring in a sizeable sum for the Household Treasury.'

Vancia was impressed, but she was also doubtful. It would be a huge undertaking. 'How could we manage the creation of such a movement? From nothing? '

Sainter leant forward. He was more enthusiastic than Vancia had seen him in a long time. 'First must come the dream. Then the finding of the sword. Those should be prominently reported and the story spread. Then work should begin on the shrine. It might take some time to design such a thing and gather the craftsmen and builders needed to construct it, but we would not wait. The processions and rituals could begin as soon as the sword is found.'

Vancia could see that it was a well-thought-out scheme. But was it ingenious and complex enough to take attention away from the present dismal situation?

'How could we spread the story?' she said. 'Gossip and hearsay? The way we got across to people that this Yukka...'

'Yalka.'

'...whoever, Peglar's whore, was being held?'

'I think that for this, something more formal is required. I suggest the appointment of a group specially briefed to do it. They might be called regents, the Regents of Farumon. The Arch-Regent would be Lord Ragul himself, and the others, twenty or thirty of them, would spread the news of Farumon, and promote the observance of his rituals. Also, they would observe the citizens, celebrate and reward examples of virtuous behaviour and punish and condemn wickedness. Oh, and they would collect the offerings to the shrine.'

Vancia could see the potential of what Sainter was suggesting. 'You say that Farumon's fifty volunteers were women.'

'So the story goes, My Lady.'

Vancia could see another benefit, something which might serve her own interests. 'Then as well as the regents there should be priestesses, fifty of them, who would be part of the parade, all wearing white.'

Sainter beamed. 'An inspiration, My Lady.'

Possibly an even greater benefit, Vancia thought, would be the effect on Ragul. Since the combat with Peglar, she had become increasingly worried about the functioning of his mind. He knew he had not won and that the City Marshal's judgement had been biased. Had she not paid him for it to be so? But it had damaged Ragul's confidence and the preposterous reward he had offered for Peglar had been evidence of that. There was more. Almost every night now Ragul came to her room in the small hours and crept into her bed, snuggling up to her and calling her mummy. When she told him this had to stop he said that he could no longer sleep in his own room because he heard the spirit of Burian calling to him in the dark. It was not only the people who needed to be distracted; her son did too.

'How long would it take to set up what you describe?' she asked.

'I think it could be done reasonably quickly. We could circulate accounts of the dream right away. We could start to appoint the Regents – I have in mind several people who would be suitable – and recruit the Priestesses. If the Assembly could be persuaded to finance the work on the shrine for the golden sword, that also could begin at once.'

'There is a problem,' said Vancia. 'We have no golden sword.'

Sainter smiled. 'Then we must acquire one. We must have one made, and bury it on the Citadel where the shrine will be built.'

Vancia nodded, and at last she smiled. 'Then please begin.'

Sainter stood and bowed, and shuffled out of the room, panting again.

Vancia watched him go. He'd come up with an ambitious and imaginative plan, but it was not without risk. She knew that public opinion was volatile and could develop a life of its own, and having begun to move against the House of the Leopard it would be hard to turn it around. Could it be done? She did not doubt that if anyone could do it, Sainter could. The little man was truly an asset; if he was not quite so physically repellent she could hug him.

19

YALKA'S HAIR

Yalka knew that her hair was probably her most striking feature. Her face was not bad. Her Grandfather always said she was pretty, but he would say that wouldn't he? Peglar had told her the same thing, and of course ever since she'd first met Meshi when she went to work at The Quiet Woman, he had been unable to take his eyes off her. But any pretensions to beauty, either of body or mind, had to compete with the birthmark on her cheek, the whore mark; some people found it hard to get past that. So her long, golden hair was often seen as her major asset, and sacrificing it would be a wrench.

She went to the kitchen, where she found a large pair of scissors. Then to the parlour, where Eylese was kneeling on the floor by the grate, blowing on the fire to get it going.

'I want you to cut my hair,' she said.

'You want me to what?' Eylese said, looking up in surprise.

'I want you to cut my hair. Will you? Please?'

'Why? It seems a funny time for either of us to be bothering about how we look.'

Yalka drew up a chair, plonked herself on it and folded her arms. She usually wore her hair bound up, but that night it was loose and it fell on either side of her face and down her back.

Eylese left the fire, came round behind her, and started to part the strands. 'You want me to level it and trim the ends.'

'No, I want you to cut it off, all of it. I want it short, like a boy's.' She swept a hand through her blonde mane.

Eylese came round to the front of her. She looked horrified. 'But your hair's lovely. Everybody says so. Why do you want it all cut off? Are you mad?'

'No. I want to get rid of it.'

'Are you sure? You can't stick it back on if you change your mind.'

'I'm sure.'

Eylese didn't move and Yalka sighed, took the scissors in one hand, grabbed a handful of her hair in the other, and hacked. The scissors were blunt and pulled and Yalka winced, but she kept going until a sizeable hank was loose and fell to the floor. 'There, like that.'

Eylese put a hand to her mouth. 'On my life, girl, what are you doing?'

'I want to be in disguise. I need to go into the city and I don't want Big Ears spotting me and putting me back in that tower. We've been talking about how we can find out what's happening, and the only way is to go there, mingle with the people, look and listen. My hair marks me out.'

'But you could cover it up. You could wear a hood.'

'It's too risky. All my life I've lived in the River Settlements so there's a good chance somebody in the city could recognise me. If Ragul or any of his gang realise I'm there they might grab me again as a way of getting to Peglar, and we'd be back where we started. That can't happen. The mark on my face is enough of a giveaway but the hair would clinch it. I can get rid of the hair. It has to go.'

Eylese looked upset and as though she was going to say more, but as far as Yalka was concerned the discussion was over. She held out the scissors, folded her arms, and Eylese started. Yalka sat with her eyes closed while she felt Eylese tugging and cropping. It took half an hour and she kept encouraging her friend to cut it shorter, while Eylese chopped and cropped, taking the golden strands, snipping them off and setting them aside. Then she stood back.

'That's it,' she said. 'Any more and you'll be bald.'

Yalka raised a hand to her head. For as long as she could remember, whenever she'd done that her hand had met long hair, thick and lush. Now it felt short and fuzzy. It didn't feel like hers at all.

'Pass me the mirror,' she said.

Eylese did so and Yalka took a long look at herself, turning her head from side to side.

'It looks a mess to me,' said Eylese. 'It's like a boy's.'

'That's just what I want. Now I want you to dye it for me.'

This time Eylese didn't question her. She simply took the dye Yalka had brought with her and dissolved the powder in warm water. Yalka bent over the bowl and felt Eylese working the black liquid into what was left of her hair. Then she bent forward while it was rinsed and rubbed dry.

She looked into the mirror again. Within an hour her hair had gone from luxuriant golden waves to a spiky, muddy brown stubble. She stared at her reflection. She looked to be a different person.

'I still think you were daft to do this,' said Eylese.

'I've told you. I want to look like a boy. If people take me to be one of the street kids they won't take any notice of me.' She laughed. 'It's a good job I haven't got tits like yours.'

Eylese gave her a friendly push. 'It's all right for you,' she said. 'I know I could do to lose a bit, but everything that goes in my mouth seems to make me put on weight. You can eat like a bear and never gain an ounce.'

It was true, but men seemed to like what Eylese had. She'd even seen Meshi taking a sly peep now again.

'What do we do now?' said Eylese.

'We go upstairs, go to sleep, and when we get up I'll tell you the plan.'

'Why not now?'

'There are still one or two things I have to think through, but it will be all right. Trust me.'

Syramos, Flynt and Myander were talking in the parlour. Eylese said goodnight for both of them because Yalka didn't feel ready for them to see her new look yet, certainly not her Grandfather.

The girls went upstairs and they huddled together in Eylese's bed. The house got chilly as the night came on and it comforted Yalka to feel the warmth of another body close. She was apprehensive about what was to come. What would happen over the following days was going to have a big effect on the rest of their lives, and on a lot of other people's too.

There was too much going on in her brain for her to sleep. She lay awake for a long time and heard the first bell, then the second, and then the third. As soon as it grew light she got out of bed carefully, so as not to disturb the still sleeping Eylese. She put on some clothes and sat at the table by the window. There was a pencil and some sheets of paper, and she began to draw. There were things Eylese needed to know.

She'd been busy for a while when there was a cry from the bed. 'On my life, I didn't recognise you! I thought some strange boy had invaded my room.'

Yalka looked at Eylese, who was sitting bolt upright and staring at her. 'A boy in your room. You should be so lucky. The disguise works, then.'

'Yes.' Eylese shook her head in wonder. 'It's not just your hair, it's your clothes. You're wearing a tunic and breeches.'

'They're Meshi's. They're baggy but they'll do.'

Eylese got out of bed, came behind Yalka and looked over her shoulder. Yalka had drawn a triangle, with some lines across it.

'What's that?' she said.

'It's Chamaris,' said Yalka. 'You don't know it so I'm making you a plan.' She pointed out the features she'd drawn. 'At the top here,' she pointed to the apex of the triangle, 'is the Citadel.' She inscribed a letter C. 'That's the oldest bit of the city. It's in ruins. I used to meet Peglar there before he got kicked out, but no one else goes there any more.' Yalka remembered but didn't say that it was also where she and Syramos had buried her brother, Verit, on the night that the fire killed him and destroyed their home. 'This,' and she ran a finger along a horizontal line just below it, 'is the street where the rich people live. There are lots of amazing houses along there, and the biggest is the Master's Palace, right at the end. That's where Peglar's family lives: his stepmother, Vancia, and his half-sister, Malina, and his father, Karkis, and of course Ragul the rat.'

Yalka felt her friend tense. Eylese had told her when they first met that Ragul had been in command of the detachment that put down the revolt in Semilvarga. Her parents had been hanged and she held Ragul responsible. She had left her home and come to Maris Partem so that she was near enough to Chamaris to find an opportunity for revenge. Yalka felt her friend's hurt and respected her need to make Ragul pay, but she doubted it would ever be possible, there were just too many obstacles. However, getting into the Palace would be a start.

She took her hand. 'We can't go after Ragul yet. Since Karkis got so ill, he's practically taken over as Master of the City. We'll never get near him. The best way forward is to get Peglar's exile lifted so he can come back to the city and help us deal with the bastard.' Yalka felt Eylese's hand tighten.

'What's that?' she said, pointing to another horizontal line about halfway down the triangle.

'It's called the Grand Parade,' said Yalka. 'It goes right across the city from the west wall to the east. It's wide and impressive, and lined with big, important buildings. It's where all the formal stuff goes on. The line that crosses it is another road that runs from the Citadel all the way down to the Great Gate.' She pointed a finger at the junction. 'Where the two roads meet is the Great Square.'

'Why is everything called great?' Eylese asked. 'Great this and grand that?'

Yalka rolled her eyes. ''Cos that's what they're like in Chamaris. They're full of themselves and they think everything they've got and everything they do is special. Anyway,' she turned her attention back to the intersection of the two roads and drew a rectangle, 'the square is here. The Hall of the Council is on one side and opposite is the Ceremonium. That's where the most important civic events take place. Between the two there's a big fountain. That's where we'll meet.'

She saw Eylese frown. 'Meet? What do you mean? You want me to go there?'

'Yes. We need to get the lie of the land. When I lived in the River Settlements I had a good idea of what was going on in the city. I knew what was happening, what the people were thinking and talking about, who was in and who was out. But I've not been there for a while now and I'm out of touch. We need information. The more we can find out the better we can decide what to do.'

'And you're going there first.'

'Yes.'

'What are you going to do?'

Yalka didn't know how much to say. She trusted Eylese absolutely. Hadn't she just rescued her from Big Ears? But she knew how determined her friend was to get to Ragul and was concerned that she might leap in and do something rash. For now, it was better to go slowly.

She took Eylese's hand. 'I think I know somebody

who might help us, but to reach him we have to get into the Palace. That's tricky. We can't just walk up to the main gate and march through. Luckily there are other ways in, but we have to make preparations. It will be best if I start those on my own.' She didn't add that she was lighter and more agile than Eylese, and would be better able to get away if anything went wrong.

'So where will you be? What will you be doing?'

'Do you trust me?' Yalka said.

'Of course I do. How can you ask that?' Eylese looked wounded.

'You're a proper friend,' said Yalka. 'A friend like I've never had before. You want to get even with Ragul and so do I, but it won't be easy. It's dangerous. Ragul has a lot of people under his thumb, and if they catch you he'll do anything to make you talk. If you don't know where I am or what I'm doing you'll have nothing to tell them and there'll be no point in them hurting you.'

Yalka knew perfectly well that Ragul would never believe that Eylese knew nothing. If he caught her he'd torture her anyway. And if he decided that she had no information of use to him he would kill her. Eylese was smart enough to know that too. Keeping her in the dark wasn't protecting her, but the truth was that Yalka herself wasn't entirely sure what she was going to do. She had an idea that the tunnels beneath the city might be useful, but she needed to do some research first.

The tunnels had been dug out in olden times by the original builders as part of the construction of the city. It was said that they ran beneath most of the larger buildings and even some of the smaller ones. As time went by the tunnels weren't needed any more but they weren't filled, they were just left. She'd known about them from an early age, all the children in the River Settlements did. There were scare stories about them being haunted, of people going into them and not coming out again, and of them being the home of monsters. They were the subject of dares. One of the kids would be challenged to go into a tunnel entrance and the others would hide and make creepy noises to scare them out. Then Scorpion came, saw the tunnels as a way of getting children in and out of the city so they could steal for him, and all the fun stopped.

Yalka had been in the tunnels often, sneaking in and exploring, but she'd stayed near the surface and never gone deep. She'd not seen anything unusual but she had heard sounds that she couldn't explain. She reasoned that if the network of passages was as extensive as she'd heard, there might be a way of using them to get within striking distance of Ragul. So the first task was to investigate and find out what their potential might be. However, she knew that if she told Eylese all this her friend would find it hard to hold back, so she must explore on her own.

She rose from the table and got her cloak. 'Just give me today,' she said. 'Then you and Meshi can join me. Meet me here, tomorrow morning.' She pointed to the rectangle she'd drawn to indicate the Great Square.

Eylese was aghast. 'You're planning to spend the night in the city? Really? What are you going to do?'

'You'll see,' said Yalka. She stabbed her finger at the map again. 'Can you be there?'

Eylese looked concerned but she nodded. Yalka wrapped the cloak around her shoulders and left.

20

THE PARADE

E ylese was on the edge of the square, in a spot that gave her a good view of the fountain so that she could watch for Yalka. Meshi stood beside her. Early that morning they'd set out from Maris Partem and walked the three miles across the plain to Chamaris. Once there they joined a crowd of people waiting for the Great Gate to open.

'Who are all this lot?' Meshi whispered.

'All sorts,' Eylese told him. 'Some of them will be servants in the big houses.'

'Why don't they live in them?'

'The ones here are the lowest,' she said, 'bottom of the heap. The higher ranking ones live in, and they're allowed to stay so long as they don't go out of the building.' She saw Meshi's puzzled expression. Didn't he know the system? 'If you're not a citizen,' she explained, 'you can't stay in the city overnight, you have to leave at curfew.'

'What happens if you don't?'

Eylese didn't know but she assumed it wouldn't be good.

'I didn't know there were so many servants,' Meshi said, scanning the sea of strained faces.

'They're not all servants,' said Eylese 'Some of them will be coming into the city to do odd jobs, like cleaning the streets, collecting rubbish, mending things. The rest are here to sell stuff, like we are.' She indicated the basket hooked over her arm.

They had one each. Yalka had told Eylese that the easiest way to get into the city without the authorities taking an interest in them was to turn up at one of the gates with something to sell in the market. Fruit had been an obvious choice and they'd gone into Maris Partem first thing and bought some cherries.

'We don't need two full baskets,' Eylese had reasoned, 'just enough to make them look full. We don't want to buy more than we have to.'

They'd carefully arranged the fruit on sacking so that it looked as though there was plenty underneath the top layer. The Guardians on the gate had to check everybody through but they were sloppy about it.

'That one,' Eylese said, and they joined a line queueing in front of the Guardian who seemed the most casual. He glanced into Eylese's basket, took a handful of cherries and put them in his bag. Then he leant over to Meshi. ''Ere laddy, tell that sister of yours that she can show me her cherry anytime.' He laughed and winked at Eylese. It was all she could do not to tell him what he could do with the cherries, basket and all. She knew that Yalka would have made mincemeat of him if he'd said that to her, but she held her tongue and the Guardian waved them through. They climbed the road up to the Great Square, found the fountain, and now they waited.

The square was busy, and more people were arriving all the time. Most of them looked to be in a holiday mood and were in high spirits, laughing, joking, and sharing snacks.

'What are all these people doing here?' said Meshi. 'It looks like a party.'

'I don't know,' said Eylese. 'I didn't think there'd be so many.'

'It's a public holiday.' A man behind them had overheard Meshi's question. 'Everybody's here for the procession,' he said. 'It's a condition of having the time off. You've got to come here in the morning to watch the parade, and then the rest of the day's your own. They do it to guarantee a good turnout.'

'What's the procession for?'

'Ah, you'll see.'

Just then a bell in the Ceremonium began a slow toll. It seemed that the event, whatever it was, was about to begin, and it would be something significant. For some minutes there was nothing except the bell booming, but Eylese could sense an air of excitement building. Everyone was looking to where the road from the Citadel turned into the square. Then other sounds joined the bell, distant to begin with but getting closer. There was a bass drum, its throbbing so deep that Eylese could feel it in her chest. It was joined by the drone of pipes, high-pitched and reedy, and along with them she could hear a rhythmical chanting.

The crowd was by now completely enthralled, with people peering around and over each other, straining to get the first glimpse of what was coming.

Eylese turned to the man behind them. 'What's it all about? What's going on?'

'Haven't you seen it before? Well, you're in for a treat. It's the Parade of the Sword,' the man said.

'What sword?'

'Just wait and you'll see.'

The excitement built and the drums and the pipes and the chants grew louder. Then, over shoulders and between heads, Eylese saw them.

First into the square were men on foot, a group of them, walking in twos. They moved slowly in step, chanting and swaying from side to side in a rhythmic crocodile. They all wore purple cloaks, and elaborate headdresses that made the wearers seem very tall, although to Eylese they looked comical, as if the headgear might at any moment topple off.

'They're the Regents,' said the man behind them, who seemed to have appointed himself their guide.

Next came another group, barefoot and dressed totally in white – white cloaks, white hoods, white face masks.

'These are the Priestesses,' the man said. 'Fifty of them. All virgins.'

The Priestesses were followed by a rider, also in purple, on a magnificent, shiny horse the colour of jet. Behind him came another eight men on foot, also in purple. They carried on their shoulders a flat platform. On the platform was a gilded throne, and on the throne sat Ragul.

Eylese hadn't seen her enemy since the day three years ago when he'd stood in the middle of Semilvarga and ordered the hanging of twenty rebels, including her parents. He looked plumper now and was red in the face. He held aloft in his right hand a magnificent sword, made of gold and encrusted with jewels. He waved it in time to the drumbeat and it caught the sunlight, scattering it in dazzling shards.

'Impressive, isn't it?' said their guide, who'd now moved beside them. Eylese saw that he was middle-aged, a little shorter than she, and he had an open, friendly face. 'I'd be there myself if it wasn't for this.' He nodded down towards where his right leg would have been, if he'd had one. All Eylese could see below the hem of his tunic was a single limb, alongside the crutch he was leaning on.

The platform bearing Ragul passed before the spectators, accompanied by a ripple of homage as people bowed. Eylese and Meshi followed suit and bent with the others. Some people knelt, and a few of the women made a strange wailing sound and prostrated themselves, lying face down on the ground. Amongst the crowd there was a low murmuring, like the buzzing of many bees.

'What's it all about?' Eylese asked as she got back on her feet. 'What are they all doing?'

The man looked at Eylese as if she was a particularly slow child. 'Don't you know? Where have you been? This is the biggest ceremony in Chamaris. It's bigger than the swearing-in of the Assembly, bigger than the annual military parade, bigger even than the inauguration of a new Master. It's bigger than anything. Every month just before the full moon, that golden sword is taken in a procession from its place on the Citadel and brought down to the Ceremonium. It stays here for five nights and the Priestesses watch over it.'

'Oh.' This seemed to Eylese odd. Yalka had told her

only the day before that the Citadel was in ruins and not used any more.

The head of the procession was now nearing the huge domed building that Eylese took to be the Ceremonium.

'That one there,' said the man, pointing to the throne, 'he's Lord Ragul, the Master's Regent. It was his vision that found the sword.'

'Some find,' said Meshi. 'What's so special about it?'

'It's Farumon's sword.'

'Which one's he?' said Eylese, scanning the parade.

'Which one's Farumon? You are new, aren't you. Farumon was the greatest of all the heroes in the history of the city, the greatest one who ever lived.'

'Oh!' Eylese watched as the bearers started to manoeuvre Ragul and his throne up the broad steps of the building. It was a slow job and a tricky one, and Eylese was hoping that the platform would tilt enough to tip Ragul and his smelly throne off, but to her disappointment that didn't happen. The crowd surged forward to follow them and the buzzing became more intense. Eylese realised what it was. The people were chanting 'Farumon, Farumon, Farumon, Farumon…' repeating the name again and again in a rhythmic mumble like a rolling wheel.

She was puzzled that when Yalka had told them to meet her in the square she'd said nothing about a procession. 'How long does this business go on?' she asked their guide.

'That's it,' he said. 'Once the sword's in the Ceremonium it stays there. I know this is a new thing but I'm really surprised you don't know anything about it. It's the talk of the city.'

'When did it start?'

The man settled down to explain. 'A couple of months ago there was a special moon. It's called a hanging moon because there's a bright star above it so the moon looks to be hanging from it, like a pendulum. And it's bigger and redder than usual. We get them two or three times a year. Well, that night Lord Ragul had a dream. Farumon came to him and told him that he hadn't been killed in battle like the stories said but he was only sleeping, and he would wake up one day when the citizens of Chamaris needed him. He said that when he did he would judge the people and reward those who had served the city well. He said that his golden sword had been buried up in the Citadel, and Lord Ragul was to go and find it.'

'And that's the sword?'

'It is. Lord Ragul was in a trance for three days after the vision, and when he came out of it he went straight to look for the sword, and do you know? He found it at once, just where in the dream Farumon had said it would be. Buried in the exact same spot.'

'But the sword looks new. It doesn't look as though it's been buried underground for hundreds of years.'

'Ah, that's the amazing part,' said the man. 'Lord Ragul came down from the Citadel with the sword, and it looked as if it had only just been made.'

The man paused, a triumphant smile on his face as if all this was down to him. Eylese did her best to look impressed.

'After that,' the man continued, 'Lord Ragul said a special shrine was to be built on the Citadel where the sword should be kept, and it was to be guarded night and day, and once a month it was to be taken in a procession to the Ceremonium, kept there, and returned on the night of the full moon.'

'What happens while it's in the Ceremonium?'

'It stays there, guarded by the Priestesses. Then there's another procession to take it back to the Citadel, and as the full moon rises it's put back in the shrine and there's a ceremony asking Farumon to protect the city and its Master for the coming month.'

'Does it then stay in the shrine?'

'Yes, till the next parade. It's a big monument a bit like a tomb. It's not finished yet, but when it is it will be a wonder. You'll be able to see it from all over the plain.'

'And who are the Regents?'

'They're the ones in purple, the ones who came first. They watch what people do, good and bad, and they write it down so that when Farumon returns they'll be able to give him an account of how everybody's behaved.'

'Was that in the dream too?'

'No. It's in the Book of Farumon, though. After his vision, Lord Ragul ordered one of the scholars from the Academy to collect together all the stories about Farumon, all his sayings, everything that was known about him and put it in a book.'

'That hadn't been done before?'

'Some of it had,' admitted the man, 'but this scholar, his name's Lord Sainter, is finding lots of fresh stuff that nobody ever knew about. The Book's not finished,' he added. 'New bits come out all the time. The Regents put things in it, too, what they find out about people.'

Just then there were sounds of exultation from the Ceremonium, and more cries of 'Farumon, Farumon'.

An ecstatic expression formed on the face of Eylese's companion and he shuffled forward on his crutch with a knot of excited spectators. She took the opportunity to slip away, and by the time the man looked back she had disappeared into the crowd.

21

A NIGHT ON THE CITADEL

Yalka arrived in the square just as the ritual was ending. She watched Ragul as he was helped down the Ceremonium steps and into a carriage. He seemed to be finding any sort of movement difficult. Did she feel pity for him? No. Probably she would for anyone else with those problems, but not for Ragul. He deserved it.

The carriage pulled away with its escort of horsemen. Ragul waved to the crowd and there was some cheering, but it was not what might be called adulation. The purple-clad Regents stood around in knots talking. Each of them had an imposing-looking ledger bound in leather, and they looked to be using them to compare notes. The Priestesses were being marshalled by a tall woman who appeared to be their superior.

Eylese was under a colonnade at the side of the square. 'What are you doing hiding here? I said in the middle, by the fountain.' It came out more snappy than Yalka meant.

Eylese was startled, then relaxed. 'You made me jump. I didn't recognise you. You look so different with your hair like that, and in those clothes too. Did you see the parade?

'Some of it. I only found out about it last night. You've got to hand it to Ragul. To set up something like this in a few weeks is astonishing. It's a complete institution, a regular observance all sewn up and ready to wear.'

'Why has he done it? What does it all mean?' Eylese asked.

'I don't know, but it will be all about him. My guess is that it's a stunt he's come up with to increase his power and control, and I bet his mother's had something to do with it, too.'

'I think it's sinister, all this stuff about writing down in a book the things people do wrong.'

'It is sinister, and it's also typical of Ragul.' Yalka looked around. 'I thought Meshi was going to come with you.'

'He did. He was here when we were watching the parade, and then I got talking to this old guy who was explaining it all to me, and when I looked for him he'd gone.'

The square had emptied quickly and there were only a few people left. None was Meshi. 'He's slipped off somewhere,' Yalka said.

'Shall we look for him? Wait for him? Or shall we carry on without him?'

Yalka considered for a moment. Meshi didn't often share what he was thinking and probably he'd disappeared for reasons he hadn't told Eylese. She guessed it had to do with keeping out of sight and avoiding anybody who might be connected to Big Ears. 'Carry on. He's a big boy now and he can look after himself. We need to get moving. It's lucky for us that the sword procession was today.'

'Why?'

'Because it seems that a lot of the time there are people on the Citadel to watch over it. But if the sword is being kept in the Ceremonium there'll be no need for that. We should have the whole place to ourselves.'

'And we need that, why?'

'So we can hide.' Yalka caught her friend's expression. 'You look surprised.'

'I am. I thought we'd come here, you would do whatever it was you had to, and then we'd go back home. It seems that you have other ideas.'

Yalka felt guilty. Wasn't pressing ahead and expecting others to keep up one of the things she disliked when people did it to her? 'I'm sorry,' she said. 'I told you I'd explain what I have in mind, and I will. Come with me.' She took Eylese's hand, and laughed.

'What's up?'

'If anyone sees us holding hands they'll think I'm your boyfriend.' Eylese laughed too.

On the way to the Citadel, they passed a gate supervised by two men. They wore grey uniforms, with leopard crests on their chests.

'That's the Master's Palace,' Yalka said. 'That's where Ragul lives. It's where Peglar lives, or rather used to.'

Eylese looked astonished. 'Peglar lived there? But it's enormous.'

'You've not seen it before?'

'No. I've not even been in the city before.'

'Well it is impressive, I'll give you that,' Yalka said, 'but don't forget: the bigger the dunghill the deeper the shit.'

They carried on beyond the Palace and up the rough slope to the Citadel gate.

Yalka was right, the place was deserted. The shrine that was being built for Farumon's sword was obvious; it was big, and the only new construction there. Everything else was ruined, stones on their sides or leaning, walls tumbled, scrubby bushes and stunted trees. But in the centre was a newly cleared area dominated by a monstrous cube of white marble. They walked across to it. The single word 'Farumon' was carved in huge, gilded letters, and below it in smaller ones, 'He lives that you may prosper'.

Yalka felt her eyes prickle and sniffed.

'What's the matter?' said Eylese. 'It's ugly but surely it's not that bad.' She put her arm protectively around her friend's shoulders.

Yalka didn't go in for crying. She thought that tears were a weapon used by women who were weak, so she shook her head and wiped her cheek with the back of her hand. 'It's just where the bastard has built it,' she said. 'It's as if he knew.'

Eylese waited for her to go on.

'This here,' and Yalka waved at a line of mounds on either side of the white block, 'is called The Avenue of the Heroes. It's where they used to bury famous people in the past. This is where Granddad and me buried Verit on the night he died, the night of the fire. Right here.' She pointed with her toe. 'That slimey dick has put this monstrosity right on top of him.'

'Oh, Yalka.' Eylese hugged her, and the two stood in silence.

'I don't know what's wrong with me,' said Yalka. 'I don't usually cry, but now I seem to be blubbing all the time. Anyway,' she said when her sniffles had stopped, 'come and see this. They haven't done anything to this.'

She led Eylese to the wall overlooking the city.

'Look in there' she said, pointing to a small opening between two of the stones.

Eylese knelt. There was a heap of rounded pebbles in the gap. Amongst and around them were the remains of dead flowers, and wedged behind was an oval of white card. She reached in and pulled it out. The image was faded but it was still possible to make out the face of a girl.

'That's Lela, my sister,' said Yalka.

'I didn't know you had a sister.'

'Well I don't. Not any more.'

'What happened to her?'

'Back in the River Settlements things were fine. We didn't have much money, but we had enough to eat and we were free and we had a good time. We didn't have all the rules and regulations that people in the city have to put up with. We were happy. And then one day Scorpion arrived.'

'Who was he?'

'We never found out. Nobody ever saw him because he had a bunch of hard men to do his dirty work.'

'What work was that?'

'They took the children. Just the youngest ones, five, six, seven years old. They had to be small enough to get through the narrowest tunnels.'

'What tunnels?'

'The tunnels under the city. The whole place is riddled with them. They were used back in olden times by the people who built the city and they never got filled in.'

'And you can get into them? How?'

'You can get into some of them, but others have collapsed. There are some openings under the city walls and a few in other places. Did you notice that monument across the road from the Palace?' Eylese nodded. 'Well, there's one that starts in there. It goes right under the Palace. I've been in that one, and a few of the others.'

'Isn't it risky? Mightn't they fall in?'

'Some of them have, but I think the ones that are left are all right.'

'So, about these children. What did this Scorpion guy have them do?'

'He made them thieve. They had to use the tunnels to get into the city after dark and break into people's homes so they could take stuff. Not the big houses, they're too well protected, but the smaller ones.'

'And did you do that?'

'No. I was too big, and they didn't want Verit because he was deaf and dumb. But they took Lela.'

'Do you know what happened to her?'

'Not for sure, but I can guess. Lela went in a few times and then one night she went in and didn't come back. I think she was got.'

'By the Guardians?'

Yalka laughed scornfully. 'No. The Guardians couldn't catch a fish if it swam up their arses. There were gangs of youths from rich families who decided they were going to clear the city of what they called "street rats". So they'd go out at night, and if they found any kids they'd kill them.'

Eylese shuddered. 'What, children? Kill children?'

Yalka nodded.

'And you think that's what happened to Lela?'

'Yes. And you know what else? I've learnt that one of the gangs was led by Ragul. The same Ragul that set fire to the River Settlements and by doing that killed my brother. The same Ragul who gave the order to murder your parents. So you see, you have business to settle with that scumbag, and so do I.'

There was a long silence.

'What happened to this Scorpion character?'

Yalka shrugged. 'Who knows? Nobody's seen him since the fire. Maybe he died in it. Maybe with his base in the River Settlements gone he just went away. Or maybe he's still around, waiting for the chance to come back and cause more trouble. Nobody except the kids knew what he looked like and none of them are left, so he could be anywhere.'

'If your sister's dead, do you know where she might be buried?' said Eylese, scanning the broken monuments.

'No. I think the Guardians burnt the unclaimed bodies. I put this here for her so there was somewhere she'd be remembered.'

'You did this? This drawing?'

'Yes.'

Eylese shook her head. 'It's lovely. I couldn't do anything like that.'

Yalka felt a flush of pleasure but it it didn't deflect

the anger that always rose in her when she thought about Lela, Verit and what had happened to them.

'The people in that house,' she said, pointing to the roof of the Palace below them, 'they did this. Them and their friends. They're responsible for the situation that killed Lela. What they did killed Verit, and now they've built their stinking shrine right on top of his grave. I'm going to see that they pay.'

She squatted on the wall and Eylese sat beside her. For a long time there was silence while they watched the plain under the almost full moon. Maris Partem twinkled in the distance, and in the darkness beyond would be Verlam and the tower where she'd been kept. She hadn't thought about it much since. What had happened after she'd left? How long had it been before Woman had been found? What did she tell them? Had the people who'd been gathering to intercept Peglar gone away now that she'd escaped? And where was Peglar? Was he somewhere out there on the darkening plain? Was he thinking of her?

Eylese shivered. 'Oughtn't we to be getting back?'

'No,' said Yalka. 'We're staying here.'

'Spending the night here?' Eylese sounded horrified. 'What on earth for?'

'Don't worry, it's not haunted,' said Yalka. 'At least I don't think it is.' Then, seeing the look of alarm on Eylese's face, 'Just kidding. That big stupid monument over there isn't going to be housing Farumon's sword tonight, so we're going to sleep in it. The temperature can drop at night, but we'll be snug enough in there. I brought up earlier the things we'll need for the night, and some clothing to wear tomorrow. There's a spring over on the far side so we can drink, wash and clean our teeth.'

'Clothes for tomorrow?' said Eylese. 'Do we have to wear something special?'

'Oh yes, something very special.'

'Why? Where are we going?'

'We going to see the Palace. From the inside.'

22

IN THE PALACE

Yalka went first. She took the route she'd followed the day before, out through the old gate of the Citadel and down the short hill to the rear of the Palace. Across the road from the rear gate was a small, neat garden. It had been planted as a memorial to the heroes so that the people could honour them there and not have to trail up to the ruined Citadel. In its centre was a tall obelisk of black marble and in the rear of that was a door, so small and overgrown that it could easily be missed. Yalka opened it to show a flight of steps.

'It's not kept locked?' said Eylese.

'No, never,' said Yalka.

'And it's a way to get into the Palace?'

'Yes.'

'You mean the Palace of the Master of the City is left open and unguarded, so anyone could walk in? Really?'

'Really. Peglar said that ages ago, when the place was built, it was left as an escape route in case of trouble. I know what you're thinking. You're thinking that if this is a secret way in we could use it to get at Ragul.'

'Yes, I was thinking that,' said Eylese. 'Weren't you? I was also wondering why anyone with a score to settle doesn't just march in.'

'It's not that easy. There are watchers everywhere inside the Palace, and anyone who doesn't look right will quickly find themselves up against the Household Guard, and there are loads of them. So the secret is to blend in, and that's what we're going to do.'

Yalka led the way down the steps. At the bottom was a dusty passage. She paused and listened.

'Hear that?'

Eylese was aware of a distant sound, a kind of echoing hiss. 'What is it?'

'I don't know,' Yalka said. 'There are often noises in the tunnels. When I was a kid and used to go in them with my friends we said it was the city breathing. But sometimes there are what might be voices, too.'

'Creepy.'

'You could say, but we never saw anything.'

The tunnel ran beneath the road and came out under a wing of the building, where a flight of steps led up to a small courtyard.

Yalka emerged first, and as soon as she was satisfied that there was no one around she beckoned to Eylese. Both of them were apprehensive. Smart in their grey servant smocks, they walked briskly across the grass towards a side door, trying to look as though they were hurrying to obey some instruction. Once inside they would be able to mingle with the other staff and not be noticed. That was the plan. However, it didn't work out like that.

As soon as they stepped through the door Yalka knew something was wrong. There were plenty of servants about so it should have been easy to merge with them. Except there was not a single grey smock in sight, not one; everyone was wearing black. Yesterday when Yalka had crept in to filch the uniforms they now wore there had been a busy buzz as people went about their work and they had all been in the usual grey. Today there was complete silence. Nobody spoke, and the hush was oppressive. She turned, ready to tell Eylese to go back outside while they conferred about what this meant and worked out what to do about it, but a sharp voice arrested them.

'You two, come here!' It was a severe-looking woman standing at the head of the corridor. For an instant Yalka considered making a run for it, but it was clear that would be a mistake, so she approached the woman. Eylese stood behind her.

'Why are you not in mourning?' The woman was tall and severe, and she was obviously in charge here. She would know they weren't genuine members of the household.

'We're sorry,' said Yalka. 'We didn't know that we were supposed to be.'

She made an effort to keep her eyes on the ground like servants are meant to do. That was not easy for her because her instinct was to face up and look a challenger in the eye.

The severe woman glanced towards the ceiling with an expression of exasperated incredulity. 'Don't you people ever listen to anything? The instruction from Lord Ragul is that until further notice all the staff are to wear black. Get along to the tiring room and get some blacks on you. Hurry, now, before anyone else sees you.'

Yalka felt a surge of relief. At least this woman

accepted them as Palace staff. She knew where the tiring room was. It was where the uniforms for all the staff were kept and where the day before she'd got the two grey smocks they were now wearing. Yesterday it had been deserted but today there was somebody there, another woman, who looked almost as sour as the first one.

She said nothing but examined the girls with a critical expression, handed them black smocks and stood back with her arms folded. It was clear she expected them to change their clothes now, in front of her, while she waited. Yalka was worried. Their undergarments were fairly basic, probably not what the staff of the House of the Leopard would be expected to wear. Moreover, Yalka was concerned that although she might look like a boy as soon as she stripped down it would be obvious that she was a girl. However, the woman didn't appear to notice anything amiss and simply held out her hands for the discarded greys.

'Excuse me, ma'am,' said Yalka, as meekly as she could.

'Yes?' the woman snapped.

'I'm sorry to ask, ma'am. My sister and I were late and we've only just arrived. Can you tell me who is being mourned?'

The woman gave Yalka a look of contemptuous incredulity. She obviously felt it was beneath her to answer such a stupid question from a skinny youth who must be at the very bottom of the domestic pecking order, but she possessed information and she couldn't resist the satisfaction of being in a position to pass it on. 'We are mourning Lord Karkis, our dear City Master. He has been unwell for some time and he died last night, in his sleep. Lord Ragul has succeeded him as Master and has ordered all the staff to wear black and to go about their work in silence.'

'Thank you, ma'am,' Yalka said. She almost dropped a curtsey but stopped herself and turned it into a bow. 'I'm sorry.'

The woman made a dismissive noise, part grunt part snort. 'You mean you are sorry for the Master's demise? Or sorry for your ignorance?'

'Both ma'am.'

It was the right answer. 'Well, get about your business. And remember, no talking.'

'Yes, ma'am.'

Now in black, the two girls emerged again into the body of the house. The servants' tiring room was at the end of a passage which led off one of the main corridors, and Yalka looked out cautiously. A little way along a girl was dusting. She had a wooden box with a handle, containing rags, cleaning cloths, jars and other paraphernalia, and when she reached a door she put the box down, polished the doorknob and went inside the room, presumably to do the same to the other side.

Yalka didn't wait to find out. She tugged Eylese's sleeve and set off along the corridor. As she passed the box she bent and picked it up. It was done smoothly and without stopping, and they were soon round the corner and out of sight. On the left was a large, imposing door. Yalka knew that this was the Library. She pushed it open, gave Eylese a duster and took another herself.

The Library was a longish room with a square bay at the far end. Peglar had described it to her and told her it was where Sainter and Malina had set up the trap for him when he was accused of assaulting her. The room seemed now to be the essence of calm but it was dead, the air dead, the sound dead, and she could easily see it as a place of deceit and entrapment.

Another servant was dusting books and shelves. She gave them a questioning look when they came in, but Yalka ignored her and she went back to her work. The fact that talking was prohibited would be to their advantage. They wouldn't be expected to chat and were unlikely to be asked who they were or what they were doing.

Yalka started on the shelves on the opposite side of the room, as far away from the servant as she could, and Eylese worked next to her.

'So can you tell me now what the plan is?' Eylese hissed. 'Or am I just to blindly follow you?'

'Yes,' Yalka whispered back. 'I'm sorry. This is what we'll do. Along from that door is the Atrium. It's a big hallway just inside the main entrance. Everybody who visits the Palace officially comes in that way. It will be heavily guarded but we've got to get across it.'

'What for? What's on the other side?'

'The Palace headquarters. Where all the decisions are made.'

'What in the world are we going there for?' Eylese was so incredulous she had raised her voice. The servant frowned at them and Yalka held a finger to her lips. She knew from Peglar that a common means of advancement in the household was to report on someone else's misdemeanour. She didn't want to give the servant any opportunity to do that, so for the next few minutes she and Eylese carried on in silence, taking the books off the shelves one by one, dusting them and replacing them.

After a little while the servant left and Yalka felt it was safe to speak again, but still quietly in case anyone else came in. She moved close to Eylese and whispered, 'We're going to find a man called Feldar. He's the Palace Steward.'

'Is he expecting us?' Yalka shook her head. 'You mean we're just going to turn up and walk in?'

Yalka nodded. 'More or less. If he's there.'

'If he's there,' Eylese repeated. 'You mean he might not be?'

'No. He's a busy man. He might have gone to meet somebody in the city. But when I asked somebody yesterday they said they thought he was free this morning, so let's hope for the best.'

Eylese didn't look impressed and Yalka didn't blame her. She couldn't deny that she had not thought much about the details of her plan.

'If he is there, what then?' Eylese asked.

'We'll ask him to help us to find Peglar.'

'Will he?'

Yalka shrugged. 'I don't know. He stuck up for Peglar when Malina accused him and he acted as his second in the combat, but he's been Karkis' Steward for years, so...' She shrugged.

Eylese seemed disappointed. Yalka wished she'd stop asking awkward questions. It was as if she expected some carefully worked-out scheme, but in reality there was none. This was the best she could do.

'We have no idea where Peglar might be, and no way

of finding out,' she explained. 'We can't look for him because if we get close we'll simply alert others. Feldar's served the family for years and Peglar rates him highly. He's honest and capable. What's more, people like him and they respect him, and even more important than that, he's no friend to Ragul. He serves him because he's loyal but I don't think he likes him, so he may be prepared to help us.'

Eylese looked serious but she nodded. 'Okay,' she said, 'let's give it a try. Let's do it, and get out of this dismal hole before somebody blows our cover.'

'Right,' said Yalka. 'I think that woman who was in here when we arrived might suspect something. She could have gone to report us.' She opened the door a crack and looked out into the corridor. All was clear. 'Come on,' and she led the way towards the Atrium.

They heard the noise before they got there, but even so neither of them was prepared for what they found. With the rest of the house so quiet the din seemed louder than it probably was. The Atrium was packed with a swarm of people, all men, all wearing black armbands, most of them talking. Even though nobody was speaking particularly loudly the sound was amplified by the high space. The main entrance was supervised by Household Guards, who looked stern and forbidding as they scrutinised the press of people trying to get in. In the middle of the wall opposite the entrance was a large door, which Yalka could see led into a large hall. The Guards were directing people into queues to get in there. She glimpsed stained glass, rich hangings, and a gilded throne occupied by a woman who was veiled and dressed in black.

'That's where official visitors are received. It's where

Granddad and me were taken for the rhyming that Ragul wanted. That woman must be Ragul's mother, Vancia.'

'What do all these people want?'

'I think they've come to pay their respects and offer their condolences. Most of them are probably hoping that there's something in it for them, too.'

'If this Feldar guy's so important, won't he be in there?'

Yalka didn't reply. That hadn't occurred to her. It was possible, she supposed, but she didn't know. She felt anxious.

'How can we get to the other side of the crowd?' Eylese whispered. 'We'll have to cross the doorway to the hall in front of the queues, or go around the other side. Either way we'll have to pass the Guards.'

'Or we could just go through the middle,' said Yalka, and she dived into the eddy.

It was never going to work. They kept their heads down and murmured apologies, but the throng was so dense that they were bound to cause a disturbance. People grumbled, they stumbled over feet, Eylese caught somebody with the cleaning box and they cursed her. They were less than halfway when they heard a shout.

'Stop!'

They froze and the people around them took a step back, as if the intruders had suddenly become toxic.

'What do you think you're doing? Guards, arrest them. Take them to my office.'

Giant hands seized Yalka's arms like pincers and dragged her across the Atrium. The crowd parted for them and closed behind. She was angry. She hated being manhandled. The Guard's grip was hurting her and it was all she could do not to lash out. But there was more than that. She felt her head spin and her stomach hollow. The man who had shouted, who was now following them, limping along on two sticks, was familiar. She would know that chubby face and bullying attitude anywhere.

She glanced at Eylese. Her face was twisted in fear. They were being pushed towards the corridor. Colours and images whirled before her.

Out of the Atrium, they were faced by the man who had stopped them: Ragul. He was flanked by Guards and he was livid. 'What are you doing?' he shouted. 'How dare you push through here. The household is in mourning. This is the Atrium. There are citizens here. It's no place for servants.'

He didn't look well. Spittle flecked his lips and he was breathing heavily. His eyes were puffy and his face flushed. He was about to start on the girls again when Yalka heard a voice behind them.

'My Lord, I apologise for this disruption to the normal functioning of your household. You should not have to concern yourself with matters such as this. The conduct of Palace staff is my responsibility. Please allow me to deal with these wretches.'

Yalka could see Ragul's struggle. He wanted to punish them, he would enjoy it, but it was true that to do so was beneath him.

'Very well then,' he said, reluctantly. 'You discipline them. Find out who they are.' He pointed to Eylese. 'I've seen the fat one before, and there's something about that boy's face that's familiar too. I want them soundly whipped and thrown out. I never want to see them in this house again.'

'Yes, My Lord.'

'And I hold you accountable for this, Steward. I shall speak to you later.'

'Yes, My Lord.'

23

FELDAR

'I don't know who you are or why you're here, but I don't believe you're servants.'

Feldar had ushered the girls into his office, dismissed the Household Guards, and told them to sit down. Yes, sit down. Then he had spent several minutes simply looking at them. He frowned at Yalka, as though something about her puzzled him. She was tempted to speak but thought it best to keep quiet, for now.

'Yes, that's it,' said Feldar. 'I remember. I saw you in the tavern down by the Great Gate, the day after the fire that burnt the River Settlements. You were with an old man.'

'Yes,' said Yalka. 'That was my Grandfather.'

Feldar looked at her closely. 'Your hair was different then. It was fair, and long. And I saw you once before that, when you ran out from the crowd and tried to hang onto the Master's carriage on the day of Lord Peglar's initiation.'

That was true, she had. She'd been protesting about Scorpion and the way he forced children into the city to steal, and about the children who were killed by the vigilante gangs. She'd felt she had to because Karkis and the Guardians were doing nothing about it. She'd gripped the edge of the open carriage and tried to talk to him, but she'd been grabbed and flung back into the crowd. This man had a good memory. She was encouraged that he referred to Peglar as "Lord". He'd been stripped of the title when he was exiled. The fact that Feldar still used it suggested he might be sympathetic.

'Yes, sir,' she said.

'You lived in the River Settlements.' It was a statement, not a question.

'Yes, sir. We were burnt out, Granddad and me. The day you saw us we'd stopped on our way to Maris Partem after we'd buried my brother. He died in the fire.' There was a pause. Then she added, 'My name is Yalka. I'm a friend of Peglar.'

Feldar nodded. 'I guessed that. He talked about you. And who's this?'

'My name is Eylese, sir. I'm from Semilvarga and I met Yalka in Maris Partem. We're friends. And you're right, we're not servants.'

Feldar was still weighing them up, and at last he asked the obvious question. 'Right then, if you're not servants what are you doing here in the Palace wearing the uniform of people who are?'

'We've come to see you, sir,' Yalka answered.

If Feldar was surprised he didn't show it. 'We need help,' she went on. 'Peglar needs help. He's in trouble.'

Feldar put his elbows on his desk and leaned forward. 'Do you know where he is?'

'No.'

'Then how do you know he's in trouble?'

How? thought Yalka. Peglar was an outlaw on the run, with a huge price on his head and people scouring the plain searching for him. Wasn't that trouble enough? 'Ragul, I mean Lord Ragul, I suppose I should call him, doesn't seem content with just sending Peglar away. He wants him dead. He's setting traps for him. I was one of them. They took me and shut me up in a tower in Verlam just so they could grab Peglar when he came to get me out. I escaped, so that failed. But Ragul and his men will try something else. They'll keep on trying until Peglar's luck runs out.'

'What makes you think either that I want to help, or that I could?'

'You've helped Peglar before,' said Yalka. 'He told me about it. You took his side when Ragul bet that he wouldn't be able to complete the things he had to do before he could claim his inheritance. You believed him when Ragul and Malina cooked up that pack of lies about him assaulting her. You helped him when Ragul challenged him and they had to fight in the cage. And you helped him again when he was exiled and had to leave the city. He respects you. He says you're one of the few people in the Palace who's honest. He thinks of you as a friend.'

Feldar looked embarrassed. 'Well, a lot of that is returned. I think Peglar is a fine young man who's been very badly treated. I'll help him if I can. But what's in this for you?'

There was a long, long pause before Yalka answered. She had hinted this to Eylese, her Grandfather would certainly know it, Meshi had probably guessed it, but she had never said it out loud to anyone. 'I love him,' she said.

Feldar looked at Yalka with an expression she found hard to read. There was understanding and sympathy, but there was also regret.

'There are two futures for Peglar,' he said. 'Either he's caught and is brought back here, and Ragul will have him executed, or he goes far far away and never comes near this place ever again. I can see something for you in this second possibility if you go with him.'

'There is a third,' said Yalka. 'He's pardoned and returns.'

'That's highly unlikely, and even if it were to happen there's nothing there for you.'

Yalka looked at him bleakly. 'I know that,' she said. 'Peglar would be a leading member of the House of the Leopard. He would have a large slice of the family's fortune. He would be required to pair with a daughter of one of the wealthy houses, and their fathers would be queueing up to get him. I know I wouldn't figure in that, a poor girl from the slums. But why would I want the life of a great lady? There is nothing in Palace life for me. I have my friends, my drawing, my Grandfather and my rhyming. If I could have Peglar too, that would be perfect, but at least so long as I knew he was safe it would ease the hurt of being apart.'

Feldar looked moved at this. Eylese dabbed at a tear.

'Well,' said Feldar, 'before any of that can happen we have to find out where he is. I expect that everyone now knows that you escaped from Verlam. My agents tell me that most of the people who were waiting along the road so that they could ambush Peglar have gone. We need to think about the possibilities. If Peglar got the first bit of news, that you were a prisoner in the tower, what would he do? And if he's heard you've escaped, what then?'

'If he thought I was still in the tower he'd try to get me out. But he wouldn't just walk up to the tower. He's much too wary for that. He'd probably watch it for a while first, so he could make a plan.'

'And what would he do when he realised you were not there?'

Yalka shook her head. 'I don't know. He'd probably go back to Semilvarga because it's beyond the single day's journey limit and in theory he'd be safe there. But Ragul and his scumbags would still be looking for him.'

Feldar turned to Eylese. 'And what about you?'

Eylese hesitated and Yalka could see she was wondering how much to say. To tell her story would be a risk. She had come to Chamaris to take revenge on the man who was now the city's principal and Feldar's master. To admit to this in the Palace would be treason. She had formed the impression that Feldar was on their side but she wasn't yet sure how far she could trust him.

Yalka sensed her difficulty and stepped in. 'She's my friend,' she said. 'Eylese has come along to help me.'

Feldar nodded and got up from his desk. He reached for something on a high shelf behind him. It was a whip.

'Don't worry, I'm not going to use it,' he said, seeing the scared look on Eylese's face. 'But I'm supposed to be disciplining you, so you'd better look as if that's what's happening.' He opened the door and called for a Guard. 'Oh,' he said, turning back to the girls, 'it would help if you could cry a bit.'

There was still a crowd of people waiting to get into the Palace at the main entrance so they left by a side door. Feldar marched them out and down the thoroughfare from the Palace, across the square where the day before Eylese had watched the Parade of the Sword, and into the lower city. Feldar walked behind the girls, driving them like a couple of sheep, with a pair of Household Guards at the rear. He made threatening plays with the whip but he didn't actually touch them.

They were near the bottom of the hill, close to the Arena, when he told Yalka and Eylese to stop and turned to the Guards.

'You can go now. I'll see these two sluts out of the gate and then I have some business here in the city.'

'Lord Ragul said they were to be beaten, sir,' one of the Guards said.

'And so they shall be once they're out of the city,' said Feldar, tersely. 'I don't need your reminders and I don't need you any more. Your job is to do what I tell you. Get back to the house.'

The man looked rebuffed and bowed stiffly. They both turned and left. Once they were out of sight Feldar pointed towards the Arena. 'This way.'

They walked along a quiet, broad avenue lined with trees to a group of stone benches outside the entrance, where Feldar told them to wait.

'I'm going to get somebody who I think can help us. He knows Peglar and he has good contacts in some of the other cities. You two stay put and keep in the background. It's best if you're not seen.'

'What now?' said Eylese, once Feldar had disappeared into the Arena building.

'We wait,' said Yalka, 'like he said. We've got no choice.'

'Who's he gone to find?'

Yalka shrugged. 'Dunno. A friend, someone to help, he said.'

'Do you think he's really on our side? Perhaps he's just dumped us. Or gone to report us.'

'Don't be daft. If he wanted to do that why would he bring us all the way down here? Why not just deal with us at the Palace, like Ragul wanted?'

The mention of Ragul made Eylese seethe. '"The fat one" he called me! He's one to talk. Lord Lard himself.'

Yalka grinned and put her arm around her friend. 'You're not fat. You're just bigger than me, that's all.'

'Everyone's bigger than you, skinny minny!'

Yalka gave her a playful punch. 'And no one's fatter than you, chunky monkey!' They both laughed then, till Yalka said. 'Shush, we'd better calm down. We don't want to attract attention.'

She needn't have worried, there was nobody around. Nevertheless, they waited in silence for what seemed like an age, so long that even Yalka began to wonder whether Feldar was coming back or had abandoned them, as Eylese feared.

When he did return it was with what she later said was the most handsome boy she had ever seen. Feldar introduced him.

'This is Cestris. He's the friend of Peglar I told you about.'

'I know you,' said Yalka. 'We've met. My Granddad, Syramos, did a rhyming at The House of the Raven. You were there. We talked about Peglar. You told me he was in trouble and you said I should help him.'

'Yes, I remember. You were the Rhymer's acolyte. But you were blonde then. I think I like you dark.'

Yalka nodded, unable to believe that he preferred the

muddy, mousy colour her hair was now to the glorious gold it had been. She didn't like what she thought of as empty flattery but she bit back the sharp retort that was on the tip of her tongue.

'Peglar needs help again,' she said. 'He really does need it now.'

'Yes. Feldar's told me. I've been away and I didn't know about the trap that had been set for him, but Big Ears is a nasty piece of work so it doesn't surprise me.'

'It's Ragul too,' said Eylese. 'He ordered him to do it.'

Cestris pulled a face. 'Yes, Ragul's another story. And now he's Master of the City he'll be hard to control.'

Yalka was surprised. 'Won't the Assembly choose a new Master?'

'No,' said Feldar. 'That's how it used to be but not anymore. When Karkis got ill the normal thing would have been for him to resign and make way for somebody else, but the Assembly agreed to Ragul acting as his Regent. Karkis had served the city with distinction over many years and the Assembly loved him, so Ragul, or rather Vancia, exploited this and got them to agree to let him name his successor.'

'Yes,' said Cestris. 'It's a surprise that the other powerful families agreed to it because the position of Master might have been given to any one of them, but there was always a lot of argument and plotting at election time, and sometimes violence too. They decided they didn't want that, and provided they were left alone to do what they wanted the House of the Leopard could carry on providing the Master.'

'And that lets Ragul in. Don't they know what he's like?' said Yalka, disgusted.

'No, I don't think they do,' said Feldar. 'Ragul is very

plausible. He comes across in public as open and straightforward and it's only in private that you see his true nature.'

Eylese had been quiet and was thinking about the new situation. 'So if the office of Master is to be held by the House of the Leopard and something happens to Ragul, then Peglar would take over.'

'Yes,' said Feldar, 'he would. That means Ragul will see him as an even greater threat now. So you see,' he turned to Cestris, 'we must find him before anyone else does.'

'I think the place to start is Verlam,' said Cestris. 'Let's start there.'

24

THE TOWER

Peglar hadn't thought that leaving the farm would be as easy as simply walking off, but it was. He didn't even say he was going. He went as usual to his work on the stones and as usual towards the end of the morning Wossly brought the basket of food. This time he told her that he would eat later and she was not to wait. She looked chastened as she crept away, as if he'd found fault in her. He was unhappy about that. He had no great liking for the girl but he didn't want her to feel hurt.

He felt worse about Reddall. That scythe wound was nasty. He was not a physician, and while he was happy that the treatment he had given and prescribed would do no harm, he was not convinced that it would do much good either. The damage looked far too serious for honey poultices. If he'd been confident in his ability to effect a cure he would have stayed, but he was not. The injury needed the attention of someone who knew what they were doing, but there didn't seem to be anyone in that category available locally, Jorion didn't have enough money to bring anyone in from further afield, and Peglar himself had absolutely nothing. He was pretty sure that gangrene had already set in, and if it was not dealt with Reddall would die. That made him very sad, but there was nothing he could do to change it. And Yalka needed him more, so he had to make a choice. Somehow he had to go to this place called Verlam, find out where she was being held, and free her. Beyond that he hadn't thought, but he made a silent promise that when he could he would return to the farm for Alendur and Beldrom.

As soon as Wossly was gone Peglar unpacked the basket. He fed Safren and he ate something himself. Then he filled his pockets with what was left, put the basket against the pile of stones, took Safren's rope and set off towards the Maris Partem road. He reckoned that if he could keep behind the low line of rocks until he got close to the road, and then dash across the open area until he reached the shelter of some trees, he had an excellent chance of not being seen from the farm. Safren could see no urgency in this and it was hard to keep her moving, but eventually she agreed to what was going on and co-operated, although there were frequent short halts to explore interesting scents.

Peglar had been comfortable at the farm. The work had been easy and the food good. He could have coped with the Wossly issue. He was sorry he'd not been able to make himself known to Alendur and Beldrom. He'd overheard that they were now on loan to another farm and he would have liked to have stayed until they got back, but the description given by the rent collectors had unnerved him. Tall, skinny, dark hair, nineteen or so. It would fit any number of young men, but he was the only one around and the chance of five hundred golds might tempt Jorion to let Ragul's men know he had someone like that, just in case.

The rent collectors had said that Verlam was not far from Maris Partem, a little way off the road to Semilvarga. He didn't know the area, but the whole business had been set up to trap him so the tower should be easy enough to spot. Finding the place wasn't the problem. The rent men had also said that there were a lot of people hanging around waiting for him to turn up so that they could grab him and get the reward. He couldn't risk running into them.

Having Safren with him would be a help because the searchers wouldn't expect him to have a dog. Also, she might come to his aid if anyone attacked him. Or she might not. Had the sausages been enough to buy her loyalty? Some sort of disguise would help. He could use an old cloak, and if he could find a hat somewhere and pick up a fallen tree branch to use as a staff he would look older. He cursed himself for not thinking about taking something of Jorion's before he left. Maybe he'd be able to get what he needed from one of the farms on the way, but he had hardly any money and he would need to eat, and so would Safren.

Working in the field heaving stones had done something to improve his condition. Over the days spent pretending to sort Ryker's papers he'd become torpid and listless, but now he felt better. He made good progress on the road and by evening he reckoned he was well over halfway to Maris Partem. He hadn't come across many people on the way and no one had paid any attention to him, but he thought that as he got closer to the tower it would be a good idea to get off the main road where there was a chance of being ambushed and try to approach Verlam in another way. The plain was as flat as a plate. He should be able to see the tower from some way off, but there was also a strong possibility of being seen.

He found a spot a little way from the road to settle for the night, and he shared the rest of the food with Safren. She wasn't convinced he was being fair because she kept sniffing around what he was eating and trying to lick his fingers. There was an animal drinking trough nearby, and although the water had a green film it tasted all right. Once more he lay down next to Safren and the two of them slept.

He woke before sunrise. He was stiff and sleepy, but if he could make some progress before daybreak he might be able to avoid anyone who was on the lookout for him and get close to the tower. He stood up, dusted himself down, pissed, and set off. 'Yes, I know, breakfast,' he said to Safren. 'I'll see to that when I can.' Dogs can't shrug their shoulders but Safren came close.

He struck out towards where he thought the tower would be, avoiding the road and using what cover he could find. Then he saw it, in the far distance. At least he assumed that was it. It was the tallest building he'd seen for some time, three storeys, with a squat steeple on top. It must be the place. There could be no doubt about it.

Although the land was flat it was uneven, full of ruts and holes, and that meant the going was now slower. The tower didn't seem to be getting any closer and in the end he stopped looking at it because the view was too depressing. It took him a couple of hours to get close enough to see it properly.

It was an imposing building, but rather dilapidated.

He took cover among some olive trees where he had a good view of it and the immediate surroundings. There was no sign of any life. He watched the windows, hoping to catch a glimpse of Yalka. He willed her if she was there to look out, but there was nothing. He watched and watched, losing track of time, but nobody came and nobody went. He was hungry, and so was Safren. She'd found something recently dead a little way back and devoured it enthusiastically but she would need more.

It was the end of the afternoon before he was satisfied that the tower was deserted. There had been no movement of any sort near it and nothing appeared to be going on inside. Surely if anyone was being held there he would see jailers of some sort, but there were none. He hadn't seen any sign of Yalka but that didn't mean she was not there. What if she was tied up and unable to move? What if she'd just been left, abandoned? Starving? He couldn't walk away without finding out.

He looked around for a weapon and found a piece of old olive wood, gnarled and heavy. It made a useful club. He gripped it in one hand, took Safren's rope in the other, and performed a crouching walk across the piece of scrubland towards the building.

The door was unfastened, and it opened with a push. There was a hallway with rooms on each side and a staircase ahead. He could feel the emptiness of the place at once and knew that no one was inside, but he called anyway.

'Yalka. Hello. Yalka. Are you there?'

There was no reply. One glance was enough to confirm that the two downstairs rooms were empty. One of them was a kitchen. There was a large pan of some sort of soup. He sniffed it. It smelt foul, but Safren seemed enthusiastic. He put it on the floor and she gave it her attention.

He climbed the stairs. Although he was sure now that the tower was empty he told himself that he couldn't be too careful and he went slowly, cudgel in hand.

There was a heavy door at the top. That too was unfastened; he pushed it open and went through. It was a day room. Some of the furniture had been knocked over and something spilt on the rug. There was a broken plate and a pile of what looked like bandages on the floor. It was empty, and he could see nothing to indicate that Yalka had ever been there. In the corner, he found more stairs up to the top floor. All he found was a low bed and a chair. There was a closet that contained a few clothes. He picked some up and held them against his cheek. Did they say Yalka to him? He thought that maybe they did, but he couldn't be sure. He froze for a moment when he heard a sound on the stairs but it was only Safren. She did an olfactory circuit of the room, concluded there was nothing there of any interest, and came to sit alongside him.

The question was, if Yalka had once been in these rooms where was she now? And if she had been used as bait to lure him into the open and was no longer there, what did that mean?

He left the building and walked to the road. It was deserted. There was no ambush, no one looking for him. He waited at the roadside to be sure. A peasant with a donkey approached and passed. Peglar was going to ask him if he'd seen anyone else on the road but thought better of it. He didn't want to draw any attention to himself. He looked towards Maris Partem. That might be a likely place to look for Yalka because that was where he'd seen her last. However, it was well within a day's travel of Chamaris, and the sentence passed on him by the City Marshal declared that anyone finding him inside that limit was obliged to apprehend him and take him to Ragul. That and the huge reward offered meant that if he went there he would have no peace at all and he would most likely be finished.

He turned his back on Maris Partem and began walking away, back in the direction of Semilvarga. He was weary and he was dejected. Where was she? What had happened to her? Was she all right? When would he see her again? Would he ever? And if he did not, how could he live with that?

He heard the sound of wheels on the road behind him and turned to see a cart approaching. There were three men on board. If there had only been two he reckoned that he could have managed. He would have had an excellent chance even against three if he'd realised sooner what was happening. And if Safren could have been persuaded to come down to earth she might have defended him, but she was in another world, strolling along at his side while no doubt dreaming of her next sausage.

'Going far?' said the driver as the cart drew level.

'Semilvarga,' said Peglar.

'That's a long walk,' said one of the others. 'When do you plan to get there?'

Peglar didn't know. He'd never travelled that road and he struggled for a sensible answer, but he didn't need one because the third man said, 'Nice dog. Yours?'

'Yes,' said Peglar. He supposed she was now.

'Friendly?' said the first man.

Peglar nodded. Something felt wrong and he wished to move on but the cart was blocking his way and the men wanted to talk. 'Yes,' he said, 'she is.'

'What does it eat?' said the third man, getting down from the cart. 'Does it like rabbit?'

Peglar didn't know. He'd never seen Safren eat it, but he hadn't yet found any food she didn't like so he said yes.

The man lifted a bag from the cart and took out of it a tin box. He opened it to show several pieces of raw, pale meat. Safren's nose twitched and her ears pricked up. She licked her lips. The man held out the tin and Safren ambled towards him. He put it on the ground and she started to eat.

Peglar was watching this when suddenly he felt one of the other men very close behind him, and something pricking his neck.

'That's my knife,' said a voice in his ear. 'You cause any trouble and it will go right in. My friend has a zirca. The best, made in Rasturoth, sharp as a witch's tit. If there's any trouble from that dog he'll slice her in half. Understood?' Peglar nodded. 'Now I want you to very slowly climb onto the cart. Do it quietly and don't call or speak to the dog. Just get on.'

Peglar had no choice. He could see that Safren was still licking out the tin and was unaware of anything amiss. He scrambled onto the cart and two of the men settled beside him. The man who had been feeding Safren eased himself away from her, leaving the tin behind, and got into the driver's seat. He cracked his whip and the horses moved off. He cracked it again and they quickened their pace and then began to gallop. Safren raised her head from the tin, looking puzzled, then alarmed. She started after the cart and kept up for a short way but she was no match for the horses and she soon fell behind.

The last Peglar saw of her she was standing in the middle of the road looking forlornly after him. Then she turned and went back to the rabbit.

25

MESHI

'Moon and stars, Meshi, where have you been?' said Yalka.

'One minute you were with me at the fountain in the square, and the next you were gone,' said Eylese. 'What on earth happened to you? We thought you were lost.'

Meshi faced the two girls, looking from one to another. 'I was,' he said. 'Well, a bit. I knew where I was but I was still kind of lost.'

'So what happened to you?' said Eylese.

'Well, I was with you in the square, and we were watching this great long procession with all those people and the sword and that, and I saw this kid staring at me. He was by the wall against that big building everybody was heading for and he kept looking. Every time I turned round he was watching me. Well, I thought he was watching me but it turns out he's blind, but I didn't know that at the time.'

Yalka sighed. Meshi wasn't much of a talker, but when he started it always seemed to take him a lifetime to get to the point. 'All right, so this kid you didn't know was blind was watching you. Then what?'

'Well,' said Meshi, 'he looked weird, this kid. You know, strange. He was white. I mean really white, not just not black or brown, but white like he'd been painted. His skin was the colour of milk, and his hair too. I've never seen hair like it. I mean, your hair was fair,' he said, glancing at Yalka, 'but that was kind of golden fair.'

Meshi stopped talking and Yalka looked at him and saw that he was blushing.

'Right,' said Eylese, 'you saw a child with very white skin and white hair, and then what? How come that made you go off?'

'He wasn't really a child,' said Meshi. 'More sort of our age really, but very small, like he hadn't grown properly. And I didn't know he was a boy because he had long hair and I thought he was a girl, but it turns out he was a bit of both.'

Yalka thought her brain was going to explode. She took Meshi's hands. 'Meshi. Dear, dear Meshi,' she said. 'Please please please get on with it and tell us what happened.'

Meshi went scarlet. Yalka sensed that he didn't want to pull his hands away but thought he should. She felt cruel for embarrassing him in such a way but, she told herself, he asked for it. She released her grip on his hands and Meshi looked down.

'Yes. Well. All right,' he said. 'Well this kid, he/she was looking at me, except he/she wasn't and I thought his/her skin colour and hair were weird…'

'Meshi,' said Yalka.

'What?'

230

'You've told us that this person you saw was both a boy and a girl, so can we keep it simple? Just call him her?'

Meshi frowned. 'What? Oh yes, I see.' He paused and thought, clearly trying to remember what point in his story he'd reached.'

'You've told us that the colour of her skin and hair was unusual and then…?'

'Oh. Yes. Right. Well, it was the whiteness of him, I mean her, that I noticed first, but then I saw the eyes. They were pink. I don't just mean pink like the whites of your eyes go sometimes when there's been a dust storm or when you've been swimming in the sea, or if you've been crying. I mean the bits in the middle…'

'The pupils,' Eylese offered.

'Yes, the pupils. They weren't really pink, they were more, kind of, red. I've never seen anything like it.'

'She's an albino,' said Yalka.

'Where's that?'

'It's not a "where", it's a condition. People who have it are unable to produce any colouring in their skin or hair, and that's why they're so white. They're missing what protects them from the sun, so if they go out in it they don't tan, they just burn.'

'How awful for them,' said Eylese.

'That must be why this kid lives underground,' said Meshi.

'Underground? Where underground?' said Eylese.

'I was just telling you that,' said Meshi, looking pained, as though she hadn't been listening.

'In the tunnels under the city,' said Yalka.

'Yes,' said Meshi, looking at her in wonder. 'How did you know?'

'Never mind, I just guessed,' said Yalka. 'Tell us what happened. You saw this albino kid who you thought was watching you, then what?'

'Right. Well, she was a bit of a way off, on the edge of the square, by a door into one of the big buildings there. I'd never seen anyone like this kid before and I was curious. I didn't know she couldn't see and I started going over to her, and then she suddenly turned and ran through the doorway.'

'How come?' said Eylese. 'If she was blind.'

'Well yes, she is,' said Meshi, 'but somehow she must have known I was going towards her because that's what she did. She went through the doorway and I followed.'

'You just walked into one of the civic buildings without authorisation, in broad daylight?' said Eylese. 'There were Guardians everywhere. You could have been thrown in jail.'

'I didn't think,' said Meshi. 'I just followed. Anyway, there was this passage and I could see the kid going down it and then she came to another door and went through that and I followed there too. I went through it and the door slammed behind me. I just about wet myself 'cos it was pitch black and I couldn't see a thing. I tried to open the door but it was stuck, and I was scared then, real scared. I heard somebody laugh and I felt someone take my hand. I was properly freaked out now, I tell you. I tried to pull my hand away but this thing, whatever it was that had got it, held on tight and started to pull. I thought, I'm for it now, but there was no choice, I had to go. But here's another weird thing, as I went I started to feel a bit less stressed. It didn't seem like I was being threatened or set up or anything.'

Eylese shook her head in wonder. 'I'd have been scared out of my wits,' she said.

'And you were in the tunnels?' said Yalka.

'Yes. How do you know about them?'

'All of us who lived in the River Settlements did. I've been into a few of them myself. Go on, what happened next?' She was thinking that she'd never heard Meshi say as much as this since he'd described the night when he followed Big Ears and saved her from his attack, and possibly even saved her life too.

'I couldn't see a thing,' said Meshi, 'but there were a lot of sounds. Like you say, I was in a tunnel and there were whispers and echoes, and somebody called, and somebody laughed. I don't think it was the person who was leading me, there were others. I don't think they were trying to scare me, it was just what they did. The ground seemed to be quite smooth and we felt to be going pretty quickly, but I didn't feel in any danger or anything. Then I could hear the sound change and I guessed we were in a bigger space. It was still pitch dark and I couldn't see nothing, and then there was a spark and somebody set fire to a torch.'

Meshi stopped. Yalka doubted that it was for dramatic effect because Meshi wasn't like that. He was probably working out how to tell the next bit of his story.

'And?' she said.

'Right. Yes. Well, I'd been struggling trying to see in the dark and the sudden light dazzled me, but when I got used to it I could see it was a circular room with a stone bench around the edge of it, and there were about twenty of them all sitting on the bench and all looking at me, and I was in the middle, like some sort of exhibit or something. The kid I'd seen first was there but she was hard to pick out because there were three or four of them all like that, all of them white and all of them about her size. There were some other kids too, and a couple of older ones, our age or a bit more, but nobody older than that.'

'Who are they?' said Eylese, who seemed awestruck.

'They're the people who live in the tunnels,' said Yalka.

'You know about them?' Eylese was astonished.

'Sort of. When I was in the River Settlements there were stories about a family who'd gone to live in the bowels of the city. Some of the kids Scorpion sent in there to thieve, when they came back said they'd seen people in there, but we thought they were making it up, or just confused, and nobody believed them. But they must have been right.'

Eylese shuddered. 'But you've never seen anyone else when you've been in the tunnels?'

'No. I've heard things, and so have you. There's all manner of sounds in there. When the tunnels run close to the rooms in some of the buildings they can be separated by, maybe, just a small grill, and so noises from the room can get into the tunnels and are somehow made louder. You hear bits of conversations sometimes, and music, and laughter, and perhaps even crying and people quarrelling. But I thought all the sounds were coming from people in the buildings, not from inside the tunnels themselves. I thought the stories of people living down there were just that, stories.'

'How do they manage?' said Eylese. 'How do they live?' She was mystified.

'There's plenty of food,' said Meshi. 'They told me.

It's easy to get in and out of the big houses and raid the kitchens and food stores. They fed me, gave me a huge plate of roast duck.'

'They were friendly, then,' said Eylese.

'Oh yes,' said Meshi. 'As soon as they found out that I wasn't from one of the posh families or somebody sent to spy on them they were really nice. It turns out they call themselves Underlings. They're proud of the name 'cos they say it shows they're outsiders.'

'And are there a lot of them?' said Eylese.

'Only those twenty, and they go all over the city. The white ones stay underground all the time – well, almost – but the others come out and join in what other people in the city are doing. Underground they have places to eat, and places to sleep, and there's the room with the stone bench where they meet. All the white ones were born in the tunnels. The others have come in from outside to hide or escape from someone. Like Yalka said, a few of the kids, I don't know how many, were sent in from the River Settlements by this Scorpion guy and they hid there and never went back. They just came across the Underlings and stayed there.'

Yalka froze. 'Did you get to know any of their names?' she said. It was hard for her to speak and her voice was very quiet.

'Some,' said Meshi.

'Was one of them a girl called Lela?'

Meshi frowned. 'No, I don't think so. I didn't hear that name. Why?'

'Oh, just, I thought...' Yalka shook her head, 'Never mind.' It was a disappointment, but also a relief. The idea of her sister living like some burrowing animal was unbearable. Suppose Meshi's answer had been yes, what then?

'What do they do all day?' said Eylese.

'They explore. They tell each other stories. They listen in to things. There are tunnels under the main buildings and some go right through the Palace. They say you can see and hear a lot of what goes on in there. Sometimes they have fun trying to spook people.'

'How do they do that?'

'Well, they've been having a go at Ragul. They wait until he's alone and then they make scary noises in the space under his room. They wake him up in the night by calling his name. There was a chariot race and his best friend got killed, and sometimes they call out his name and pretend they're this guy talking to him. They say that he gets in a right state sometimes. Bales out and crawls into his mum's bed.'

26

NEWS FOR VANCIA

Vancia knew that it probably seemed silly to others that this turret room with its balcony was one of her favourite places in the whole Palace. After all, there were far grander spaces and she could have any of them for her own, but this was the one she wanted; she had from the moment she accidentally discovered it.

She'd been a new bride and had only lived in the Palace for a few weeks. She found the entrance at the end of the women's wing, partially hidden by a wall hanging. She pulled it aside and revealed a spiral staircase. The steps were of worn stone and so narrow that it was a squeeze to climb them. At the top was a large, circular space with windows all around. The stairway was the only entrance, and opposite was a large double window, and a balcony from which she could see most of the rest of the Palace and the whole of the plain. She'd known at once that this place must be hers, her very own.

Karkis had been puzzled when she told him.

'I can't think where you mean,' he said.

She'd explained, describing the room and its location.

'Ah, yes, I remember. I think I was in there once. But it's an old storeroom, full of junk. And it's hard to get to. I can't think why you'd want that as your private room when the one you have in the women's wing is so much more comfortable.'

Vancia had wrapped her arms around her husband's neck, pressed herself against him, and gently nibbled his ear. 'But it's beautiful, so romantic, like a fairy's castle. And the windows! We could lie in bed together and look at the stars.'

'Very well, then,' Karkis had said, indulgently. 'If that is what you've set your heart on I'll see that it's done.'

And it was. The room had been emptied and scrubbed and painted, and after struggles and a great deal of swearing from the servants who had to get furniture up the stairs, it was ready for Vancia to move in. She and Karkis did lie there together, and some of the time they had looked at the stars, but once Chalia arrived in the palace his visits became rarer and as the years passed they ceased altogether.

Vancia watched, studied, and learnt. It was perfect for her purposes. She could see, but she could not be seen. From the windows at the front she could observe her husband riding out at the head of a column of his men, or leaving to hunt on the plain, or watch his carriage as it took him down the hill to the Great Square and the Assembly. From those on one side she could see the endless stream of officials, petitioners, and lobbyists who came to the Palace in their droves, and she began to identify who they were. From those on the other side she could look down into the women's garden, where she could see her son, Ragul, and her daughter, Malina at play with their nurses. And she could watch, too, that whore Chalia and, in due course, her bastard son, Peglar. It was a place to plan and plot, to scheme and contrive. A place in which she could lurk and a place from which she could slink out and attack. For Vancia it was not a lady's day room; it was the lair of a tigress.

The feature that she probably liked the most was that the space was difficult to enter. The uneven steps made it necessary for anyone climbing them to watch their feet. This meant that a visitor would rise into the room head first and eyes down, like an animal emerging from its burrow. They would have to take similar care when leaving. It was impossible to make either a graceful entrance or a dignified exit.

That was particularly true of the man who was squeezing up the stairway now. Sainter was neither graceful nor dignified in any place, and certainly not here. His huge bulk only just fitted the space, and Vancia was sure that as time passed and his girth grew he would one day become stuck, unable to move up the stairs or down. He would block the passage for good, like some vast cork. That would be a shame, because whatever his faults, which were many, and however much he irritated her, which was a great deal, he was useful. Probably more useful than anyone else.

He eventually reached the top and stood for a moment puffing and swaying. Sweat stained his armpits and back, and his forehead glistened. Vancia pushed a chair towards him.

'Sit down,' she said. And when his breathing had steadied, 'Your message said you have news for me.'

'Yes, my lady, I have. Indeed I have.' He beamed,

enjoying the moment. When Vancia didn't respond he continued, 'It's Peglar.'

Vancia froze. It was a name she hated. 'What is Peglar?' she said slowly.

'He has been taken.'

She rolled her eyes. The little man was so tiresome. 'Taken where?'

'I mean taken, as in captured. Peglar has been captured.'

This was better news than Vancia could have hoped, so much so that she could have hugged Sainter. She might have done were he not so sweaty, so greasy, so repellent.

'Where was he captured? How? Where is he now?'

'That I do not know. Actually, I know none of those things. Only that he is no longer at liberty.'

The warmth Vancia had been momentarily feeling for Sainter evaporated like a raindrop on a hot stone. She sighed and turned to the waiting woman behind her. 'Forta, kindly go to Steward Feldar and tell him that I require him here, urgently.'

Forta nodded and left. Sainter mopped his brow. Vancia went to the balcony and looked in the direction of Verlam. Peglar was a danger and a threat but he was not stupid. Had he really been rash enough to come so close to the city? Verron's plan must have worked. He must have heard of the girl Yalka's imprisonment and attempted to rescue her, not realising that she had already escaped. The fool! Vancia glowed with self-satisfaction. The last piece in her puzzle was slotting into place.

Feldar arrived sooner than she had expected,

climbing the stairs easily and, as he reached the top, offering a smooth bow.

'My lady, you summoned me. How may I be of service?'

Was there a trace of irony in the Steward's tone? Perhaps she was imagining it, but she had never liked him, or wholly trusted him. He did what he was told but she often felt there was something else going on behind the scenes, a different life of which she was not a part. It troubled her.

'Sainter has just brought me news,' she said. 'He tells me that Peglar has been apprehended. Is that so?'

Feldar glanced at Sainter and nodded. 'Yes, ma'am, it is. I had my own people out searching for him but before they could locate him a trio of three fairly disreputable characters spotted him on the coast road. He was on foot and heading towards Semilvarga. They almost failed to notice him because he had a large dog with him and they didn't expect that. They were also wary of it, but they managed to distract it and they captured him. They were still not sure until they got him to Maris Partem, where his identity was confirmed. They have now put in a request for the reward.'

Was it her imagination, or did Vancia detect that the Steward was disappointed to be telling her this? 'And he is being held secure? And they're sure it is him?'

'Yes to both those questions, ma'am. There is no doubt that it is Peglar.'

'Where has he been all this time? And how did he get so near without being spotted?'

'He's clearly managed to find a good hiding place, and as I said, having a dog with him helped.'

'Whose dog is it? Where is it now?'

Feldar shook his head. 'I am sorry, My Lady, but I can answer neither of those questions.'

'I want Peglar brought to the city.'

'He is already here. He is being held in the city jail. Marshal Thornal is putting him on trial and plans to hold the first hearing tomorrow, preparatory to him appearing before the Assembly.'

Vancia let out an expression of annoyance. 'Why? There's no need for a trial. When Peglar was sentenced to exile it carried the condition that if he were to come within a day's journey of the city he should be killed. Thornal himself read it out so he of all people ought to know this. A trial is unnecessary. Peglar can be disposed of now.' She paced the room like a caged animal. She was so close to securing the last of her enemies. 'Go to the jail, Steward Feldar, get Peglar, and bring him back here.'

'Yes, ma'am, but I shall need authorisation. I doubt if the Marshal will hand Peglar over to me just on my say so.'

It was a nuisance, but Vancia assumed he was right. 'Very well. Go to your office and wait for further instructions,' she said. 'I'll get you the authorisation you need.'

THE STUDY that Karkis had used for his administrative work as the Master of the City was a sombre place. It was dark, with the curtains habitually closed and feeble lamps struggling to lift the gloom on even the brightest day. There had been an imposing chair and an enormous desk, in front of an alcove containing paintings of family elders. The carpet was threadbare, and even in the middle of summer a fire had always burned in the grate. Books had lined the walls, and piles of papers had crowded every surface, all jostling unsteadily for attention.

It was different now. The curtains were still drawn and the room depended on lamplight, but there was no fire. The worn carpet had been removed and so had the books, although their shelves remained. The paintings in the alcove had been replaced by a large wooden board. A human figure, female, was crudely painted on it, with enormous breasts and an exaggerated vaginal opening. Four throwing axes were embedded in and around it. Splinters and gashes on the wall were evidence of attempts to hit the target. There was not a document in sight.

Ragul was at the desk, playing cards with a man Vancia didn't recognise. There was a pile of coins between them. He beamed as she came in.

'Mummy,' he said, and struggled to get up. She gestured to him not to bother. The damage Peglar had done to his knee in the combat had been serious and his condition seemed to be getting worse. It was something else for which Peglar would pay, she promised.

'You have heard the news of your half-brother,' she said.

'No, Mummy. What news?'

Vancia didn't like being called mummy. It made her feel matronly and old. She'd told him many times not to do it but still he persisted. She put it aside to deal with later and went through what Feldar had told her.

'Oh, Mummy, that is splendid.' Ragul beamed and turned towards the man at the table. 'This is Silon,

Mummy. He's my new friend. My very special friend. Hear that, Silesy?' he giggled. 'Pegleg's for the chop.' He turned back to his mother. 'We'll go to the trial, Mummy, all of us. We'll make a day of it.'

Silon grinned, which seemed to Vancia to be all he was capable of, the faculty of speech having bypassed him.

'There is no need for a trial,' she said. 'Peglar's guilt in defying the order of exile is undisputed, and he has already been condemned. I've instructed Steward Feldar to go to Marshal Thornal and bring Peglar to the Palace so we can deal with him here.'

Ragul clapped his hands in delight and Silon looked towards the board with the throwing axes.

'Feldar needs a letter from you that he can present to Thornal, instructing him to hand over Peglar into your custody.'

Ragul showed an expression of distaste. He found any sort of paperwork unappealing. 'Crestyn deals with all that sort of thing,' he said. 'Here, Silesy, pop along the passage and tell Crestyn what's needed. Then bring it back here for me to sign.' Silon seemed reluctant to take this instruction and didn't move. 'I'll give you twenty pieces start on the next game,' Ragul said, gesturing towards the cards. Still Silon didn't move. 'Thirty?'

It was enough, and the man left.

'Who is he?' said Vancia.

'Who is who, Mummy?'

Vancia sighed. How could this lump of a son be so witless? 'The man who has just left. The man you call Silon.'

'Oh, he's a friend,' Ragul said airily. 'After I had to

end my relationship with Burian I needed a new companion.'

'End your relationship,' said Vancia. 'I suppose that's one way of putting it. Where did you find this man? How do you know he's honest and can be trusted?'

'He's from a very good family. Not top drawer, but very reliable. He sleeps with me, in my room. Since he's been with me I haven't been troubled at all by the voices, not once.'

Vancia had to admit that her son looked in better spirits than she had seen him in a long time, and it was good that he had not come to her room for several nights. If that was due to this new creature she supposed she should be thankful.

She gave him the benefit of one of her broadest smiles when he returned with the letter from Crestyn. He gave it to Ragul, a servant came forward with a pen and inkpot, and Ragul signed it. He didn't read it, didn't even glance at it, he merely added his name in an untidy scrawl and pushed it away. Careless, thought Vancia. And dangerous, too. This was a situation that she would need to watch. It was one she could exploit. However, she was also aware that she would need to watch Silon, too.

'Pick out half a dozen of your best men and send them with Feldar,' she said.

'Half a dozen?' said Ragul scornfully. 'For Peglar? Who do you think he is? Farumon?'

Silon produced what sounded to Vancia to be a fake laugh. Laughing at Ragul's clumsy jokes had been one of Burian's main duties, and Silon seemed to have inherited it.

'It's not Peglar that concerns me,' said Vancia. 'There

are others in the city who see him as wronged and want to make him something of a martyr. We must be prepared. I want Peglar brought back here safely so that we can ensure that Marshal Thornal's sentence is carried out. Six good men from the Household Guard will ensure that happens.'

'Ah,' said Ragul, understanding. 'Very wise, Mummy. See to it, Silesy.'

27

SENTENCE

Peglar's cell was hard and cruel. There was no furniture and no comforts at all. The only place to sit was the floor. The tiny barred window was too high for him to see through and only good for admitting a dirty yellow light. He was thirsty and he asked for water but none came. He needed to relieve himself but there was nowhere to do it. This was worse even than the slave market.

Time was contorted and he couldn't tell how long he had been there. On the journey to Maris Partem he'd been bound, and his captors had forced his head down in case anyone saw him in the cart. They had taken him straight to the Guardians and he'd been put in a room while he listened to arguments outside. As far as he could tell his captors expected the reward for his capture to be handed over on the spot, and were angry when they learnt that this was not possible and that a Guardian's outpost didn't have five hundred golds lying around. The situation was at last resolved and the three men went away.

There was a long wait, and then another journey, this time in a closed cart to Chamaris. As he was bundled out in front of a few onlookers and taken into the jail building, Peglar glimpsed the dome of the Ceremonium and remembered the lavish parade that had taken him there for his initiation. It had seemed such a wonderful day, such a triumph and so full of promise. Now he wished it had never happened.

He sat on the floor thinking about Yalka and hoping that she was safe. Was she in Maris Partem? Semilvarga? She'd escaped from the tower in Verlam. What had happened to her after that? He thought about Safren too. Where would she go? Who would feed her?

The painful hours passed, the light faded and his cell grew dark. No water appeared and there was no food either. He lay down on the stone floor and waited for what might happen the next day. He wanted the night to pass but he didn't want the new day to come.

But come it did, and there were sounds from outside. However, no one came to his cell. He was beginning to think that this was to be his manner of execution, that he would be left there to starve to death or die of thirst, when he heard a commotion, muffled conversations and calls, in the passage outside the cell. Then there was the noise of a key in the lock and the door opened.

It was not food or water. It was two Guardians. One carried a rope and the other a zirca. Peglar tried to get to his feet and found that was nowhere near as straightforward as it had been. He staggered, half fell, and put a hand to the wall to steady himself. There was a pounding in his ears and he seemed unable to balance. The room tilted, his knees buckled, and a black cloud wrapped around him.

He woke, and he was in another cell, a different one. This one was marginally more comfortable than the last because he was on a low bed and not the floor, but his eyes were fuzzy and it was hard to see clearly the figure bending over him.

'Hold his head up,' he heard someone say. It was a voice he knew. Feldar.

His head was lifted and a beaker raised to his lips. It was water and it tasted like the sweetest thing he had ever drunk. He clutched at it and gulped greedily but the beaker was pulled away.

'Take it slowly,' Feldar said. 'You've been deprived of water. I don't know what they could have been thinking of. You can have some more in a few minutes. It's not good to drink a lot quickly when you're dehydrated.

'Where... where... where am I?' It took two or three goes before Peglar could get his voice to work.

'You're in the Palace,' Feldar said. 'You were unconscious when they transported you from the jail. They got you in through the rear gate and brought you down here to the cellars.'

The Palace. That could not be good. 'Why am I here?' he said.

'Ragul's orders,' said Feldar. 'He doesn't think there's any need to bother with a trial so he's had them transfer you here.'

That sounded ominous. 'What's going to happen to me?'

Feldar looked away. 'I can't pretend it's good,' he said. 'Ragul wants to get rid of you and he won't delay trying to do that. But you have friends in the city. Cestris is contacting Lembick and Malina to see if they'll step in and try to talk Ragul down.'

'Malina? She won't help me. Look what she did. It's because of her that I'm in this mess.'

'I think she's starting to regret that. Anyway, all we can do is wait and see. Nothing will happen tonight but I expect Ragul will be down here in the morning. Have some more water.'

Peglar took the beaker and this time he was allowed to drain it. He handed it back.

'What about you?' he said. 'Aren't you putting yourself in danger talking to me like this?'

Feldar shook his head. 'I'm all right. The warden who was with me when you woke up didn't hear anything before I sent him away, and the one outside thinks I'm interrogating you. See if you can get some sleep. You'll need all your strength tomorrow.'

Feldar left and the cell door slammed behind him. Sleep? He didn't think there was much chance of that. Some more water had been left for him, and a couple of dry biscuits. They were the first things he'd eaten in a long time and he made himself chew them slowly. He lay back on the bed. It wasn't too bad. At least it was better than the previous night. Even so, he was wide awake and he thought that going to sleep would be impossible, but in the end he fell into a restless drowse.

The Household Guards who woke him were not hostile. They were not even unfriendly. They were neutral, treating him as no more animate than the extravagantly decorated chair they brought into the cell with them. Two of them carried it and another stood at the door, his hand on the zirca at his belt. Peglar stood up shakily, but the Guard waved him back and he withdrew to the wall furthest from the door.

He felt wretched. His head ached and his body

itched. He couldn't remember when he'd last washed. He'd not been to the lavatory either, but he supposed that if he wasn't eating or drinking anything there was nothing to come out. He reached for the water jug, filled the beaker and drained it. The two Guards with the chair placed it against the opposite wall and stood one on each side of it. He guessed that something would happen soon.

It did. There were more sounds in the passage, the Guards snapped to attention and there was an air of anticipation. The doorkeeper indicated that Peglar should stand, and he then moved aside. There was a pause, and Ragul appeared in the doorway. He had a stick in each hand, but even so it was a struggle for him to get through the door and into the cell. It would have been amusing, except that there was nothing funny about the situation. At least, Peglar thought, he would now find out what was in store for him.

Ragul hobbled over to the chair. There was someone with him, a man that Peglar didn't recognise. He'd expected Burian, but perhaps he'd been replaced. It took Ragul some time to settle himself and for his companion to help him get his lame leg comfortable. All the time he grunted and grimaced, clearly in pain. When all was done the new man went to stand with the doorkeeper and Ragul turned his attention to Peglar.

'Well, little brother,' he said, looking at him with an expression of utter disdain. 'It looks like you've come to the end of your brief adventure.' His lips parted in what was probably meant to be a gloating smile but looked to Peglar more like a rictus of agony. 'I'm surprised you made it so easy for me. My plan worked. I dangled your little whore in front of you and you came scuttling back to get at her like a rat on heat.'

Peglar said nothing. It hadn't been simple at all. He'd been aware of the trap all along and had very nearly escaped it. After he'd found the tower empty he should not have gone on the main road towards Semilvarga. There were plenty of places to hide and he should have made use of them. But for that silly misjudgement he would still be free, free to continue the search for the girl that he knew now he could not live without.

'I intend to keep this simple,' Ragul continued. 'Marshal Thornal made it clear when he exiled you that the penalty if you returned to the city would be death, so we do not need to trouble legal minds about what should happen to you. You are to die, and as the Master of the City it's my responsibility, no,' he smiled again, 'my pleasure, to see that the Marshal's sentence is carried out.' Ragul stroked his chin and looked at the man who'd come in with him. 'What do you think, Silesy? Poison, like his mother? A knife to the throat?'

'We've got that board in your study,' said the man he'd called Silesy. 'And the axes. We could do with a bit of target practice.'

'Nice idea,' said Ragul, nodding with enthusiasm. 'I'd like that. Think of his screams as we cut off a hand, or split his balls. Mummy thinks it should be public, though. The people must witness his execution so his death can be in no doubt. Justice must be seen to be done, and all that business. Yes,' he rubbed his chin again, 'a public execution so that the people can be sure that the law has been applied, even to a member of my own family.' He looked to the ceiling and spoke quietly as if thinking aloud. 'How should it be done? We could still use the axes, but maybe that would be a bit too gory. Beheading, too, is messy. After all, we want the crowd to see the whole thing, we don't want the ladies passing out so they miss the best part.'

'There's the Citadel,' said Silesy. 'In the past weren't criminals thrown off the precipice at the back, so they were smashed on the rocks below?'

'That would be appropriate,' said Ragul, smiling at him. 'There's a problem, though. If we did that it might be hard to retrieve his miserable carcass. In the olden days they used to just leave them on the rocks to be eaten by wild animals and birds, but I want this one's corpse on display.' He turned to Peglar. 'I want people to see that you're really dead. So I think that on the whole it would be best to hang you, on a high scaffold so that everyone can watch it, and afterwards your body can be put on display in the Great Square. And I have the perfect time for it. Tomorrow is a full moon, and every full moon I lead the Regents and Priestesses in a procession to return the golden sword to Farumon's tomb. So you could be part of the ceremony. All process together, hang you, deposit the sword, and process again back into the city with your carcass.' He looked to have a sudden thought. 'And do you know? The astrologers predict that tomorrow it will be what they call "a hanging moon". That's when it rises big and bloody and looks to be suspended from a star. Appropriate, don't you think?'

Silesy guffawed, but Peglar noticed that only one of the Guards was joining in. The other two looked uneasy.

Ragul pointed his stick at Peglar. 'What do you think, brother mine?'

Peglar had no words. He was horrified. Was this

really happening to him? It was ridiculous. A farce. Ragul couldn't be serious. But he was, and so as well as being unreal it was also very frightening. He had just been told that there were only a few hours of his life left. His legs trembled and his stomach was in a tight knot.

'The good news for you,' Ragul said to him, 'is that hanging is painless. Or so they say, although how anybody knows beats me.' He turned to Silesy and they both laughed. 'I'm told that the secret is in positioning the knot. If the hangman gets it in the right place the jolt as the plank gives way and your body drops will break your neck, and death will be instant. Well, almost instant. The problem is that if it's not done properly the noose will strangle you. That will be very slow and very painful.' He leant forward and assumed a confidential tone. 'I'll send the hangman to see you. He needs to weigh you anyway, so he can work out how to fashion the knot and the right length for the plank. You might want to slip him a few golds to encourage him to take particular care.' Ragul sat back and let out a savage laugh. 'Of course, you'll have to trust him because if he doesn't do a good job you won't be in a position to ask for your money back, will you?'

Silesy thought this was hilarious, clearly finding the prospect of Peglar's death entertaining. It was hopeless. There was no way that Feldar, Cestris, or any of the people who he thought of as friends could help him now. This was it. He had a sudden flashback to Reddall, lying unconscious in the farm shed, his leg rotting away. He was under sentence of death too. At least his own would be quick.

Ragul banged his staff on the ground. Silesy and one

of the Guards took an arm each and helped him get onto his feet. He took one final look at Peglar.

'I win, I believe. I'll see you on the Citadel tomorrow evening, your date with the hanging moon.'

He limped out of the room, the door closed and the key was turned. Peglar was left alone to contemplate what the next twenty-four hours held for him.

28

PREPARATIONS

Yalka began to weep, and once the tears came they turned into a flood. She was not given to crying, she thought it pointless and she would always prefer to channel her emotions into action. So when her younger sister was killed by a gang one night in the city, she responded by making a shrine for her. And when Verit, her deaf and dumb brother, was killed in the fire that ravaged the River Settlements, she and her grandfather took his body that very night up the hill to the Citadel to give him a hero's burial. But there seemed to be no action she could take here. There was absolutely nothing she could do.

She supposed that despite what her Grandfather told her he foresaw, despite what she herself had felt, it was never going to work out. They'd met by accident, a rich boy who liked to be alone and wanted to get away from his insufferable, suffocating family and a poor girl who'd found a lofty spot from which she could look down on the unfathomable comings and goings of a society for which she had no time and even less respect.

The bond between them had formed slowly. It wasn't the dazzling flash of love at first sight that Eylese seemed to be searching for. It was gradual, and it had surprised her when she found herself increasingly hoping that when she went up to the Citadel he would be there. She remembered the surge of elation when he was, and the doleful dejection when he wasn't.

It had not all gone smoothly. There had been misunderstandings, quarrels, and anger. There had been the time when she'd blamed him for Verit's death. There had been the time when she'd misunderstood his motives for a lavish present he'd given her, assuming that he'd done it to get her to have sex with him. That had been embarrassing. And there was the occasion when she'd learnt that he was accused of sexually assaulting his half-sister. To her shame, for a second she had wondered if it might be true. Malina was devastatingly beautiful, and coquettish too, and there were lots of stories in the Settlements about the things that posh boys got up to. And then she had put the tale against the Peglar she knew and had no doubt that he'd been set up. But all that had been in their early days and was long past. Since then the knowledge that Peglar was in the world, even if he wasn't with her, had been like a warm wrap on a cold night.

Peglar's exile should have made things easier for them. He would have no more demands from the Palace and she had always been free. They should have been able to go away and build a life together in another city. They had been trying to do that but something always got in the way and their paths diverged. When she'd asked her Grandfather about their future he'd told her that he could see a time when they would be together.

Her own visions as she flexed her developing talents as a rhymer said the same.

But rhymers could never tell exactly when an event would happen, or predict the precise steps on the way. And they could be wrong. There was no way out of this. Peglar was a prisoner of his half-brother and lodged somewhere secure in the Palace. He'd been sentenced to death by hanging. He would be watched all the time. It would take an army to free him, and Ragul would make sure that if Peglar's liberty seemed possible he would be rapidly dispatched by one of his guards before a rescuer could get near him. There was no hope. This was the end.

'There's got to be something we can do,' said Meshi, his adoring gaze fixed on the distraught girl. 'Can't we get into the city by using the tunnels? We could find him, and then we could get him out the same way.'

'I don't think it would be that easy,' said Yalka. 'The Palace is huge. Even if we could get in, we've no idea where he's being kept and there might not be a tunnel anywhere near. And if we did find him, we couldn't just walk out with him.'

'What about the Underlings?' Meshi persisted. 'They seem to know everything. They'd know where he is.'

'They might, but then how could we get him away from his jailers?'

'And you can be very sure,' Flynt added, 'that Ragul the rat will have made sure there are plenty of those.'

'So what do we do?' said Meshi.

There was silence. For perhaps the first time in her life, Yalka had no idea how to act. Her plan had been simple. After Eylese had rescued her from the tower they would watch the road from Semilvarga. News of her captivity and its location had been spread energetically by Big Ears and his men, and it was inevitable that Peglar would hear it. Then he would come to find her. All she had to do was wait until he did and intercept him, and then they would be together. And yes, Peglar had come, but others on the road had found him first and the insane reward that Ragul had offered had done its job. Oh, what had possessed Peglar to use the main route? Why hadn't he stuck to the tracks and byways that linked the villages of the plain? He would have had a far better chance there. There was nothing they could do. It was hopeless. She let out another sob, loaded with frustration, anger and hopelessness.

'I think you ought to go,' said Flynt.

Yalka looked up and tried to clear the tears from her eyes. 'Go? Go where?'

'I think you ought to go tonight, to be at the… the… event.'

Yalka couldn't believe what she was hearing. 'You think I should be there when they hang him?' She had a vision of Peglar swinging from a rope, clutching at his throat while his feet flailed frantically in the empty air. She shuddered. 'You're mad. I couldn't. It will be terrible.'

'Listen,' said Flynt. She sat at the table opposite Yalka. 'Look at me, and listen. This is what Ragul has arranged. Tonight is the full moon, the time when every month there's the procession and Ragul and his Regents and Priestesses parade up to the Citadel to collect Farumon's sword. It's predicted to be a hanging moon and therefore Ragul has decided to carry out his threat against Peglar at the same time as the moon rises.'

Yalka shook her head. She knew this.

'What I'm saying is this,' Flynt continued. 'The Palace is like a fortress. There will be guards everywhere. There is no chance at all of rescuing Peglar from there. But tonight, at the ceremony, it might be different. Ragul wants a big crowd. He's had heralds all over the area announcing what's going to happen and telling people they're expected to attend. Then there are the politicians and other bigwigs, the representatives of the tribute cities, the family hangers-on, and don't forget the fifty Priestesses. It will be heaving. There'll be pushing and shoving, and lots of distractions. It might be possible to arrange something.'

Yalka shook her head. She knew that Flynt meant to be kind and comforting but she also knew that there was no way Ragul would let Peglar out of his clutches now. A milling crowd would make a rescue more difficult, not less. Also, there was the bleak vision of her Grandfather. After Peglar's capture she'd asked him for a rhyme to show the future. He'd taken armanca, a double dose, and gone into a trance, but the rhyme he'd uttered was even vaguer than usual and meant nothing. Her own prophetic gifts had deserted her. What was to come was like a blank wall. It was as if the seizure of Peglar was a watershed. Before it they could feel harmonies from future worlds; on this side of it neither of them could foresee anything.

'You have to be there so that if there is an opportunity to save him, we can. Lots of people are grumbling about Ragul. Say the crowd suddenly turns against him and takes the side of Peglar. Or say there's some sort of mix-up. We could take advantage,' said Flynt.

Yalka said nothing. Flynt was trying to be positive but there was no chance of what she was suggesting.

'There is another thing,' said Flynt slowly, 'and I'm not sure of the best way to say it. I know that if Peglar's...' She hesitated.

'You mean his execution. His murder. You can say it,' Yalka interrupted.

'Yes, right, well if it does take place, you won't want to watch it, of course you won't, but it would comfort Peglar if he knew that you were near. That you were with him at the very end. If something like that was happening to you, wouldn't you want him to be close?'

Yalka didn't know. It was an impossible question. She couldn't imagine being in that situation. Would she feel better if she was in danger and Peglar was nearby, even if it was obvious he could do nothing to save her? Yes, she supposed she would. Yes, she certainly would. She nodded. 'Yes, you're probably right.' She wiped her eyes with her sleeve. She would be there for him, but there was no way she would be able to watch.

'We'll get you ready, then.'

Eylese started first with her hair. Some of the black dye had washed out and blonde roots were already showing. Eylese soaped and rinsed, soaped and rinsed until as much of the remaining dye as she could shift had gone. Then she turned to her face and began shaping Yalka's brows. The hair was one thing, but it felt intolerable to Yalka to be giving such attention to her appearance at a time like this.

'What's wrong?' Eylese said, looking hurt.

'The whole thing is wrong. For me to be pampering myself just to stand there while Peglar dies is obscene. I can't bear it.'

Eylese took her hand and sat on the bench beside her.

'I know,' she said. 'But it's important you look your best. I know it. Trust me.'

Yalka thought about it. She couldn't understand why Eylese was saying this, but she did trust her and she doubted that she herself was in a fit state to make sensible decisions.

'Okay,' she said.

Eylese smiled. 'Good. You'd better dry your eyes or you'll smudge the makeup I'm going to put on.'

Eylese finished her brows and treated her lashes. She moved on to her face and lips and painted her nails. Finally, she rubbed scented oil into her neck and shoulders, her arms and legs. She helped her into a fresh gown, silken and deep green, and fastened her sandals on her feet. Yalka had to admit she felt better, but it still seemed to her to be an inappropriate way to prepare for the terrible thing that was going to happen.

Eylese stood back, and with her head tilted to one side she surveyed her work.

'There's one more thing.' She took a wooden box from a shelf and put it on the table.

'What's that?' said Yalka.

'It's your hair.' Eylese opened the box to show a harvest of golden braids, nestling in a silk wrapping. 'When you got me to cut off your hair, I kept it. All of it. I saved it and I plaited it into strands. Here they are. I can weave them into your hair now and you'll be back to your old self. Well, not quite, but nearly.'

Yalka took one of the tight, glossy braids and ran it through her fingers. 'I can't believe you've done this. It must have taken you ages. It's....'

'Now you're not to cry,' said Eylese. 'Not after I've just spent all that time on your make-up.'

Yalka took her hands. 'Thank you,' she said.

She sat patiently while Eylese worked. Occasionally it tugged and she winced, but that was nothing. Her hair had always been special, everybody said so. It was the thing that people noticed first about her, even before the birthmark on her cheek. Tonight she would get near the front of the crowd to make sure she was in Peglar's eyeline, remove her hood, and he would see her. He would know she was there, with him. She hoped against all reason that she might be able to find a way to free him, but if that was not to be, hers would be one of the last faces he would see. If that did happen, if there was no miracle, she didn't know how she would survive. She knew now that there would never be anyone else.

When Eylese had woven in the last strand she again stood back. 'You're beautiful,' she said.

Yalka shook her head. She had never thought of herself in that way.

'No, I mean it,' said Eylese. 'You really are very beautiful.' She came close, sat on a chair beside Yalka, and put an arm around her. 'Be brave and stay strong. Don't let Peglar see you're upset. And keep your hopes up. You can never be sure how something will turn out until it's over, and I have a strong feeling that tonight things might turn out to go differently from the way everybody expects.'

Yalka knew that her friend was being kind and she forced a smile. The advice was sound. Yalka had never been a gloomy person. She had in her time often known joy, sadness, disgust, fear, anger – rage, even – happiness, elation, and love. But never depression or despair. That just wasn't her. Except for now, when it was hard to shift the dread that had settled like something hard and indigestible in her stomach.

Eylese took her hand. 'I think you should give it another hour and then leave. The crowd will be forming in the square, and you want to be near the front.'

'What about you?'

'You go ahead with Meshi. I'll be there later. There's something I have to do first.'

'What's that?'

Eylese gave a grim smile. 'It's nothing to concern you now, but this evening it might help. Don't worry, I'll be there on the Citadel, I promise.'

Yalka watched her put on her cloak and let herself out.

29

EXECUTION

From Maris Partem to Chamaris is a distance of about three miles. On her own Yalka could have run it in twenty minutes, but Myander had an ingrowing toenail which made walking painful, so the journey took them over an hour. At first there were only a few others on the road, but as they approached the city people joined from side roads and by the time they reached the Great Gate there was a crush. Yalka was astonished to see families with children. Had they come thinking that there would be no more than the Farumon ceremony? Didn't they know that someone was going to be hung? Surely they wouldn't want their sons and daughters to see that. Or perhaps they would.

There was a queue at the gate because Guardians were checking each entrant, confiscating anything that they thought was suspicious or inappropriate and putting their finds in a bin. Yalka glanced at the collection as she went through the process. A few knives, a couple of Zircas, a heavy-looking club, and even a horseshoe. It appeared Ragul was taking no chances.

Despite what Eylese had said there was no hope. Where was she? And where was her Grandfather? She needed his steadiness and his comfort, but he had spent the day on his own, evasive when she asked him what he was doing.

Eventually they were inside the city, and they joined the crowd swarming up the hill towards the Great Square. With every step Yalka's fearful apprehension became more intense, settling over her like a heavy, black shroud that blotted out any hope of happiness and choked any gleam of light.

'How long until moonrise?' she said. She was so tense she could hardly speak.

'I'm not sure,' said Flynt. 'About an hour I think.'

An hour. Was that all Peglar had left? Was that all there was before her own life, too, shut down?

The shuffling crowd grew slower and came to a stop. The entrance to the square was jammed with people.

'We have to get to the front,' said Flynt.

'What about Eylese?' said Myander. 'She said she'd be here.'

'I expect she will be. And Syramos too. They're probably in the rumpus at the gate. Here, Meshi, wait on this corner. When you see Eylese and Syramos coming up the hill, meet them and bring them to us. We'll be as close to the procession as we can get.'

Meshi didn't look happy to be left but he obediently took up a place where Flynt had indicated.

Flynt turned back to Yalka and Myander. 'Right you are,' she said, 'follow me.'

Flynt set out to make a way through the melee, exploiting gaps and chinks wherever she could see them. She was a burly woman and not to be denied. She led with her elbows, smoothing their passage with 'excuse me', 'may I pass?', and 'thank you so much'. Yalka came behind her, grateful that Flynt was taking the lead and she didn't have to do anything herself except follow. Myander brought up the rear.

There was some grumbling but most people gave way with a good grace, and Yalka was astonished when they got to the front row. There was a line of Guardians keeping the crowd back, but she was close to where the procession was forming. A dozen Household Guards were at the head. They were in ceremonial dress, the golden leopard gleaming on their chests, and their spears and zircas looked deadly serious. Thornal, the City Marshal, was already there, talking to a man she recognised. It was Feldar. She was surprised to see him looking so calm. He was a friend of Peglar. Surely he could do something to stop this. Resting on the ground behind them was a stately bier. It was gold with crimson cushions and looked to Yalka to be the one that had been used at Peglar's initiation. A line of serving men waited on each side of it.

There was a commotion to the right.

'It's the Priestesses,' said Myander. 'Fifty of them.'

'All virgins,' said Flynt. 'Or that's what they claim.'

The Priestesses formed a group behind the bier and waited, heads down. They were all wearing white cloaks that hid their figures, and they had hoods and face masks of the same material. The effect was to make them look like statues, still and sexless.

'They cover their faces so that the men can't see them and take a fancy to any of them,' Flynt said.

Then came the sound of a trumpet. It was some way off, further up the hill towards the Palace.

'That will be Ragul,' said Flynt.

As soon as Ragul arrived the procession would start, Yalka thought. Time was running out. Where was Peglar? Where was Eylese?

The trumpet sounded again, closer this time, and a carriage pulled by black horses came slowly into the square, surrounded by a group of men in purple robes and wearing huge, pointed hats. Each carried a large leather-bound ledger,

'The Regents,' said Flynt. 'Those are the books that record people's lives, their deeds and whether they were good or bad. Oh my stars, look.'

What she had seen made Yalka's heart plummet. Walking behind the carriage and tethered to it by a rope was Peglar. There was a guard on each side of him and following him was a big man bearing a large hammer on his shoulder.

Peglar was stripped to the waist. Yalka had been afraid that he would show the marks of beatings or torture, but he seemed fine. His hands were tied behind his back but he stood erect. His body was unmarked but he looked starved. He also looked older. His hair was longer than when she'd seen him last, and he had the beginnings of what could have turned into a fine beard.

'What's the hammer for?' said Myander. 'Surely they're not going to strike him with it.'

'Keep your hood up for now,' Flynt said to Yalka. 'You don't want Ragul to see you, or that Big Ears creep, if he's around.'

The carriage door opened and Vancia appeared, stepping down gracefully and lightly. Ragul followed. He seemed to be in pain and several people hurried forward to help him. He shuffled the few steps to the bier and clambered on, again with help. Vancia joined him. Thornal placed the golden sword in front of Ragul. The bearers pumped themselves up, and counting down from five they raised the poles supporting the bier onto their shoulders. Ragul was now above the crowd, and he waved graciously. There were a few cheers, but not many.

'Let's hope they drop them both,' said Flynt.

A drummer had appeared and he started a slow, solemn beat. The guards and the bier-bearers took up the rhythm on the spot and then, at a signal from the Marshal, they began to march. Peglar and the man with the hammer followed, and the Priestesses and Regents after them. At the very back were some distinguished-looking men in the robes of Councillors. A piper began a wailing tune and the Priestesses took it up, chanting words that Yalka couldn't understand.

'What are they singing?' she said.

'Who knows?' said Flynt. 'Some nonsense of Ragul's, I expect. Come on, now. We need to be at the front of the crowd.

The throng shuffled forward after the procession, and Flynt again used a combination of elbow and apology to get them to its head.

Yalka looked anxiously around for Meshi, Eylese and her Grandfather but couldn't see them. The single bright star that would soon be the pivot of the hanging moon was already high and there was a faint glow on the horizon. Moonrise was imminent. What was she doing here? Her best friend in the world was about to be hanged. In an hour, perhaps less, he would be dead. Flynt and Eylese had both said that in all the hubbub and crush it might be possible to free Peglar. She hadn't believed them at the time and could see now what nonsense it was. There was no way a rescue could be attempted; there were just too many people around and it was impossible to get near Peglar. She doubted he would even see her.

Some words of her Grandfather's haunted her. She'd written them down as he'd said them, his speech blurred by the armanca, and she'd learnt them by heart like a mantra, hoping to make sense of them. She repeated them in her head now.

The tracks we make in our lives are narrow
Sometimes deep but often shallow
A rhymer may tell where they go
But even she can't stop time's flow
At the end of life, we all face death
A happy escape or a sad last breath
But the way through that door can always change
Prepare yourself to examine its range

It made no sense, and when she'd grumbled to Syramos he'd said that the truth was in there somewhere if she worked at it, and anyway, he'd added irritably, he wasn't a fairground fortune teller.

Something struck her.

'How many Priestesses did you say there were?' she asked Flynt.

'Fifty.'

'What, exactly fifty? Or about fifty?'

'Exactly fifty. According to that silly book that keeps appearing, Farumon's army was fifty women and he must be served by fifty virgins.'

'I think there's more than fifty.'

'Perhaps they're training some new ones. Does it matter?'

'I don't know.'

Yalka had seen the Priestesses line up. They'd been in rows and she'd started to count them, but then they all moved about and she'd lost track. It was just that she had a strange sensation, the sort of fluttering she had when she felt a rhyme coming. Something didn't seem right. Somewhere one of the strings was out of tune. But the feeling went and she couldn't be sure. And as Flynt said, did it matter how many Priestesses there were?

The procession swayed up the hill to the rhythm of the drumbeat and the onlookers shuffled behind. Yalka glanced over her shoulder. The crowd was huge. Had all these people really turned out to see a boy put to death? She still couldn't see her friends and her Grandfather and her spirits fell further. It would have been a comfort to have them beside her when the time came.

The procession passed the Palace and halted at the beginning of the rough track up to the Citadel. The path and the gate were narrow and the procession was squeezed. She caught sight of the bier-bearers struggling to get Ragul and his mother through the opening while keeping the contraption level. Now indeed would be a good time to cause a distraction, and in the ensuing chaos free Peglar. But it wasn't possible to get near them and in a moment the bier was through and the rest of the troop – Peglar and the man with the hammer, the Regents and the Priestesses – followed.

Guardians were channelling everyone towards the rear of the Citadel, beyond the huge white marble shrine dedicated to Farumon and above the near-vertical face away from the city. Yalka blindly followed Flynt and found herself near the front. A line of Guardians had formed to hold the spectators back and she managed to find a spot where she could see between them. Peglar's back was towards her. The Priestesses were to the side, their covered heads bowed.

The scaffold was a timber platform at the very edge of the drop with an upside-down 'L' mounted on it. The arm of the L was over the abyss, and a noose hung from it. A plank stretched out from the platform to beneath the noose. It was obvious how it would work. Peglar would stand on the plank, which was secured at the other end and the noose would be put around his neck. Then whatever was holding the plank would be released, the plank would drop, and that would be it.

'There's a wedge that holds the plank in place,' Flynt explained. 'When the moon rises and Ragul gives the word the man with the hammer will knock it out and it will tip over.'

And Peglar will fall. It was unthinkably horrific and Yalka felt sick. The moon would soon appear over the far hill. The crowd was quiet, the slow, steady drumbeat the only sound. It seemed as though time had stood still.

The drumbeat ceased. Attendants helped Ragul descend painfully from the bier. Vancia followed. He stood on a low plinth with his back to the chasm so that he could address the crowd. The Priestesses formed a semi-circle in front of him.

The trumpet sounded, reverberating in the gorge. When the fanfare had died away Ragul spoke.

'Citizens, friends,' Ragul declared. 'We are here on the night of the full moon to remember and pay tribute to Farumon, the great leader of the golden age of Chamaris, who will rise again to serve us in our hour of

274

need. But before that ceremony, we have a duty to perform. Some time ago my bastard half-brother, Jathan Peglar, instigated a plot against the rulership of the city. It was prevented and as a punishment he was outlawed, on pain of death. However, such is his pride that he returned to promote his evil plan. Loyal citizens became aware of this and apprehended him.'

Yalka was consumed by such fierce hatred that she thought she would burst, and it took an effort to stop herself from screaming filth at this loathsome creature. Ragul and his sister had smeared Peglar. Ragul had bribed Thornal to declare him the winner of the contest in the cage, to outlaw him and pass a death sentence on him. Ragul was now going to carry that out by hanging the boy she had come to love. Ragul had murdered Eylese's family and Eylese had vowed revenge. Yalka pledged herself to do whatever she could to help her friend bring that about.

Ragul waited as if he was expecting some acclaim, but there was none. The crowd was still. There was silence apart from the occasional cry of a child.

Ragul turned to his side. 'Marshal Thornal.'

The Marshal came forward and Ragul turned on the rim of the chasm to face the opposite hill where there was a reddish glow in the sky, and raised his arms. The moon was about to rise.

'Jathan Peglar,' said Thornal. 'You have been sentenced to death and that sentence will now be carried out.'

The man with the hammer, the executioner, pushed Peglar ahead of him along the plank. When he was in position he slipped the noose over his head and pulled it tight. Then he came back to the platform, leaving Peglar standing alone. He seemed all right, Yalka thought. He wasn't shaking. He simply stood there, waiting. What was going through his mind? What could he possibly be thinking at such a time? She threw off her hood. Would he see her? Would he know she was with him? At that moment he turned. The gap between them was wide, but it was nothing. Their eyes met, and for a second each gazed deep into the other's soul.

The executioner picked up his hammer and gave it a practice swing.

Ragul dropped his arms and turned around. 'No, not you,' he called. 'Him.' He pointed to Feldar. 'You do it, Steward Feldar. You strike the wedge and release the plank.'

Feldar looked horrified and stared at Ragul as if he'd gone mad. The executioner held out the hammer to Feldar.

The drumbeat started again. It beat twenty, thirty times. The rim of the hanging moon crept over the hill.

'Now,' shouted Ragul. 'Do it now.' He turned back to the gorge and raised his arms. 'Farumon, we do this for you. Accept this sacrifice from your people.'

Feldar hesitated, weighing the hammer. What could he do? How much time could he buy?

The people were silent. Time froze. Suddenly there was a commotion among the Priestesses and one of them darted forward. Someone shouted.

Ragul turned to find out what was happening in time to see a white shape hurtling at him. There was an instant before the Guardians reacted and it was just time enough.

The Priestess cannoned into Ragul and for a second they both swayed on the dizzying brink of the drop.

Ragul toppled and clawed at the edge. Vancia leapt forward to save him but he was already slipping. He threw an arm around her ankle, grabbed the Priestesses gown, and then, almost in slow motion, Vancia, the Priestess, and Ragul all disappeared over the edge of the precipice, into the ravine.

The gasps from the crowd accompanied the cries of the fallers.

30

AFTERMATH

The crowd was in turmoil and there was such a surge forward that it was all the Guardians could do to stop a lemming-like rush to follow the fallers into the ravine. Some people were horrified, others were rejoicing. There was weeping but there was also jubilation. Some of those in the press were shouting Peglar's name and trying to get to him. The Guardians had no idea what to do but felt they should be in charge. Some of them were attempting to shepherd the people out of the Citadel while others tried to stop them from leaving. The Priestesses were huddled in a white clump. They seemed stunned. They had been only a few paces from the drama and one of their number was responsible, but they were unable to work out who it had been.

Yalka broke through the frantic herd and rushed towards the scaffold. Feldar had already removed Peglar's noose and pulled him back off the plank and as he stepped to safety Yalka clung to him and kissed him on the mouth, hard. His hands were still tied so he couldn't return her embrace.

Feldar peeled them apart. 'There'll be time for that later. You have to go,' he said to Yalka, 'and I've got to get Peglar out of here.'

Somebody pulled her away and she was carried along by the crowd. Gradually a sort of order was established. Yalka wanted to stay to see what had happened, to look over the cliff and confirm that Ragul and his mother were dead on the rocks at its base and perhaps see who had put them there, but everyone was being corralled towards the gate and she had to go too. Surprisingly quickly the Citadel was emptied and the pandemonium and disorder gave way to a desperate determination. The priority for most people was to get away from the place as quickly as they could.

'Why do you think that Priestess went for Ragul?' Yalka said as she caught up with Flynt and Myander.

'I don't know,' said Flynt. 'She must have had a score to settle. It was probably a girl he'd screwed and dumped. There are plenty.'

'Perhaps she was just trying to scare him and didn't intend him to go over the edge,' said Myander.

'I don't know,' said Flynt. 'To me, it looked as though she meant it.'

Halfway down the hill, on the edge of the square, they ran into Meshi. He hadn't seen Eylese. Or Syramos.

'Do you think you might have missed them,' said Flynt.

Meshi was sure that he hadn't. He'd watched very carefully and was sure he would have seen them if they'd taken the route to the Citadel.

'Well, we might as well go home,' said Flynt. 'We

won't find them by standing here. And although it's the one night of the month when the curfew's lifted I expect that after what's happened the Guardians will want to clear everybody out.'

Myander said she couldn't walk to Maris Partem and it took Flynt some time to locate a carriage and a driver and by the time she had most of the visitors to the city had gone. They spoke little on the journey. What was there to say? Each of them was trying to process the event in her own way and to fathom what had occurred. It had all happened so quickly it was hard to be sure of the events.

Once in Flynt and Myander's home they went to the parlour. Flynt took a bottle from the cupboard. 'I think we need this,' she said. She drew the cork and filled four glasses. She took one and raised it. 'This will sound insensitive,' she said, 'and what we saw tonight was horrific, but I'm glad it happened. So here's to the riddance of Ragul and his mother.'

'And to the sister who gave her life to do that,' said Myander.

They both drained their glasses. Meshi did too, but Yalka only sipped hers. Her head was already spinning. She had been in the depths of despair, then the heights of elation, and now she was exhausted. Peglar was safe, but what did that mean for the two of them? Feldar's warning haunted her. Ragul had gone, and that meant Peglar would be Master of the City. What chance did she have of being with him now?

'Don't think I'm crazy,' Myander said, 'but I have an idea who it was who pushed Ragul.'

'Who?' said Yalka and Flynt together.

'Well, and I know you'll think I'm mad, and it all

happened so fast that I can't be sure, but there was something different about the Priestess who rushed at Ragul.'

'Different? How?' said Flynt.

Myander shrugged. 'She looked bigger. More like a woman and less like a girl.'

'They were all shapes and proportions,' said Flynt. 'Most of them were what you'd expect for young teens but there were three or four who were quite tall.'

'It wasn't just her size, it was the way she held herself, the way she moved. She looked familiar.'

'So what are you saying?' said Flynt.

'Well, where's Eylese?'

The others were stunned by what the question implied. They hadn't seen Eylese since she'd left after doing Yalka's hair. Meshi had told them he waited for her and Syramos but they'd not turned up.

'Are you suggesting that it was Eylese who shoved Ragul?' Flynt was incredulous. 'Eylese dressed up as a Priestess? How could she have done that?'

The hollowed-out feeling which had left Yalka when Peglar was saved came back to her, with an awful apprehension. 'It might be true,' she whispered. 'Do you remember? I was puzzled about the number of Priestesses, whether there were more than fifty. I had a strange impression. It was a feeling that something weird was about to happen.'

There was silence while the rest took this in. Myander spoke first. 'Eylese said she'd be with us on the Citadel. Perhaps she was.'

Flynt wasn't sure. 'Yalka has the blood of rhymers. Her feelings and impressions matter. But Eylese couldn't get to be amongst the Priestesses. They live in a block on their own. It's heavily supervised. The girls can't go out by themselves and no one's allowed in. They can't even have family visit them.'

'I don't know,' said Yalka, 'but Granddad's missing too. It's not like him to go off without telling me. Perhaps he's had something to do with it. Maybe he's somehow helped her.'

Flynt pursed her lips and refilled her own and Myander's glasses. 'I bet she was in the crowd and we simply missed her. There were so many people there it wouldn't be surprising. She'll be here soon.'

She wasn't. The evening wore on and Eylese still didn't appear. Sleep was impossible, and they stayed in the parlour going over again and again what they had seen. There were long periods when no one said anything and each of them retreated into their own thoughts. At length the pale fingers of dawn reached through the shutters and sunlight crept over the valley. It was morning.

31

THE GREAT STONE

Yalka and Peglar sat in the moonlight on the raised slab called the Great Stone. With Feldar's help, Peglar had managed to get out of the Palace unseen by the staff. He'd got a message to Yalka to meet him there and they were enjoying the blissful peace.

The Stone was special because it was where they had first met. It was where Peglar had been the first time he saw the girl with yellow hair. Where Yalka had been when she glanced up and saw a wimpish-looking posh boy looking down on her and accused him of spying. Neither knew then what they would come to mean to each other.

The Great Stone marked the middle of a broad track that bisected the ruins. Known as the Avenue of the Heroes, it had once been lined with statues and carved memorials supposed to show the resting places of the champions who in ancient times had created Chamaris and built it up to be the chief of the cities of the plain. The statues had long been taken away and re-erected elsewhere but their plinths remained, and so did a line of iron gratings that were the entrances to the tombs of the dozen or so most important families. Right next to the Great Stone was the vault of the House of the Leopard. The ashes of Karkis, Peglar's father, had rested in there for over a month now. Already the flowers that Peglar had laid for him were dead. Had Peglar himself died, as Ragul had intended, would there have been flowers for him too?

The Great Stone had once been their regular meeting spot. One of them would get there first and anxiously await the other, and then they would talk. Peglar would regale Yalka with what it was like to be subject to the petty rules and restrictions of life in the Palace, and she would tell him that there was a sickness in the city, not a plague but a different sort of infection which arose out of an order where everything was owned and commanded by a small number of very rich men.

At those times they had looked down over the city and across the plain to Maris Partem and the sea. Now they faced the other way, towards the chasm, the hills on its far side, and the full moon climbing slowly in a graceful arc. Although not a hanging moon it was nevertheless bright, and they could easily see the white block of the monument to Farumon, and beyond that the edge of the abyss into which Vancia, Ragul and their assassin had tumbled. The wooden platform erected for Peglar's execution was still there but the scaffold had been removed, and there was the start of what would eventually be a wall, a parapet, intended to prevent the scores of visitors who came every day to see the site of the drama from completing their trip as a heap of broken bones on the rocks below.

They held hands but they were not together. Safren

lay between them like a gigantic brown hearthrug, her chin on her paws and their arms resting on her woolly back.

'It was clever of you to find her,' said Peglar.

'It wasn't hard,' said Yalka.

'I didn't think it would be, for a rhymer.'

She grinned at him. 'It was nothing to do with rhyming, it was just common sense. People in Maris Partem were talking about a huge animal that looked like a bear and was haunting the wharf. Feldar had told me about this big dog you'd lost when you were snatched on the road, so I went to have a look, and there she was. The fishermen had taken a fancy to her and they'd leave her titbits in the bottoms of the fish boxes.' Yalka rubbed the dog's ears. Safren didn't lift her head but a low rumble came from deep in her throat and her tail flapped a couple of times.

'I know about the seafood diet,' Peglar said. 'When she came back to me her breath was enough to blow your hat off.'

They both laughed, and for a time they watched the moon in silence. It was a calm evening. Up here on the Citadel it was pleasantly warm, but down in the lower city where Yalka and Syramos had their home it would be uncomfortably hot. That meant sleeping with the windows open and letting the mosquitoes in. Something nocturnal rustled in the scrub behind them and the cry of an owl echoed in the gorge.

'Does being up here again bother you?' Yalka said.

Peglar looked over to where the scaffold had been. 'A bit, but it seems unreal. And such a long time ago, far longer than a month.'

He had so far said little to her about what he'd felt

and experienced under the last full moon, when he'd come so close to death, but he had nightmares about it and Yalka knew that visions of that night haunted him. Her rhyming told her that the dreams would remain to torment him until he faced them. 'Are you ready to talk about it?' she said.

He became thoughtful. His face showed pain and his eyes closed. He held her hand more tightly. 'You'd think it would be burnt into my brain,' he said, 'but it's hard to remember everything properly. I didn't sleep at all the night before. In the morning the jailers asked me what I wanted for my last meal but I told them nothing, so I didn't eat during the day. They were trying to be kind and offered me armanca because they said it would make the whole business pass more easily for me, but I didn't want that either. I wanted to feel my life right up to the final second.

'I'd been scared witless during the night, but when daylight came I felt calm. Not in control exactly, but reconciled to what was going to happen to me. The day seemed to pass so quickly, and I was led out of my cell and brought up here behind that platform thing that Ragul and Vancia were on. Feldar was with me and he was trying his best to help me stay cool but I knew he could do nothing. I was surprised at the number who'd turned out to watch. Ragul was waving to the people but I think a lot of them were actually cheering me, not him. I was patted on the back by a few at the front and some of them were calling my name. I felt all right, and then I saw the scaffold and it hit me: it was all over. I was terrified. There was no way I was going to get out of it. It was the end.'

He shut his eyes. 'I can see the scaffold now, and that

big guy with the hammer. The plank was so narrow that I thought I might fall off before they got the chance to hang me. In fact I thought about doing it, you know, jumping, deliberately. It would have been easy, and I don't know why I didn't. They put the rope around my neck and I turned my head to look at the crowd, and then I saw you. You looked so sad and so beautiful, and I cried. I wanted your face to be the last thing I saw and I shut my eyes, tight. That meant I didn't see what happened. I didn't see your friend save my life.'

'She wanted to save you, of course she did, but the main reason she was there was to kill Ragul for what he did to her parents.'

'Whatever it was, I'm grateful to her, and to your Grandfather for making it possible for her to get in with the Priestesses. How did he manage to do that?'

'Easy. He knows the woman who was in charge of them, the Corporate Mother. He did a rhyming for her once. She was grateful, and happy to agree to his request to get Eylese into the group.'

They both looked towards Farumon's memorial. Eylese's name had already been carved on its outside and the jar with her ashes placed within. That had touched Yalka, and she had been moved even more when Peglar had ordered that Verit's name should be inscribed there too.

Peglar rubbed his eyes. 'If it wasn't for her I wouldn't be here now. I wish I'd seen what she did. I wish I could thank her. All I know is that I heard a terrible scream from the gorge and a gasp from the crowd and then I felt somebody grab me and pull me back off the plank and then there you were, and Feldar pulling us apart.'

'Spoilsport,' said Yalka.

'Yes, but we've made up for it since,' said Peglar, and squeezed her hand. 'And if you'd move into the Palace with me we could make up for it more.'

Yalka shook her head. They'd been over this before. 'You know I want to be with you, but Palace life isn't for me. And having me there isn't right for you. What would the people say? "Look at Peglar, installing his whore in the Palace." You'd lose respect and it would delay the changes we both want. Get those done and then we can live our own lives.'

Peglar knew she was right. He was avoiding the pressures on him to choose as a pair a daughter from one of the wealthy families by saying that in memory of his murdered mother he'd taken a five-year vow of celibacy. Openly living with Yalka would sink that. For now they had to be content with his occasional visits to her home by way of the network of tunnels. And at least that had got him to meet the tunnel dwellers, and to set Meshi on to finding ways to make them more comfortable.

It was time to change the subject. 'You met my half-sister,' he said.

'Malina, yes.' A couple of days before Yalka and her grandfather had rhymed for her and Lembick, her pair. Malina had recently learnt that she was pregnant, and it was fashionable to commission a rhyming at such a time.

'What did your Grandfather foresee for her? Peglar asked.

Yalka gave him a playful punch on the arm. 'You know I can't tell you that,' she said. 'A rhyming's confidential to the person who asks for it.' She wondered whether to say more, then decided that she would. 'She wants to make up with you.'

'Oh yes?'

'Yes. She says she knows what she did, what she said about you, was wrong.'

'Well she's right about that.'

'She says it was Ragul who persuaded her to do it. He sold it to her as just a prank, a stunt that would be a bit embarrassing for you at first but would be funny when everybody was let in on the joke. It turned out in a way that she didn't expect, and as soon as she'd done what Ragul had told her, Vancia took her away, which meant she couldn't put it right.'

Peglar thought about this. 'It's hard to believe that. She's had lots of opportunities since then to tell the truth.'

'She says that Ragul threatened her. He said that if she ever changed her story he'd tell everybody that it had gone further than she'd said and that you'd raped her. She knew that if he did that she'd never be able to pair with anyone from one of the top families.'

Peglar sniffed. There were some differences between what Malina had told Yalka and the way he remembered things, but perhaps she too had been a victim of Ragul and Vancia's scheming. 'So she wants to be friends.'

'She wants to be forgiven. And we need her.'

'We do? Why?'

'Suppose Malina was not your half-sister. Suppose she was a boy, your half-brother. What would be her position now?'

'It's obvious. She's older than me. If she was male she'd have taken over after Ragul was killed. If she was male she'd be Master of the City.'

'And you?'

'I wouldn't be, of course. I wouldn't have the responsibilities I have now, or the privileges.'

'And us?'

Peglar saw what she was getting at. 'We could be together. I'd be able to move out of the Palace and live with you.'

Yalka leant across the hot body of Safren and rested her head on Peglar's shoulder. 'Flynt and Myander and me are working on the wives, mothers and daughters in the city, just like you and me agreed. We're forming them into women's groups and they're putting pressure on their fathers, brothers and husbands to get the Assembly to change the laws so that women are equal to men and have the same opportunities and rights. Malina has a lot of influence. With her on our side we can get it done. By the time we do, most of the changes you're working on to turn the city into a fairer and more honest society will be in place. Then you'll be able to hand over to Malina. I think she'll do a good job.'

'I think so too.' He did, despite everything Malina had done to him.

'And then we can live our lives. Together. As we want.'

He put his arm around her shoulder and squeezed. Sometimes he felt there were too many things to think about and he didn't know where to start. But his enemies were in retreat. He had Feldar as a right-hand man and Cestris to help him, and he had the wisdom of Syramos to call on when he needed advice. Crestyn was working on restoring the Household Treasury, and Yalka, and now it seemed Malina too, were mobilising the city's women. Sainter and Silon had disappeared and that was a concern, but he'd set Halnis, a Gate Guard he trusted, to find them, and Alendur and Beldrom, recently freed from the farm, would be on that too. And most of all he had Yalka; not an assistant but a true partner. He felt strength, and energy, and joy, and he knew that if the two of them set their minds to it they could achieve anything. But he knew it wouldn't be easy, and he knew it would take time.

'There's a lot of work if we're going to achieve everything we want,' he said. 'It could be ages before it's done. Maybe five years.'

'Perhaps,' she said. 'I suppose it could be less but it could be more. Rhymers like Granddad and me can often tell what will happen, but we can never say when.'

There was a long pause while they thought about the road that lay before them. Then Yalka squeezed his hand. 'Yes, a long time,' she said. 'But hey, here's the thing about time; it passes.'

PHILL FEATHERSTONE

Phill was born and brought up in West Yorkshire and has worked in several areas in the south and midlands of England. He has a Bachelor's degree in English Literature from Cambridge and a Master's in Education from Leicester. He has two children, four grandchildren, and now lives with his wife in Sheffield, South Yorkshire.

It was not until he retired that Phill found the time, energy and mental space to realise his long-held ambition to write a novel. His first was finished in 2015 and he has since written another eight, and a collection of short stories.

Phill's books have received widespread recognition and he has been a finalist in the Page Turner Book Awards, and in the Wishing Shelf and the Chill Book Awards. Five of his novels have received Indie B.R.A.G. Gold Medallions.

Phill Featherstone's writing and plotting are as enjoyable as almost anyone else doing the job. In this ambitious new project, The Leopard's Bane series, he introduces us to a fascinating world of mystery, intrigue and adventure.
www.scintilla.info

Scan the code below to subscribe to Phill's newsletter. Once a month you'll receive a chatty email containing information about what he's working on, what he's been reading, and news of events and activities. There's also a chance to **win signed copie**s of various titles, and all subscribers get a **free download** of his book of short stories, *Undiscovered Countries*.

<u>Novels (all available as hard copies and eBooks)</u>
Paradise Girl (REBOOT series book 1)
After Shocks (REBOOT series book 2)
Jericho Roase (REBOOT series book 3)
REBOOT - the complete collection
The God Jar
I know What You're Thinking
What Dreams We Had
The Poisoned Garden (Leopards Bane Book 1)
The Rhymer's Daughter ((Leopards Bane Book 2)
A Hanging Moon (Leopard's Bane Book 3)

<u>Short Stories</u>
Undiscovered Countries (exclusive to subscribers to Phill's emails)

<u>Education</u>
Various books for teachers of very young children, written in partnership with Sally Featherstone and published under the Featherstone Education imprint by Bloomsbury Publishing plc.

ACKNOWLEDGMENTS

When you write nine novels and a book of short stories in less than ten years it means that the people who know you have had to put up with a lot. It's not just the hours spent bent over a computer or a notebook. It's the many occasions when you've been physically present with them but mentally somewhere else, in an imaginary world dealing with people who only exist in your head.

So my warmest, deepest thanks and appreciation go to my friends and social media contacts, and especially to my long-suffering family.

Among loyal readers and friends, I want to thank in particular Helen & Rod Collett, Emma Dunmore, Theresa Anafi, and Mags Schofield for their careful reading of ARC versions and their thoughtful and helpful feedback.

As always, I want to express my special gratitude to Sally, my most perceptive critic, my unraveller of plot knots and character foibles, my wife, companion and soulmate of many years.

THANK YOU

Thank you for reading my book. If you enjoyed it would you leave a review on Amazon? And if you can on Goodreads too? Reviews are very important to independent authors because they let other readers know about our work. And if you did like it, please tell your friends, both in person and via social media.

You can find details of all my books on my website, together with plot summaries, book covers, buying options, and questions for book discussion groups –

www.phillfeatherstone.net

Finally, I'd love to link with you on social media. Would you follow me on Facebook, Instagram and Twitter/X?

facebook.com/PhillFeatherstone-author

twitter.com/@PhillFeathers

instagram.com/phillfeathers

Printed in Great Britain
by Amazon

36824679R00175